GETTING A LIFE

GETTING A LIFE

The Downshifter's Guide to Happier, Simpler Living

Polly Ghazi and Judy Jones
Illustrations by Colin Wheeler

Hodder & Stoughton

British Library Cataloguing in Publication Data
A record for this book is available from the British Library

ISBN 0 340 68485 2

Typeset by Hewer Text Composition Services, Edinburgh

Printed and bound in Great Britain by
Mackays of Chatham PLC

Hodder and Stoughton
A Division of Hodder Headline PLC
338 Euston Road
London
NW1 3BH

This book is dedicated to our parents

ACKNOWLEDGEMENTS

Grateful thanks to Ian Christie, Associate Director at the Henley Centre for Forecasting, London. This book is the richer for his personal contribution, insights and support, and for kind permission to draw upon research carried out for the Centre's *Planning For Social Change* service.

Special thanks also to Allan Thornton for his unstinting support and enthusiasm.

We are indebted for their help and encouragement to: Ray Pahl, Research Professor of Sociology at the University of Essex ESRC Centre on Micro-Social Change; Dr Maurie Cohen, of the Oxford Centre for the Environment, Ethics and Society; Duane Elgin; Professor Juliet Schor of Harvard University; and Vicki Robin, of the New Road Map Foundation. We are grateful to *Home Run*, the magazine for the self-employed, whose material we drew upon in Part Four. Last but not least, thanks to Colin Wheeler for his illustrations.

Many thanks also to all the downshifters who told us their stories for this book. Penelope Dunn at A.P. Watt and Rowena Webb at Hodder & Stoughton gave us invaluable assistance and advice. Thanks also to John Malam, our copy editor, and to Arvind Anand for printing out various drafts of the manuscript at almost no notice, without complaint.

A TALE OF TWO DOWNSHIFTERS:
ABOUT THE AUTHORS

Judy Jones

When Polly and I were staff journalists on *The Observer* newspaper, sitting at adjoining desks, we used to chat about whatever we were writing at the time, and all sorts of other things besides. It was good for our morale. There weren't many women on the paper, so we were a sort of mutual support system.

The newspaper business is fraught with insecurity – like many others these days – and as two of the front-line troops, we felt we were constantly having to perform at our peak. In journalism, you are only as good as your next story. There is no safe and predictable employment any more, and in some senses that is as it should be. Anyway, I felt I did my job pretty well and worked hard at it.

Early in 1996, I first heard the word 'downshifting'. Duane Elgin, the American author of a book called *Voluntary Simplicity,* came to the UK to take part in a debate in Oxford about the downshifting movement that was sweeping America. He forecast that it was likely to become an important trend in Britain too. I only knew all this because Polly was writing an article about it for the paper. I remember saying to her: 'That's it, that's what I want to do. Now Polly how do I do it exactly?'

We mused upon the subject at some length. Meanwhile, fate intervened. Our employers at the paper announced that they were offering redundancy packages, and that anyone interested in volunteering should make themselves known so that they could find out how much they would get. Polly and I made early calls on the company's head of human resources. I think both of us thought that we would never get a better opportunity to downshift. I had toyed with the idea of going freelance before, but had never done anything about it. It looked like one of those 'now or never' moments.

The morning I found out that my application for voluntary redundancy had succeeded, my emotions vacillated between two extremes. I set off at lunchtime at a brisk pace, head down against the light drizzle, for the Ironmonger Row Baths, in Finsbury, London, my pillar-box red swimming bag slung over my shoulder. As usual, I was in two minds. On one level, I felt piqued, almost shocked, that I should be considered so dispensable by my employers. After all, I was a vital cog in an extremely important wheel, the health correspondent of a national Sunday newspaper. I was widely respected in my field (so I liked to think), liked and admired by my fellow hacks. How on earth would they manage without me? Did they realise what they were doing, letting me go?

My bluff (was it a bluff?) had been called. After nearly two decades working as a staff journalist on local, regional and national newspapers, a jack of all trades and a master of very few, I was out of the door – literally – and already getting rained on. I was not at all sure that I was happy about my bosses giving me what I had so publicly asked for. Perhaps if they had haggled with me a bit more, flattered me more, I might have stayed. Or, more likely, I would have found myself on the very cusp of self-employment a slightly more poised and confident woman. Redundancy means they don't need you any more.

Would I be needed again, I thought as I leapt into the warm, over-chlorinated water of the pool and started to propel myself back and forth, and if so by whom? Then, I suddenly felt slightly elated. I realised I hadn't been counting the lengths I'd swum, as usual. My mind had been too busy racing with vivid images and exciting speculation about what could loosely be described as my future.

Normally, at this sort of time, I would have been thinking to myself: 'Come on, get a grip . . . one more length. Right, now get dressed, get back to your desk, have another go at tracking down that contact. You need him for this story you're trying to write. Remember?'

The next day I walked into my back garden early and saw the first of my daffodils were coming into bud (this was March 1996). The visual metaphor unleashed a cascade of clichés about life beginning at 40, and today being the first day of the rest of my life, which was not the most promising start to my career as a freelance writer and journalist. Later, I took my old newspapers to be recycled (always a strangely satisfying experience) and saw the cream petals of my neighbour's magnolia bursting forth. The visual metaphors were gathering thick and fast, and were starting to annoy me.

Why had I done it? Well, it was probably overwhelmingly due to the fact that I was approaching the age of 40, and the realisation that dawns on almost everyone at some stage that time appears to shrink as you get older. One minute you feel young and your life is before you. When you next have the chance to think about it – which might be several years later – you realise: 'Good grief, I am middle-aged.' In my case, it hit me like a fist from the dark.

You think of all the things you never quite got round to because you were too busy establishing yourself in your career and getting on: things like getting married, having children, becoming an Olympic standard horse-rider, or even just horse-owner or, in fact, dog-owner. Progressively and without realising it, I had become a rather one-dimensional person. All I had got round to being was a health correspondent for a national paper. When I wasn't working, I was more than likely travelling to or from work, worrying about work, or planning work – journalists often find it hard to 'switch off' because they are always looking for new ideas for articles, weeding them out and bouncing them off other people.

So how has downshifting been for me? Touch wood, it's been going pretty well. Mostly, I am having the time of my life. When I left the paper in April 1996, the first two weeks just felt like a holiday, which is how I treated it. The next fortnight felt much as I imagine a sabbatical to be – making some modest moves to set up freelance work, starting to research this book, but mainly just pottering, relaxing, doing my garden, seeing more of friends and family.

During the second month I felt slightly disoriented, not exactly missing the office, but feeling slightly uneasy about working from home, like I was playing truant somehow. However, once I had converted my spare bedroom into an office, made and painted my bookshelves (jade green), got to grips with my computer and fax-modem and got an extra phone-line installed, I felt myself again. Having fixed myself up with an accountant and registered for VAT, I no longer felt in limbo – hovering somewhere between employment and unemployment – as I had done before. Now I feel exactly what I am – a self-employed journalist and writer.

As time goes on, the more I realise what the missing ingredient was in my past employment. No employer was to blame, and nor was I. The missing ingredient was a sense of *control* and this missing link was a product of my previous *mode* of employment. It was a structural flaw, and my personality was finding it ever more difficult to tolerate this missing link as time went on.

Some colleagues were surprised that I had volunteered to have my job made redundant, but most wished me well and said: 'Good for you!' One or two thought I was making a big mistake. Someone flagged me down as I was disappearing into the lift one day and asked me anxiously why I wanted to leave. As the doors closed, I struggled for a brief but accurate reply: 'Well, you know . . . I just want to *get a life*, basically!'

Polly Ghazi

When I first joined *The Observer* full-time in October 1989, aged 27, it was the fulfilment of every young ambitious journalist's dream. Getting to Fleet Street, as it was then still called, and working on my favourite national newspaper was hugely exciting. For the first four and a half years or so, I loved every minute of it. The buzz of front page stories, the travel opportunities which came with my environmental brief, even the pressure of constant deadlines. I thrived on it all.

Slowly, however, I began to be ground down by the high pressure, high stress lifestyle. I had begun by working very hard to prove that I deserved a place on the paper, and found it hard to step back once my position was assured. At the same time *The Observer*, its sales declining, was coming under increasing financial pressure. Between 1990 and April 1996 I lived through five rounds of redundancies among the journalists. Like much of the corporate downsizing which went on in the late Eighties and early Nineties, many respected and long-serving staff members lost their jobs and some absences were keenly felt by those who remained. In my six and a half years, the editorship of the paper also changed three times. When the offer of voluntary redundancy came up, I decided to apply.

Why did I choose to go? For many reasons, personal and professional. First, my health was suffering from the stress of the constant upheavals and uncertainties at work. Second, I was a year into my marriage and beginning to resent working every Friday night and 9.00 a.m. to 6.30 p.m. on Saturdays. Third, I felt ready for a change of direction in my career. I wanted to switch from being a news reporter to concentrating more on comment and longer, more analytical articles. This was a role which I thought I could more easily carve out for myself by writing for a range of different publications. Fourth, the voluntary redundancy scheme was generous – and I felt that such an opportunity might not arise again.

All these arguments, particularly those on quality of life, won the day. But it was a very tough decision. Four months later, my life transformed for the better, I look back and wonder how I could have agonised so long and hard.

The first few weeks after leaving the paper were an emotional roller-coaster. The voluntary redundancy scheme was sorted out fairly quickly and I left only about six weeks after applying. After spending years with *The Observer* occupying most of my waking hours (and many of my dreams too!) it was a tremendously abrupt parting.

Nevertheless, the first week I was euphoric. Sleeping late in the morning had never felt so sweet, and ordinary chores like cooking or going round the supermarket became much more enjoyable. It may sound silly or simplistic but what really made the difference was having the time to take things slowly and enjoy the experience. I suddenly realised how much I had been living in 'absent' time when at home, my mind constantly on something else (work!) instead of enjoying the present moment.

The second week my husband Allan and I went on holiday to the Canary Islands and I collapsed in a heap. Swimming, sunning and sleeping helped to rejuvenate me a little. But when we got home I found myself rushing around like a mad thing for the next fortnight. Suffering from the terminal insecurity that most journalists feel as soon as their name has not been in print for a couple of weeks, I rang up various newspapers and magazines and fixed up and wrote two or three stories.

After these appeared, I calmed down a little. But then came an attack of the blues. For about a month or so, I felt dislocated, claustrophobic at home, and often tearful. When my husband went out of the door to work in the mornings, I resented the fact that I wasn't doing the same. I was very excited about writing this book, but I found it hard to get going on such a mammoth task.

Thankfully, six weeks or so after starting my new life, this feeling lifted. I became used to working at home and began to appreciate its benefits. When the sun shone, I took my laptop computer into the back garden and worked there. When I needed to sleep in I did, and then worked in the evenings. If I had one very busy week, I could take it easy the next. I began to see my friends more often, to do more exercise and eat more healthily. My quality of life began to improve daily.

I have certainly been working less hard than on *The Observer* and am on course to earn roughly half of my last year's salary in my first twelve months as a freelance. But I don't consider this a problem. Firstly, I cannot stress enough what a difference receiving a large redundancy cheque makes. Without it as a cushion, I would not have left without another job to go to. Secondly, the amount Allan and I are spending has fallen dramatically. We haven't yet got round to doing a proper audit of the four months since I left the paper, but we estimate that we've cut our spending by around 40 per cent without even trying! How? Because my change in employment has brought us a whole new lifestyle.

Firstly, we now have the time and energy to cook and eat *in* five times a week instead of *out* five times a week. Secondly, I no longer speed around in taxis because my life is so busy I don't want to waste time walking or waiting for the bus. Thirdly, my deep need for retail therapy has abated dramatically. I used to buy a new item of clothing once a fortnight or so, and when I was particularly unhappy at work this would rise to once a week. I also indulged in frequent massages to relieve tension and stress. Now I don't look or feel so tired, the necessity has vanished. When I go these days, it is to indulge in a rare treat rather than to have my body de-stressed so that I can leap back into the fray.

Is there anything I miss? Of course. I miss the buzz of writing a major news story. I sometimes miss the high level contact-making which goes with a correspondent's job on a national newspaper. I miss my colleagues and friends in the office. But the compensations are enormous. The stress that used to consume me daily has lifted and, although I get tired, I no longer feel exhausted most of the time. I find life as a freelance stimulating and exciting and only a little daunting. Above all I feel back in control of my life whereas so often in the past couple of years I have felt swept along by an uncontrollable tide of events. It is a sweet feeling.

Will I jump back on to the treadmill and take another full-time job? Quite possibly at one stage or another in my life. I would be a hypocrite if I said otherwise. But one of the main lessons of this book is that it is just as possible to influence people and even events from outside the traditional career structure as within it. For me, downshifting is categorically *not* about opting out. It is about creating the circumstances for a thriving, balanced life which enables us as individuals to give the best of ourselves – at home, at work and in the wider world.

CONTENTS

Contents

PART ONE

OVERWORKED, OVERLOADED, OVER HERE

Life is about more than just maintaining oneself, it is about extending oneself. Otherwise living is only not dying.

Simone de Beauvoir (1908–1986), French socialist, feminist and writer

'Consumption became the thing . . .'

PREFACE

If Life Is So Good, Why Do We Feel So Bad?

Britain is increasingly an over-developed, dysfunctional and unhappy nation. Have a good hard look at the people around you next time you are in the supermarket queue or sitting on a bus. How many look content and in command of themselves, or strike up conversations with the person next to them to pass the time of day? Now see how many faces look puffy-eyed or stiff with tension. How many just staring blankly ahead, avoiding any eye-contact? If the number in the first category outnumber those in the second and third, count yourself lucky. Life, for too many of us, has become lopsided, one-dimensional. That dimension is our work: we either have far too much, or we do not have paid work at all. We are worn down by work or, for large chunks of the population, the lack of it. From early this century until the late 1980s, the length of the working week fell for the average Briton. But in the 1990s, people in jobs have rarely worked harder or longer. The average employed Briton works 43.8 hours a week in his or her job, more than any of our counterparts in the European Union. At least 3.3 million of us work 50 hours a week or more. The treadmill turns faster and faster, and we have to exert ever more effort to maintain our place on it. And if you don't work hard enough, there is a fair chance you will join the ranks of the unemployed, who are also stressed out. Around a quarter of men and a third of women in Britain are in an anxious or depressed state at any given time, surveys have shown. We are all brought up to believe that if we work hard and apply ourselves diligently, life will be good, or at least better than it otherwise would be. But for many, the Protestant work ethic, evolved over 500 years, is beginning to look like a hollow credo, shattered by contemporary market forces. We can get thrown on the scrapheap of unemployment, having played by the rules of all our established institutions, just as easily as those who never chose to or who never had the chance. All bets are off. Rarely since the Industrial Revolution has a generation of children left school or college so uncertain about their own prospects, and those of our damaged planet. Rarely have their parents' generation felt so insecure about their jobs and careers, and so confused about how they – and their *own* parents – will live out the rest of their lives. For their insecurity is boundless. We now live in an increasingly self-help society, where not only the boundaries of government, but also our much-cherished Welfare State, are fast retreating.

On the very cusp of a new millennium, Britain and the world face unprecedented uncertainty and bewildering choices. Overpopulation and overconsumption are threatening the planet. Many of us feel our lives are truly on the edge.

How did we end up in this predicament? In the euphoria of post-World War II economic and technological advance, we came to despise almost *anything* that was from an earlier era, whether it was a piece of furniture or a set of values. We wanted to throw it out, and replace it with something a bit more modern. Consumption became the thing: a refrigerator, a front-loading washing machine, a TV set for the sitting-room, a nice car for trips out at the weekend. All mod cons: that's what we wanted. We aren't so sure now whether the twin gods of capitalism and rampant consumerism have landed us quite where we want to be. Perhaps more than ever before, we are wondering what life is all about, what it's for. We are searching for meaning and balance. Many are turning to alternative ways of living, and downshifting is one of them. Indeed, in Western societies downshifting is one of the fastest-developing social trends of the late 1990s, as more of us yearn for simpler, more fulfilling lives and the time to enjoy the good things in life.

Crisis? What crisis?

Life crises tend to be regarded as negative experiences, particularly by those who have not had them. But what they often present are opportunities not simply to come to terms with life, but to recast it in a new and more liberating mould. It is a time when you allow yourself to start becoming the person you always wanted to be, before you got side-tracked by other more immediate goals that took priority at that time.

4

The mid-life crisis is one of the most common and most widely discussed. In some ways it is the perfect point in the life-cycle for people to start moving their own goalposts. It is a shame that we wait so long to do this. Ideally, we would all have our mid-life crises in our twenties so we could spend the rest of our lives doing what we actually *want* to do, rather than what others expect of us. But few people in their twenties have the confidence, the knowledge borne of experience, or the luxury of financial security to change tack radically and decisively. We go through childhood and our teenage years, yearning to be grown-up or at least a few years older. As students at college or university we are told that all this hard study will be worth it in the future, because it will help us to find satisfying careers that will reward us with ever more status, power and material success. Then we start on the first rung of the career ladder, and we find ourselves once again at the bottom of the pecking order, doing menial or less than satisfying work. Power, influence, wealth and status still seem to lie on a rather indistinct horizon.

So we spend the first years of our lives constantly trusting that one day our promised gratification will no longer be deferred, and look forward to tasting the sweet fruits of all our youthful energy. Then we reach the middle years, and find that if anything life is full of even more obstacles to fulfillment and happiness. At which point you start behaving like a plane coming towards a landing strip: your psychological engines go into reverse thrust, and you start looking wistfully backwards and wish you were young again. From here on, the regrets can easily pile up unless you shift your way of thinking into a different gear altogether.

People readily find excuses for their lack of happiness. They find it easier to cast themselves in the role of victim or martyr to some constellation of events and circumstances that they see as fateful and uncontrollable, rather than to try to develop a *new* mind-set, that could liberate them from this 'no-win' dependence.

None of this needs to mean abandoning collective goals and social expectations of how each individual should behave. But it does mean working out which goals and expectations really matter to you, and developing your own personal philosophy that transcends the material world around you.

There is a theory of happiness called 'flow'. It's about using your concentration and being totally absorbed in an activity, by a thought or by a sensation. Crucial to the creation of 'flow', particularly in adversity, is the use of imagination. A rich fantasy life – fragments, sensory images, narratives that we cull from the depths of our subconscious – has sustained people through the most severe deprivation, the worst kind of degradation, as many prisoners of war and hostages have testified throughout history.

We needn't feel forever chained to our past or present misfortunes, nor dependent on the promise of some future fulfillment to make sense of life and to enjoy it now. We can live our lives proactively or reactively, we can put all our psychological energies into positive thoughts or negative ones. We can bury ourselves in work and activity that we don't enjoy. We can sacrifice our chance of happiness by always playing by the rules, and doing what is expected of us. Often, we believe we are simply responding to the needs of those around us, but they may not always notice still less thank us for our effort. The choice is ours.

CHAPTER ONE

Our Consuming Passion

The avarice of mankind is insatiable.
Aristotle (384–322 BC)

As you move around your home take a good hard look at its contents. It's likely that your living-room will have a television set and a video, and your kitchen a washing machine and tumble dryer, maybe also a microwave oven and electric toaster. If you are a typical British householder, your bedroom drawers and wardrobes will be stuffed with almost three times as many clothes as you or your parents wore in the 1950s. You almost certainly own a car and possibly a home computer, holiday abroad at least once a year and eat out at least once a week. If you could see the volume of rubbish in your dustbin over a year, you would be horrified.

The typical British household now enjoys a luxury of lifestyle beyond the grasp of any previous generation. And we are not alone. The lucky 70 per cent of Britons who live above the breadline are members of a global consumer society which embraces most North Americans, West Europeans, Japanese and Australasians, together with the inhabitants of the Middle East oil sheikhdoms and the city-states of Hong Kong and Singapore. As we hover around the cusp of the twentieth and the twenty-first century, the consumer class is on the rise, too, in Eastern Europe, Latin America and South and East Asia. Germans bought one million used Western cars in 1991 alone, while in Chinese cities, two-thirds of households now own washing machines.

So powerful is this worldwide urge to buy and consume that it is easy to forget how recent a phenomenon it is. In his book *How Much is Enough?*, Alan Durning of the Washington-based Worldwatch Institute traces the birth of the consumer age to 1920s America. It was then that brand names first became household words, that packaged foods became widely

7

available on shop shelves and that the motor car, consumerism's ultimate symbol, began to take its place at the heart of modern American culture.

But the consumer society really came of age after World War II. With the basic survival needs of most of the population catered for, American politicians and business leaders needed a new formula to drive the engine of economic progress. Their answer was to aggressively promote mass consumption. One prominent American retailing analyst of the post-World War II era, Victor Lebow, summed up the new credo: 'Our enormously productive economy . . . demands that we make consumption our way of life, that we convert the buying and the use of goods into rituals, that we seek our spiritual satisfaction, our ego satisfaction, in consumption. We need things consumed, burned up, worn out, replaced, discarded at an ever increasing rate.'

The formula succeeded beyond Lebow's wildest expectations. Almost half a century after the end of the Second World War, the American consumer society provides the model to which ordinary citizens in every corner of the globe aspire. In America itself, the average couple owns twice as many cars, covers 25 times as much distance by air, and uses 21 times as much plastic as their parents did in 1950. Today, the consumer society can be summed up by 'shopping mall mania' and 'fast-food frenzy'. Some 60 per cent of the food Americans eat is bought ready-made in supermarkets, at take-away outlets or in restaurants. In 1992 the world's largest shopping mall in Bloomington, Minnesota, was opened amid great fanfare, in the confident expectation that it would attract more visitors a year than the number of pilgrims who flock to either Mecca or the Vatican. In 1996, the so-called 'Coca-Cola Olympic Games' in Atlanta, USA, underlined the grip which commercialisation now holds over the American soul. Many felt the Olympic ideal had been eclipsed by the huge number of commercial sponsors at the Games.

Japan, Western Europe and Australasia are not far behind. In the last half a century the British, French and West Germans have tripled the amount of paper per person they consume. In the 1980s the amount of processed and packaged food eaten per individual doubled, while consumption of soft drinks per person shot up by 30 per cent between 1985 and 1990. Meanwhile, the choices laid before us have proliferated to a bewildering extent. Take something as simple as buying a toothbrush. It used to be simply hard brush versus soft. Now the Boots chain stocks 75 different varieties. In Japan one of the most striking expressions of growing affluence has been in foreign travel. One million Japanese travelled abroad in 1972, whereas 11 million did so in 1990.

The global spending spree triggered by the rapid growth in affluence has encountered little effective resistance in either America or Europe. Consumption strategies now underpin the entire global economy. Money, and the goods and services we buy with money, have become the yardstick by which we in Western nations judge each other's social worth. Economic imperatives form the bedrock of relationships between governments, and with the people they govern. Why else is it that at every general election, the economy, and what in 1967 the former British prime minister Harold Wilson called 'the pound in your pocket', becomes the only issue that mainstream politicians end up talking about?

Advertising: the dream machine

By the age of 18 the typical British teenager will have already been bombarded with about 150,000 television advertisements. Nor is he or she alone. From Moscow to Seoul to Dhaka, Western-style billboards and television commercials provide the raw fuel that drives the relentless expansion of mass consumption.

The world of advertising well understands human nature, and ruthlessly exploits human frailty. It generates new needs, so that it may endlessly sell us new products. Advertising fuels our wants and desires. For it to succeed, it must persuade large numbers of people that enough can *never* be enough. It works by making us feel unhappy or insecure about our diet, appearance and possessions, in other words, every aspect of our lives. Nine times out of ten it is selling us something we don't really need. But it often proves irresistible nevertheless. One such invention was 'Fun 'n' Fresh' deodorant for 7–12-year-olds, dreamed up by American entrepreneur Philip B. Davis. Condemned by American paediatricians as wholly inappropriate on the grounds that perspiration odours don't usually manifest themselves until puberty, it sold well all the same.

Some sociologists have argued that clever advertising exploits our vulnerability and our uncertainty about life's most fundamental dilemmas; that it has come to eclipse religion in shaping people's ideas of what they expect and want out of life. Nevertheless, there are limits to the advertisers' powers. The huge gap between the images and desires which agencies conjure up to sell their products and the reality that consumers experience is becoming harder to reconcile.

When less is more

We don't want more anything any more. What we want now is less.
More and more less.
Faith Popcorn, American trendcaster

As we straddle the new millennium, there are signs of a small, but growing backlash against the stranglehold of mass consumption. The spend-spend-spend culture has plunged many Britons into debt and negative equity. Insecurity over jobs and pensions has made us more cautious in our approach to spending. For some of us our possessions are becoming a burden. And a new uncomfortable feeling is also beginning to emerge: that society is paying a high price for the benefits of ever-increasing spending power for the majority.

Since 1979, the gap between rich and poor in Britain has widened dramatically. The legacy of 20 years of deregulated markets, individualism, and profligate spending has left Britain with the unenviable title of most unequal country in the Western world. The chasm between rich and poor is also deepening across the globe.

One-fifth of the world's population, some 1.1 billion people, now takes home 64 per cent of world income. This amounts to 32 times as much as that earned by the world's poorest fifth. In 1990, the average person in the richest one-fifth of the world's countries earned $15,000, whereas those in the poorest fifth earned $250 – an income gap which has doubled since 1960. But perhaps the most shocking indictment of growing inequality came with the publication of the 1996 United Nations Human Development Report. Even the toughest of cynics blanched at its extraordinary revelation: that the world's 358 billionaires now own as much wealth as the poorest 2.3 billion people – almost half the global population.

Greater spending power has brought Westerners previously undreamed of lifestyles and travel opportunities. We have become understandably wedded to our comfortable houses, foreign holidays and cars. But many people are beginning to sense that indefinitely expanding the boundaries of our lifestyles is likely to take a heavy toll on ourselves, our society and the environment in which we live. A Mori poll conducted in September 1995 suggested that eight in ten Britons believe our society has become too materialistic. As we grow increasingly uncertain about the future, so our values and attitudes are starting to shift.

In 1987, John Elkington and Julia Hailes, authors of *The Green Consumer Guide*, founded SustainAbility, a London-based environmental research consultancy. Eight years later, it advised its corporate subscribers that there is a 'sustainable lifestyles revolution' taking place in Britain. This phenomenon, founded on the principle that we in the West must consume less of the world's finite natural resources, will be one of the most powerful trends of the next half century. While the trend so far remains 'at best embryonic', SustainAbility has devised the following table to demonstrate how our values are expected to shift between old and new world views.

Values for the Future	
From 'Global Consumer'	To 'World Citizen'
Global Consumer	**World Citizen**
Me	We
More	Enough
Materialism	Holism
Quantity	Quality
Greed	Need
Short-term	Longer-term
Rights	Responsibilities

Source: 'Who Needs It?' SustainAbility, 1995

We are, of course, a very long way from such a wholesale shift in values. But the advertising industry, ever-sensitive to changes of public mood, has picked up on this almost tangible, *fin de siècle* malaise. A windswept young man in a sweater and jeans clutching his toddler son and looking wistfully towards Stonehenge was the image chosen by Barclays Bank in the summer of 1996 for a newspaper campaign advertising their new business banking service. Another young man, a stressed and lonely-looking rat racer with his head in his hands, was featured in a TV advert for the Bristol & West Building Society. The slogan went: 'To make time for the more important things, we have to decide to do less.' Adverts like these reflect the changing aspirations of consumers to spend their time and money more rationally. Whether they generate extra customers remains to be seen.

CHAPTER TWO

Happiness – The Missing Link

Unless a person learns to enjoy it, much of life will be spent desperately trying to avoid its ill-effects.
Mihaly Csikszentmihalyi, 1992

One of the most powerful reasons why we are losing faith in consumerism as a guiding light is the realisation that money does not buy happiness. The truth of this maxim, which we are fond of quoting, is borne out by rigorous academic research. Trying to answer the question 'What is Happiness?' has become a growth industry for think-tanks and psychologists. The more they delve into our psyches, the more evidence they uncover that the link between money and contentment is a tenuous one for all except the poorest in society.

People achieve happiness when they have eliminated inner conflicts between their achievements and aspirations. The contemporary political and economic debate assumes that there is a strong correlation between income and contentment, that extends beyond the basic need for survival. This assumption is applied to individuals and societies. Politicians, economists and media commentators extrapolate from these assumptions to conclude that the 'feel-good factor', of which we hear so much, consists of making money, and being secure in the knowledge that one will go on making money, in ever larger proportions.

The economic and social policies of Britain's main political parties are constructed around these assumptions. Yet happiness has little to do with economics, unless you are unfortunate enough not to have the money you need to buy the essentials of life: food, clothing, adequate shelter, heat and light. But when basic material or survival needs have been met, what then?

We need meaning and purpose in life to feel good about it. Oxford psychologist Professor Michael Argyle, who has spent more than a decade researching what makes people happy, argues, in his seminal work *The Psychology of Happiness*, that many influences can trigger this feel-good factor. A fulfilling job or leisure activity, gardening, sport, a loving relationship, a close network of friends or bringing up children can all do the trick. Extra spending money comes way down the list of factors that people actually find important. As we focus relentlessly on working and earning, Argyle's book suggests, so two of these three crucial spheres, social relations and leisure, have begun to suffer and our happiness levels to wane.

Recent data collected from around Britain, including depressed inner city areas, bear out Professor Argyle's arguments. After analysing 24 separate studies on quality of life, Professor Gordon Mitchell of Leeds University found in 1994 that income levels did not feature among people's top two concerns. Our highest personal priority, he found, is good health, followed by freedom from crime. Personal and economic security came third, just ahead of individual development through learning and freedom from pollution.

Earlier and in the same vein, a series of nationwide polls by the University of Strathclyde (1991) found that more people rated their health (70.3 per cent) and security (68.7 per cent) as 'very important', above standard of living (58.8 per cent). When the New Economics Foundation, a London-based think-tank, sent questionnaires to the 100 householders in the far from affluent Scottish borders villages of Long-formacus and Cranshaws, asking for residents' top priorities, 'living in a clean, pleasant and safe area' came out first. Improving the local natural heritage came next with 'adequate income to cope with heating, transport and food' relegated to third place and local jobs trailing in fourth.

In his new book *The Social Psychology of Leisure*, Professor Argyle argues that 'serious leisure, an activity that absorbs our whole being, is the best guarantee of long-term contentment'. Yet most of us feel we have too little time, opportunity or money to take his advice.

Research from around the world supports the evidence from Britain that the direct link between money and personal happiness is a weak one. According to Dutch psychologist Dr Ruut Veenhoven, the happiest man in the world is not the richest (Microsoft owner Bill Gates), nor the most powerful (Bill Clinton, USA president), but the average Mexican citizen!

After conducting an exhaustive survey of happiness data from across the globe, Veenhoven concluded that, beyond a certain prosperity level, rising incomes no longer affected well-being. In the poorer countries, which cannot afford welfare safety nets, income remains a life and death issue. But in the richer consumer nations, Veenhoven found that money no longer plays a central role in individual well-being. He discovered that the more affluent the nation, the smaller the correlation between people's bank balances and their personal happiness. And he calculated somewhat controversially, that the income of the typical Mexican, at roughly half the average British income of £18,000 a year, provides an optimum level to enjoy life. Above that threshhold, he argued, earning more money does not create extra happiness.

Exactly the same conclusion was drawn by Norwegian sociologist Dag Hareide, after a similarly comprehensive study in 1993. Whereas Veenhoven drew on people's own perception of happiness, using answers to questions such as 'How satisfied are you with your life as a whole?', Hareide studied the quality of life of his fellow countrymen since 1850 by looking at social trends. Using rates of violent crime, murder, alcohol addiction and suicide to judge the level of human development in Norwegian society, he found steady progress up to a peak in 1960. Since then, the Norwegian economy has expanded dramatically, but happiness indicators have slumped. The number of suicides and violent crimes have tripled in 30 years, while Norwegians now drown their sorrows in as much alcohol as they drank in 1850.

Even in the poorest countries, it is a mistake for economists or anyone else to assume that people measure their quality of life merely by the income they can scrape together. In 1988 the Indian academic N.S. Jodha asked farmers and villagers in two villages in Rajasthan to list their own criteria for being well-off. They produced 38 examples, including quality of housing, wearing shoes, eating a third meal a day and sleeping in a different room from the family animals. Jodha found that 36 households which ranked themselves as better off on their own terms had actually suffered more than a 5 per cent drop in hard cash income over the previous year!

In the Western world, Veenhoven and Hareide's views, shared by a growing band of international economists, have enormous implications for the status quo. Rising economic growth and consumption levels have been the twin mantras of Western politicians for decades. But if growth doesn't deliver extra well-being to the citizens these politicians serve, then what is the point of it? And what message does all this hold for us as individuals?

When people are asked about what makes life rewarding and enjoyable for them, they often recall events that enabled them to achieve more than was expected of them. It can be something as simple as expressing views during a conversation that you never realised you had, playing tennis, or finishing a particularly challenging task well and on time. 'After an enjoyable event, we know that we have changed, that our self has grown; in some respect we have become more complex as a result,' writes Mihaly Csikszentmihalyi in his book *Flow: The Psychology of Happiness.*

While the sensation of pleasure requires no psychological effort, the enjoyment of an experience comes from concentration and total absorption in an activity. This is a state of 'flow'. It can be achieved by taking control of your own consciousness, and in doing so taking control of the quality of your experience. 'Flow doesn't require education, income, high intelligence, good health or a spouse. It requires a mind,' says Csikszentmihalyi.

His argument is essentially this: sooner or later in life, you are likely to ask yourself: 'Is this it? Is this all there is to life?' As disillusionment sinks in, some respond by renewing their efforts to acquire more of the things that they believed would make them happy, such as a bigger car or house, more power and status at work; others take a more piecemeal approach by tackling problems one by one, such as going on a diet, taking more holidays, retreating into a hobby, drugs or drink. None of these individual actions are likely to work on their own. We have to change the way we think, and if we can do that we can change the way we experience the quality of our lives.

CHAPTER THREE

Mission Impossible: Living Against the Clock

It was going to be one of Rabbit's busy days. As soon as he woke up he felt important, as if everything depended on him. It was just the day for Organising Something, or for Writing a Notice Signed Rabbit . . .
A.A. Milne, *The House at Pooh Corner*, 1928

Modern man suffers from a 'hurry sickness' induced by a 'time famine', wrote Michael Young in his book *The Metronomic Society*. The advent of electric lighting enabled and encouraged people to work longer and longer hours round the clock, upsetting the natural rhythmic cycles that were a feature of our evolution. Industrialisation also made us more reliant on the clock as a regulator of daily lives. Young wrote: 'We are continually having to start this or stop that at the appointed moment. Life is strung between a whole series of precisely-timed beginnings and ends which have a lot to do with man and little with nature.'

Moderate amounts of stress are essential to motivate us and make us feel challenged, but above a certain threshold they make us feel anxious and unable to cope. Thresholds will vary from one person to the next. When we encounter more challenges than we can cope with, or else too few to stimulate us, stress is the result.

Too much stress raises blood pressure, which increases the risk of blood clots forming. Over time that makes you more vulnerable to strokes and heart attacks. It interferes with the immune system, the body's natural defence mechanism that protects you from bugs and viruses. Most doctors now accept that stress can be a major contributory factor to the development of some forms of cancer. We are remarkably resilient in keeping going under stress for short stretches. But eventually we pay the price. How often have you gone on holiday only to be laid low

16

on the first day by a cold or flu or worse? It's because the pressure is suddenly off. There's no adrenalin surging around keeping the show on the road, and your brain on red alert.

Stress and overwork doesn't just make us ill by undermining our natural defence systems. It makes us behave differently, unnaturally and unhealthily. We drink too much coffee to wind ourselves up, and too much alcohol to wind down. We rush our food instead of savouring every mouthful. We graze on junk food and pre-packaged convenience food instead of sitting down to proper meals, made with fresh and nutritious ingredients. Then we're more likely to flop in front of the television (or carry on working) with a bottle of wine or a six-pack of beer rather than engage in some active pursuit.

Stress has become the great epidemic of the modern age. It accounts for 90 million working days lost a year. It costs the British economy £7 billion a year in terms of lost production, sick pay and demands on the NHS, according to the 1995 Labour Force Survey. Unemployment and fear of losing your job, head the list of the top ten causes of stress. Financial worries, especially debt, ranks second, and being stuck in a job you hate ranks sixth, behind single parenthood, divorce and housing problems.

The magazine *Men's Health* surveyed its readership on stress in 1996. Four out of five felt their work caused them stress, and nearly half were beset by money problems. Health and fears of unemployment were also prime causes of angst.

So in today's Britain we are a long way from achieving Michael Young's more civilised approach to life and work. Thirty years ago, the image of the lazy British worker, forever downing tools to enjoy a tea break, was a popular stereotype. Since the end of World War II, working weeks had been getting progressively shorter year by year. But over the last two decades the screw has been tightening once more. Employers of blue collar workers demand 10 or 12 hour shifts in return for much sought-after jobs in service industries or on factory floors. Between 1983 and 1991 the average working week for full-time service sector employees went up from 41.9 hours to 43.1, while falling from 40.3 to 40 hours in the rest of Europe. Meanwhile, millions of office workers and professionals have become addicted to the long hours culture where everyone competes to be the last one out of the door. Chancellor Kenneth Clarke, one of the rare politicians who has interests outside politics, was reportedly so appalled at the competitive long hours culture at the Treasury that he began instructing his officials to finish their work on time and go home.

The charity Parents at Work declared 21 June 1996 'National Go Home on Time Day' to highlight the heavy toll on health, productivity and efficiency exacted by excessively long working hours. It published a poll of over 2,000 members, mostly women in white collar jobs, funded by the Gulbenkian Foundation. It found that two-thirds routinely worked for longer than their contracted hours, and admitted they did not see enough of their children. Most were exhausted by the end of each day and never had any time to themselves. Some 42 per cent worked over 50 hours a week, and 27 per cent of workers were clocking up over 60 hours a week.

How worried is the UK government about the consequences for our health of our deeply-ingrained long hours culture? The omens aren't encouraging. British ministers have implacably opposed a European Union plan for a legally-enforceable maximum working week of 48 hours.

The empty promise

If economic progress means that we become anonymous cogs in some great machine, then progress is an empty promise.
Charles Handy, *The Empty Raincoat*, 1994

All around us we see evidence of the fragmentation of work, community and relationships. Redundancy is now commonplace. There have been more than 5 million redundancies in the UK between 1990–96; some 870,000 were made redundant in 1995–96 alone. With growing automation and competition from other manufacturing economies, particularly the 'tiger' economies of the Far East, the job shedding in Britain is unlikely to abate in the foreseeable future.

Only a third of adults now have full-time jobs, as a plethora of alternative less secure working arrangements – self-employment, part-time working, temporary and seasonal jobs – take their place. The proportion of self-employed people in the labour force nearly doubled in the 1980s to 11.6 per cent. Some 5 million people, most of them women, work part-time. Most of the new jobs created over the next decade or so are likely to be part-time. In parallel with the decline of the full-time job has been a steady fall in employment protection, as trade union powers have been eroded by systematic legal curbs introduced by the Conservative administration.

According to the left-leaning Employment Policy Institute, nearly a third of the workforce are in insecure jobs. Moreover, half of all households have less than £450 worth of savings, leaving them only a pay cheque away from disaster.

We are not only insecure about the jobs we hold here and now. When we have time to stop working and think about it, we are also worried about the future of the whole world of work as we know it. Most economists and trendwatchers believe that the job for life, if not yet dead, is fast becoming a thing of the past for all but the luckiest small percentage of employees. Even traditionally protected careers like the civil service, teaching and the armed forces have seen huge lay-offs in recent years. In his gloomy book *The End of Work*, the American alternative economist Jeremy Rikfin argues that new technology will only leave enough jobs for a small elite and the only employment the rest of us will be able to find in future will be in voluntary and community work. This may be an over-bleak picture, but it reflects our feeling of helplessness in the face of the global economic forces that seem to be determining our collective fate.

Two powerful new forces, the globalisation of the world economy and the advent of the age of information technology, are changing the world of work as never before. The explosion of information technology, exemplified by the Internet, has produced a wonderful tool for instant global communications. But it has also served to widen the gap between haves and have-nots, both within individual societies and between rich and poor countries. In Britain, the unemployed youth or recently sacked worker living on benefits struggles to afford the computer know-how he or she needs to give him or her the skills required for a decent job in the information technology age.

The disconnected citizen

The stresses that have accompanied these radical changes in employment patterns and the penetration of insecurity deep into all socio-economic groups have wrought immeasurable harm on social and personal relationships, and child rearing. Four in every ten marriages in the UK now end in divorce. Women are bearing fewer children, and the proportion of women who remain childless is expected to double to 20 per cent within a generation.

The traditional stereotype of an average family – a breadwinning husband, a wife in part-time employment or none at all, with two children – is disappearing as fast as the notion of the full-time job. The idea of the same partner for life is going the same way as the job for life.

In his landmark book, *The State We're In*, Will Hutton argues that family breakdown and the break-up of traditional employment patterns are closely linked. Hutton argues that Britain's deepening social divisions are turning the country into a 'thirty, thirty, forty' society. The first 30 per cent are the *disadvantaged*: they include more than four million men out of work, which includes those who are not officially counted as unemployed because they do not receive unemployment benefit or have not looked for work to the satisfaction of the authorities. The second 30 per cent is made up of the *marginalised* and *insecure*, people in part-time work, or on fixed contracts, newly self-employed, and those in full-time jobs which are low paid or have few employment rights. Hutton's final category is the 40 per cent of people whom he calls *privileged*, those in relatively secure full-time jobs.

Amid such widening gulfs, between rich and poor, secure and insecure, it becomes ever harder for marriages to withstand the constant strains. 'Britain has the highest divorce rate and the most deregulated labour market in Europe, and these two facts are closely related,' he writes.

'The doctrine of enough'

Hutton places great emphasis in his book, not simply on the centrality of work, but on the importance of collective work*places*.

Charles Handy, guru of the 'New World of Work', has located himself on a very different wavelength, one which foresees and celebrates an entirely different world of work. He promotes the concept of 'portfolio' working, where individuals sell services to a variety of customers, but also make time for 'free work' or 'gift work'.

Charles Handy used to be an oil company executive. Now he spends his time writing best-selling books about how we can integrate paid work more sustainably with the rest of our lives. He contends that the first step to personal freedom is to define what is enough, in terms of money, promotion at work or professional renown. Those who cannot do so will always feel dissatisfied, because they will always want more. The engines driving the portfolio philosophy are redundancy, the growth of home-working and tele-commuting, and the trend towards early retirement. Those who embrace the 'portfolio' concept do enough paid work to cover their bills, but make time for other kinds of work as well.

'Portfolio money is a way of thinking,' Handy writes in *The Age of Unreason.* 'Portfolio people think in terms of barter. They exchange houses for holidays, babysit for each other, lend garden tools in return for produce, give free lodging in return for secretarial help in the evenings. Portfolio people know that most skills are saleable.'

Hutton vs Handy – who is right?

Hutton's description of the workplace as a social centre as well as geographical location for most paid work is an accurate summary of traditional practices. He also stresses the sense of identity and meaning that most people derive from the conventional image of the workplace, indeed from conventional ideas of work itself. Hutton's book is an excellent diagnosis of Britain's collective economic ills, but it is Handy's vision of portfolio living that provides the inspirational and insightful prescriptions for what really ails us as *individuals* as well as what troubles us as a society.

The brushstrokes that Handy propels on to the canvas of work in the twenty-first century have the more flair, colour, conviction and radicalism. Handy's philosophy teases out a much more informal but exciting series of connections between an individual worker and a whole *variety* of employers, or customers if that person is self-employed. This vision may well offer that individual far more control, choice and satisfaction over how he or she earns money.

In terms of conventional analyses, one could contend that the prognosis of the portfolio worker is poor because of its inherent insecurity and implied notions of self-reliance. But as *we* have argued, conventional full-time employment is also profoundly insecure, and it lacks the advantages of worker control. Perhaps now, more than ever, we need to think seriously about challenging the status quo, to consider the potential benefits of self-employment, and part-time or flexible working, and of building new types of mutual organisations or unions to represent and to promote their interests. The creative energy and imagination that such moves could spark in so many thousands, perhaps millions, of disappointed souls is infinite.

CHAPTER FOUR

A New World View

And there is no greatness where there is not simplicity,
goodness or truth
Leo Tolstoy, *War and Peace*, 1865

It is not only time and happiness that elude us in the West, but peace of mind. As we look beyond the year 2000 we are afraid for our children's future and for the planet's too. In 1995, separate surveys by Mori and Gallup revealed that, for the first time since World War II, British parents believe they will not be bequeathing to their children the better life their parents bequeathed to them. We appear to be suffering a national crisis of confidence.

Look around you and it is not hard to see why. Many of us are confronted daily by polluted cities, car-choked streets, homeless teen-agers, neighbours who are strangers and exhausted friends and collea-gues. Most of us now earn more than enough for our basic needs, yet yearn for more from life than work and money. We worry about the path down which society is leading us. We fear that over-work is making us ill and damaging our relationships. We are anxious about crime levels and uneasy at the growing gap between haves and have-nots.

Only four in ten British adults (mainly the optimistic under 30s) were looking forward to the turn of the century, according to a study by Mintel in 1995. Two-fifths of the full-time workers questioned said the hours they worked were affecting their family lives. When interviewees were asked what would concern them most ten years hence, fear of crime rose five-fold and social and emotional worries, including fear of loneliness, six-fold.

Although Britain remains one of the world's most affluent nations, and most of us are comfortably off, we only have to open our eyes to see how our quality of life is deteriorating.

A new benchmark of national wealth, devised by former World Bank economist Herman Daly, suggests that quality of life in Britain has indeed been declining for 20 years, even though the traditional, official measure used, our Gross Domestic Product (GDP), remains one of the world's highest. Known as the Index of Sustainable Economic Welfare (ISEW), this measure of wealth in its broadest sense differs from conventional GDP by building into the equation quality of health and education services, pollution clean-up costs and loss of natural resources.

Recently applied to Britain by the New Economics Foundation, the index calculated that social and environmental costs were cancelling out our rising incomes. The cost of pollution of water, air and noise alone, for example, came to over £22 billion a year. Thus, while income per head has more than doubled since the 1950s, our quality of life rose steadily only between the 1950s and the mid-1970s and has been in a downward spiral ever since. A league table of six Western nations compiled by economists using the ISEW index has produced startling results. The USA, the world's conventionally richest nation, came out bottom with Britain trailing in second last. Sweden came out top, with Austria placed second; Germany and the Netherlands were ranked joint third.

In 1994, Lancashire County Council commissioned a series of focus groups involving local people of different backgrounds, ages and incomes, to test out the public's response to the concept of a more sustainable future, in which economic activity is held within environmental limits while quality of life is improved. What emerged was an alarmingly negative picture of both the present and the future.

Reasons to be fearful

'People display a pronounced degree of fatalism and even cynicism towards the country's public institutions, including national and local government,' says the report of the research project *Public Perceptions and Sustainability in Lancashire*. 'This is reflected in an apparently pervasive lack of trust in the goodwill and integrity of national government and in doubts about the ability or willingness of local government to achieve positive improvements in the quality of people's lives (not least because local authorities' powers are seen as diminishing).'

The report goes on: 'People express considerable pessimism about the future, with currently adverse trends expected to worsen in most fields, including the environment. It may be that such concern about the future is in part a surrogate for feelings of insecurity and unease about the present.'

Groups were asked what they thought life would be like in 30 years time. Here are some of the responses:

Working class women
- *'I don't think we look into the future for them [the children] too much.'*
- *'We've too much feeling for them, to look into the future for them because there's nothing good to look at.'*
- *'We don't think about these things, because we've all got grand-children and we'd crack up if we thought about this all the time.'*

Young professional bank manager
- *'I can't see any further than another two years, let alone thirty.'*

Young professionals
- *'Well, everyone will be self-employed.'*
- *'There will be no state pension, no NHS, no schooling . . .'*
- *'It's going that way already isn't it?'*

Retired people
- *All these cars can't keep coming on the road like this. We can't carry on the transport.'*
- *'Cars won't be allowed in town centres in thirty years time.'*
- *'More chaos on the roads.'*

The choking of our roads with traffic, one of the main topics brought up by the Lancashire focus groups, is probably the most obvious and widespread example of the self-defeating aspects of economic growth. The more people gain access to limited or fixed resources, such as roads or beautiful areas of countryside, the worse the experience becomes for everyone. As Fred Hirsch pointed out 20 years ago in *Social Limits to Growth*, even though GDP rises as more new cars are bought and used, quality of life falls as we spend more of it sitting in traffic jams.

Of course, not everybody shares such views about quality of life or what makes life worth living, and it is dangerous to make *too* many assumptions about what people perceive about their lives and the way the world is going. One young man on a Youth Training Scheme vividly illustrated this point during one of the Lancashire focus group sessions. 'Our quality of life,' he said, 'is going out and getting pissed and shagging women.' Nevertheless, it is fair to say that as a nation we are more affluent than ever before and yet unprecedentedly fearful for the future. Why? The answer is three-fold. We worry about the future of our jobs, about our relationships with partner, family, friends, colleagues and about the environment that we live in.

Costing the earth

Our environmental concerns are hardly surprising when you look at the mounting damage inflicted on our natural heritage both nationally and globally. Most of us for example, cannot fail to notice that our local beauty spots are being built over, neglected because of a lack of funds or over-run and damaged by visitors and that there is not as much wildlife as there used to be. And, as childhood asthma rates climb, many of us are beginning to question our love affair with the motor car. In May 1995, an NOP poll found that an astonishing 64 per cent of drivers wanted car use 'actively discouraged'.

The alarm has also been sounded over what we eat after a string of food safety scares. The scare over Mad Cow Disease or BSE is only the latest in a long list which includes salmonella from factory farmed eggs, pesticide-laden vegetables and the presence of tiny amounts of dioxins, a suspected carcinogen, in milk produced from farms located near incinerators. Water, too, is not immune from transmitting real or perceived dangers. There is growing concern, for example, that the presence of oestrogens may be playing a role in the falling sperm counts of British men. Found in common household cleaning products, oestrogens have already been identified as the chemical culprits responsible for changing the sex of fish in rivers.

We are also uneasy about our diet for ethical reasons. We do not like the conditions in which livestock and poultry are kept on intensive, factory farms as the furore over the export of veal calves for slaughter underlined. The message is coming home that British farm animals are paying a high price to allow us to buy cheap goods in supermarkets. While we believe in science and technological progress, and although we may be prepared to eat the genetically-engineered tomatoes already available in our supermarkets, we do harbour doubts, when we make time to stop and think about it, over where the cloning and cross-breeding of foodstuffs is leading us.

These concerns of ours are not just impressionistic, they are rooted in reality. Government statistics show that although river and bathing water quality has improved over the last five years, the most serious environmental problems facing Britain are worsening.

Think global, act local

Many of the world's biggest problems – global warming, ozone depletion, the squandering of natural resources – are products of the demands of industrialised societies. As individuals, the impact of our daily lives on the planet, sometimes known as our 'ecological footprint', is equally devastating. An American citizen's 'footprint' – the amount of food, energy, and other resources that he or she consumes – is about sixteen times as heavy as that of a Third World citizen, while a West European's is five times as heavy.

Already America's intelligence service, the CIA, is identifying environmental issues as major sources of future conflicts. In the developing world, its analysts predict, regional battles will be fought over water and food. It doesn't *have* to be this way.

We are facing a simple, unpalatable truth. If we carry on consuming and polluting as we are, we will increase the damage we are inflicting on our health and quality of life as well as the land we live on. This is not an issue which politicians with short-term agendas want to address, but it is one which every British schoolchild finds familiar. And it is one of the underlying reasons why our perspective on the future is so pessimistic.

It is commonly believed by politicians and the media that, after the flowering of green consumerism, the public no longer cares as much about environmental issues as it appeared to in the late 1980s. The fact that sales of premium-priced organic food have only increased slightly and that most of us still drive cars is interpreted by politicians as evidence that worries about waste and pollution are limited to a small sandal-wearing minority. In fact, nothing could be further from the truth.

A series of Mori polls conducted from 1988–95 reveals that green activism in Britain is not only alive and kicking, but is a growing movement. In 1995, Mori classified 29 per cent of Britons over the age of 15 as 'environmental activists', up from 20 per cent in 1989, the year that news of the destruction of the Amazon rainforest provoked banner headlines.

Since the late 1980s, opinion polls have consistently shown that environmental pollution rates third in people's lists of priority concerns behind unemployment and crime. The strength of this concern is underlined by the size and influence of the green lobby. Not counting the National Trust,

British environmental and conservation groups boast a membership of around four million. The three main political parties, by comparison, muster fewer than a million paid-up supporters between them.

Perhaps the most startling example of the dramatic shift in public values is the number of people who reject consumerism as a way of life. They have been labelled 'post-materialists'. And research by Mori for the World Values Survey suggests that the number of British converts has risen from one in 20 in 1970 to one in five in 1995, with many more leaning towards this new world view.

Mori produced its figures by asking interviewees to list the following issues in order of importance:

- Giving people more say in important government decisions.
- Maintaining order.
- Protecting freedom of speech.
- Fighting rising prices.

The 1995 results found that the post-materialist 19 per cent who chose the first and third as their top two choices heavily outnumbered the materialists (12 per cent) whose top priorities were the traditional ones of keeping order and fighting inflation. The majority held mixed views, 35 per cent leaning towards post-materialist values and 31 per cent holding more to the old order.

What this appears to herald is a significant shift in people's concerns from the economic to the democratic. Post-materialists, according to Mori, are also rejecting consumerist lifestyles by spending less and reining in their credit. A similar picture has been drawn by market researchers Mintel who now classify four in ten Britons as 'ethical consumers'.

What is more, the future appears to belong to this new world view. The World Values Survey, conducted in 39 countries spanning 70 per cent of the global population, reveals a steadily upward trend among post-materialists in industrialised nations. In Europe, their findings suggest that while pensioners across the continent are overwhelmingly wedded to the status quo, the under 45s and especially 15–24-year-olds are swinging towards post-materialist values.

Rebellion in the workplace

This emerging rebellion against the consumer work-spend culture extends beyond the high street and into the workplace. When Mori

Socioconsult questioned the employees of some of Britain's biggest employers in autumn 1995 they were surprised to find that many people were 'deprioritising' work with three in ten planning to devote most of their time and energy in the coming months to 'a better way of life'. Asked whether it was desirable for bosses to encourage employees to stop working for a certain period of time to bring up children or take up responsibilities in their community, a huge majority of 62 per cent said yes. Asked whether it was desirable for our working hours to be cut back after the age of 55 to allow jobs to be offered to the young, opinion was more split with 42 per cent in favour and 43 per cent against.

The findings appear to underline a big shift in attitudes from the workaholism of the 1980s and early 1990s. Although many people still feared for the future of their jobs this very insecurity, the researchers found, was now undermining loyalty to the company rather than strengthening it. Employees, it seems, are showing increasing reluctance to give everything to their work to try to guarantee their job. The report identified people's 'increasing demand for an almost equal balance between work and the rest of their life'. Britons today are more sophisticated in their outlook, Socioconsult concluded, and no longer define themselves almost exclusively by their work.

'If work used to be a main component of most professionals' social identity and status, a lot more roles and interests are now used by individuals to define themselves and position themselves in society. The leisure and hobbies in which you invest time, money and energy, the ethical values and beliefs you display, the lifestyles you enjoy or reject, are all various dimensions that come into the individual's self-definition. Work is no longer the main component, it even becomes a secondary denominator.' Downshifting is a more radical expression of workplace rebellion, of re-ordering our priorities between work and the rest of our lives.

Another form of rebellion, dubbed 'anti-politics' by the London think-tank Demos, is also spreading. One symptom is the rash of protest movements by deeply respectable law-abiding citizens against new roads, veal calf exports and so on. Another is the flourishing at local level of alternative economies and shoestring community enterprises. Yet another is the growing support for environmental politics we referred to earlier at a time when we as citizens are increasingly turned off from mainstream politics and politicians. Millions of individuals are taking up a spectrum of non-Establishment political activities which may, for example, include community work, involvement in a residents' group and fund-raising for Friends of the Earth or Greenpeace. Yet many of these people may well *not* bother to vote at the next election.

Of course, there is nothing new about mass protest or campaign movements. What is different in the 1990s is the depth and vitality of the new anti-Establishment backlash and the influential alliances it is beginning to foster. Roads and animal rights protests have radicalised prosperous middle class nimbys (Not In My Back Yards). Threatened middle managers, their jobs-for-life suddenly pulled from under them, are developing common interests with blue collar workers as they join trade unions in growing numbers. And in local communities, green and social justice activists are moving closer together via grassroots projects such as cash-free bartering or Local Exchange and Trading schemes (LETS). This new alchemy was recognised at a national level in February 1996 when the Real World coalition was born. Unprecedentedly, Friends of the Earth, Save the Children Fund, Church Action on Poverty and 30 more environmental, social justice and development groups signed up to a common political platform. Britain was paying too high a price, they argued, for economic growth and rising consumption. New priorities of alleviating poverty and unemployment, re-building communities and conserving natural resources must be set. Judging by the polls quoted above, a significant number of voters appear to agree with them.

It is not only our deeply-held values and our attitudes to work which are changing. Our views as voters are also in a state of flux. Traditional political allegiances, in place since Labour became a mass party in the 1920s, are eroding as the old left-right divides become less clearcut. As our lifestyles and values become increasingly complicated, so too do our personal politics. Many young people who want sexual tolerance and flexible working patterns, for example, also want low taxes and tough punishment for burglars and rapists. Moreover, many end-of-millennium concerns cross the old political boundaries. The environmental agenda, for example, is traditionally a left-of-centre cause. Yet living an ecologically-aware life also involves thrift and self-sufficiency – traditional Conservative virtues.

Out of touch politicians

All this spells trouble for politicians, as vilified in the 1990s as they were in Hogarth's day. Only 14 per cent of the public trust MPs and ministers to tell the truth, with trade union officials and the police scoring much higher on the veracity scale. Mori polls show that those British institutions Westminster, Whitehall and the law courts are now distrusted by four-fifths of the public. Nor can politicians salvage even the crumb of comfort that this is a passing trend. According to Mori Socioconsult, the 'comprehensive rejection' of national institutions is not confined to malcontents and outsiders, but is 'close to the centre of the socio-cultural map and . . . growing from roots which lie deep in the British psyche'.

Nowhere is this yawning gulf between public and politicians more apparent than when the latter engage in the pursuit of the elusive feel-good factor. To politicians it is now axiomatic that a healthy economy and low taxation is the number one public concern. The Tories were therefore alarmed and baffled that Britain's resurgent post-recession economic performance between 1994 and 1996 did not produce a feel-good boost in the opinion polls. Yet if the politicians listened more to what the public tells them they would realise that this obsession with more of the same is no longer good enough. An increasingly sophisticated and pessimistic electorate is hungry for a bolder politics which offers new hope for an uncertain future.

The smarter MPs who actually listen to their constituents are aware of all this. They know that the political parties need to re-invent themselves fast if they are not to become increasingly marginalised in early twenty-first century Britain.

Yet of the party leaders, only Paddy Ashdown, the least likely one to hold the reins of power in the near future, has acknowledged the depth of the failure of modern party political structures and practice. After a J.B. Priestley-style tour of recession-hit communities in 1993, he concluded candidly that: We in Westminster were speaking a language that only we understand, and doing things that were at best irrelevant to the people we were meant to be serving.' In *Beyond Westminster*, the account of his eye-opening travels, he describes how many communities had come up with ingenious schemes to tackle job losses, but believed their efforts had been hindered rather than helped by national politicians. Ashdown's chastening experience provides a lesson which politicians of all hues would do well to heed. The new world view which more and more of us are turning towards calls for an alternative path forward. This path would require a leap of faith by politicians but is more likely to chime with the public mood than the old mammon worship of economic growth and consumption. Its goals would include a more even distribution of work or training and income levels; the revival of creaking infrastructure and rundown communities via public-private partnerships; more flexible working patterns facilitated by new technology; and a gradual shift in taxation from income to resources. A new environmental system of national accounting, would run alongside GDP. The decline in local government, which is fostering many citizen-led community initiatives, would be reversed.

The new path would capitalise on British inventiveness and computer expertise. It would involve strengthening local democracy and injecting cash into the sleeping giant of the voluntary sector. New employment strategies could include encouraging the over-55s to work part-time in order to allow young people a bigger slice of the jobs market, a move which recent polling data suggests is already supported by half of Britain's working adults. Britain would shed its industrial dinosaur image and become a more sophisticated, forward-looking society.

How might such change be achieved? Probably in one of three ways. By strong national leadership, by a slow build-up of irresistible public pressure or with the help of a natural disaster which forced the politicians' hands. It may take severe water shortages in a warming world, for example, before Whitehall (and Brussels) takes seriously the need to tax natural resources rather than people's labour. Unfortunately, all the signs are that strong national leadership on the necessary scale is unlikely to emerge before the early years of the next century. Pressure from below, meanwhile, will continue to build.

PART TWO

DOWNSHIFTING: A NEW RENAISSANCE

Downshifters Through History And Literature

Jesus	Sister Wendy
Buddha	Robert Blatchford
St Francis of Assisi	Don Quixote
The Quakers	Tom and Barbara Good
Henry Thoreau	John Ruskin
Gandhi	The Amish
William Morris	Mother Teresa
The Wombles	The Waltons
Robin Hood	Aristotle
Robinson Crusoe	Plato
The Horse Whisperer	Winnie-the-Pooh

CHAPTER FIVE

Simple Living Through the Ages

There is no wealth but life.
John Ruskin, British art critic and social critic, 1862

Downshifting may be a 1990s word, but the concept of living a simple, balanced life is one of the oldest known to humanity. We see evidence of it throughout history, across civilisations and religions. Although in the complex, frantic late twentieth century Western world it has perhaps more relevance than ever before, simple living is far from a faddish response to end of millennium fear. Its historical roots run very deep.

The great philosophers of early Greek civilisation, Socrates, Plato and Aristotle, all emphasised the importance of a 'golden mean' through life. This they described as a middle way between wealth and poverty which involved disdaining material possessions in favour of a more spiritual, intellectual life.

People have been bemoaning the pace of urban life and withdrawing into quieter, gentler worlds at least since Roman times, possibly longer. As well as building Britain's first urban cities, the Roman legionaries and administrators who ran the country also built fine villas in the countryside as retreats from the pressures of ruling Britannia.

Life was far more hectic of course at the very heart of the Roman empire. Many authors in ancient Rome wrote about how they recoiled from the noise, the traffic and the crowds. Horace complained of 'that bit of Hell/ Known as big city life'.

The Protestant work ethic, which flourished in northern Europe in the Middle Ages also emphasised simple living virtues. It crossed the Atlantic with the Pilgrim Fathers. The culture of colonised North America in the seventeenth century was strongly influenced by the frugal, spiritual and community-centred ethics of the Puritan and Quaker settlers.

All the world's great religions embrace the simple living ideal. The need to balance the spiritual and the material underpins most of the Bible's teachings: 'Give me neither poverty or wealth,' (*Proverbs* 30:8). In an increasingly atheistic or agnostic West, the message continues to have resonance. In 1973, a coalition of American Christian groups developed the 'Shakertown Pledge' through which believers committed themselves to 'lead a life of creative simplicity, and to share my personal wealth with the world's poor'. The eastern religions, Hinduism, Buddhism and Taoism reflect the same emphasis on spiritual rather than material wealth. 'He who knows he has enough is rich,' says an ancient Taoist saying, while simplicity, balance and frugality are at the heart of the Buddhist way of life.

In Britain

Both the dream and the practice of escaping busy, noisy, polluted towns for the countryside goes back centuries. The yuppies of Medieval England, the rising merchant class, began buying country properties in the twelfth or thirteenth century, often as a way of establishing rural dynasties, based on agriculture. Many failed and were replaced by endless waves of *nouveaux riches*. There was a growing awareness that the countryside was not only a pleasant place to live, but a healthy one, away from the epidemics that would periodically sweep through the towns and cities.

In the wake of the Industrial Revolution that began in the late eighteenth century, towns and cities grew rapidly as thousands of people migrated from the countryside into the urban areas in search of work. The physical conditions in which the ordinary family lived were often appalling.

The Industrial Revolution provoked fears among many intellectuals and social reformers that the great rush to mechanisation would bring wealth to the very few and misery to the masses, spread inequality and injustice and diminish the soul of all mankind. Throughout the nineteenth century the voices raised in alarm at the impact of new production systems and the urban way of life they generated and depended on were as notable as those that greeted the new order as 'progress'.

John Ruskin (1819–1900) was one of the very first to warn that untrammelled industrialisation would prove to be morally and aesthetically harmful. Born in London, he was a man of letters, an outstanding artist and art critic and an influential thinker, whose writings inspired Gandhi and the British socialist movement. He harked back to the Middle Ages as a Utopia and his romantic attachment to an age long gone expressed itself in much of his writing: 'When men are rightly occupied, their amusement grows out of their work as the colour-petals out of a fruitful flower – when they are faithfully helpful and compassionate, all their emotions become steady, deep, perpetual and vivifying to the soul as the natural pulse of the body. But now having no true business, we pour our whole masculine energy into the false business of money-making,' he wrote in *Of King's Treasures*, a lecture published in 1865.

William Morris (1834–96) was another whose 'passion for the past' was matched by his reaction against the values of the industrialising present. He wrote a romance called *A Dream of John Ball* (1888), in which the narrator abandons the 'hurried and discontented humanity' of Morris's times for the slower, smaller scale, more humane fourteenth century England. His *News from Nowhere* (1891) conjured up a future pastoral England where the machinery worked itself, freeing men and women to work on what they enjoyed doing and at their own pace.

One of the Victorian thinkers who best harnessed ideas about ecological sustainability with healthy living and community values was Robert Blatchford (1851–1943). In his book, *Merrie England*, he wrote that England had to make a choice between the quality of men's lives and the quantity of production. His abhorrence of the factory system was uncompromising: 'It's evil in its origin, its progress, in its methods, in its motives, and in its effects. No nation can be sound whose motive power is greed.' More than a million copies of Blatchford's tome were sold within a few years of publication.

The people's revolt: the rise of the garden cities and the plotlanders

Doubts about the direction of capitalism and materialism continued unabated between World Wars I and II. The economist John Maynard Keynes (1883–1944) warned that the pursuit of money as an end in itself was the moral problem of the age. In *Essays in Persuasion*, 1932, he wrote: 'The love of money as a possession . . . will be recognised for what it is, a somewhat disgusting morbidity, one of those semi-criminal, semi-pathological propensities which one hands over with a shudder to the specialist in mental disease.'

It was all very well for middle class intellectuals to analyse the ills of the world. But how were ordinary people, and their champions, responding to the spread of urban sprawl and its impact on well-being and spiritual health? The social reformer and visionary of the early twentieth century, Ebenezer Howard (1850–1928), embarked on one of the most ambitious experiments in town planning by trying to blend aspects of the country into new urban areas. He pioneered the concept of the Garden City, an urban environment that encorporates large areas of green space, tree-lined streets and pleasant vistas. The Hertfordshire villages of Letchworth and Welwyn were the first to be expanded into garden cities using Howard's blueprints.

But some communities did not wait to be organised in such a 'top-down' fashion. The little Sussex town of Peacehaven, later dubbed 'the garden city by the sea', was envisaged in the early 1900s as a holiday resort. In fact it became a frontier settlement for working people from city and urban areas in search of a quieter, healthier place to live. In a bungalow and a little green plot, that one could buy for as little as £25, lay paradise.

In their book *Arcadia for All*, Denis Hardy and Colin Ward chart the social history of Peacehaven and the quest of thousands of working class people who become known to local authorities as 'plotlanders'. They were mainly poor Londoners in search of fresh air, peace and a sea view. Over the first half of the twentieth century, they abandoned the urban sprawl to find their own patch of paradise along the coast line of south-east England. Old railway carriages, army surplus huts from World War I, trams and garden sheds were given a new lease of life to form makeshift landscapes. The trouble was that this early and ramshackle form of ribbon development tended to horrify their neighbours living in more conventional dwellings, and ruined what had hitherto been *their* Arcadia.

So Peacehaven came to symbolise both the passionate desire of ordinary workers and their families for a simpler, cleaner life, and the horror of the better-off at the blots on the coastal landscape created by these ramshackle, makeshift Arcadian dreams.

Looking at just a few historical snapshots makes one thing clear. People from all walks of life, even those on the lowest incomes, have managed to find ways to satisfy their yearning for a simpler existence. In particular, the plotlanders' odyssey is mirrored today in the leisure habits of millions of ordinary Britons who flee the towns and cities whenever they can.

The plotlanders may have had their idyllic shanty towns shattered by the bulldozer, the town planner and the middle class preservation societies, but their aspirations, their values and their dreams live on.

How small became beautiful

The level of 'green consciousness' aroused in Victorian Britain by Morris and Ruskin, but popularised by Blatchford's *Merrie England* was not matched until about 75 years later. It was E.F. Schumacher's resonant and much-discussed attack on the economic structures of the Western world, *Small Is Beautiful* (1973) that helped to revive modern popular concern about the environmental and human price of technological and industrial progress.

He depicted this 'progress' as a kind of Frankenstein's monster, out of control, lacking any moral framework, all-powerful yet increasingly remote from basic human needs. We had become enslaved by the logic of materialism, he argued, not liberated by it. But what was far worse than this social malaise was the reckless depletion of natural resources and the environmental pollution caused not only by large corporations in pursuit of profit, but by implication ourselves – their customers.

Schumacher concluded that the only release from this self-induced slavery could come from establishing systems of smaller working units, with local accountability, and using local labour and resources. He cited a report commissioned in 1972 by the Secretary of State for the Environment which explored the profound moral choices facing humanity on an industrialised planet. It acknowledged the need to bring pollution under control, and to steer the human population and its consumption of resources towards a sustainable equilibrium. The report warned: 'Unless this is done, sooner or later – and some believe there is little time left – the downfall of civilisation will not be a matter of science fiction. It will be the experience of our children and grandchildren.' (From: *Pollution: Nuisance or Nemesis*, HMSO, 1972.)

Flower-power and 'The Good Life'

'Tune in, turn on and drop out,' the late Timothy Leary exhorted us all, and indeed millions did to a greater or lesser extent in the West through the 1960s and 1970s. They grew their hair long, and ambled around in purple loons and psychedelic tie-dye T-shirts. Fuelled by flower-power, and high on all sorts of chemical, romantic and intellectual stimulants, many found the perfect focus for their rebellious energies in America's military involvement in Vietnam. They earnestly told the world to *'Make love, not war.'* As slogans go, it wasn't a bad one.

Dropping out, or opting out, was a defining feature of the 1970s, but Vietnam was not the only focus for the cultural revolt against the direction taken since World War II by consumerist capitalism. Increasingly, opting out became associated with the modern back-to-the-land movement, pioneered by environmentalists such as John Seymour, whose self-sufficiency manuals became bibles for thousands who wanted not so much to stop the world and get off, but rather to slow it down and do their bit to make it a healthier place.

Its philosophy filtered through into mainstream popular culture. It was the theme of BBC Television's *The Good Life*, one of the funniest and most successful comedy series of that decade. Its heroes, Tom and Barbara Good, were no hippies. But their attempts to create Arcadia in suburbia, self-sufficiency through smallholding, certainly made them early, albeit fictional, radical downshifters.

The Good household's homespun Green romanticism and 'downward mobility' was a constant source of embarrassment and irritation for their snobbish, social-climbing, acquisitive neighbours Jerry and Margot.

The series captured not only superb social comedy but also a sense of unease. The back-to-the-land suburbanites were eccentric, but not as absurd as the well-heeled Jerry and Margot, forever keeping up with consumer ambitions. What if the Goods were right to be looking for another path to follow? What if, fundamentally, the joke was on those who saw them as hopeless idealists whose outlook would always be marginal?

The Goods are a caricature, but an endearing and enduring image also of a search for a more balanced life. That search has been renewed 20 years on as another generation becomes all too aware of the downside of the consumer dream. The search has become a quest not necessarily for the 'good life' of a hippy Arcadia but rather for more *balance* between work and leisure, and for consumption that fulfils *needs* rather than generating endless new *wants*.

CHAPTER SIX

Downshifting in the Risk Society

Our life is frittered away by detail . . . Simplify, simplify.
Henry Thoreau, *Walden or Life in the Woods*, 1854

Millions play the National Lottery every week in Britain. It tempts us to buy lottery tickets with the slogan 'It could be you!' against a backdrop of a big hand, its index finger pointing, stretched across a star-studded night sky. The fickle finger of fate might favour you this week. Just buy a ticket and see if it does! It could also serve as the motto of the Risk Society.

Most Western countries have become 'Risk Societies', where the state is devolving more responsibility for security down to individual citizens and increasingly becomes a regulator of services rather than a provider. At the same time, rapid technological change has made us feel more disconnected from the natural world.

This rather apocalyptic analysis of the fragility of life in advanced consumer cultures has been outlined by Ulrich Beck, Professor of Sociology at Munich University and the principal theorist of the Risk Society. The essential point here is not necessarily that the *actual* level of risk that we face individually and collectively has increased. What Beck is emphasising is the growing number and intensity of *perceived* risks.

The era of instant global communications has meant that we are better informed about what is happening around the world than at any time in history. If television is our mirror on to the world, the images it reflects can be distorted by the medium's inevitable focus on extremes, conflicts and novelty: natural and man-made disasters, terrorism, violent crime, so-called 'breakthrough' discoveries in science, medicine and biotechnology. Where once we saw and spoke of a Natural Order, we now see unnatural disorder, dysfunction and events spinning out of control. Not just our control, but anyone's.

The Henley Centre for Forecasting, London, a leading strategic research and consultancy organisation, has explored the developments in the British economy that lend weight to the Risk Society theory of change. It has taken the first look at downshifting as a symptom of the Risk Society and as a reaction against it, in favour of a 'kinder gentler' alternative model of modern life which it calls the 'Mosaic Society'. The Centre has kindly agreed to make its research available for this book. It looked at these two alternative models for future Western economies for its analysis of social and economic trends *Planning for Social Change* 'PSC', an annual service for corporate subscribers. The Centre's analysts do not rule out the continuing success of the Risk Society model of enterprise and individualism that has dominated UK and US social and economic structures over the past two decades, and which remains hugely influential in the developing world and former Eastern Bloc countries. But it does contend that consumers and citizens are becoming more aware of the downside, more thoughtful about the moral and social costs in comparison to the economic benefits in other words, more inclined to embrace the Mosaic Society.

The Henley Centre's report suggests: 'It could be you who wins the lottery, writes a bestseller, gets rich with a business idea, makes it to the boardroom, acquires the trappings of success. In theory, anyone can succeed given hard work, some good luck and the right business skills. Moreover, self-development and "personal growth" are the positive side of individualism; anyone can "re-invent" themselves. We have never been less constrained in lifestyle by where we come from and how old we are.

'However, we are also aware of the other side of the coin as never before. *It could be you* who is made redundant, sees the house repossessed, gets divorced because of the long hours you work, sees a favourite landscape blighted by a new road, struggles to pay school fees and old age care costs, as public provision becomes less attractive, or wonders: "Is this all worth it?" as you sit in a ten-mile tailback on the motorway *en route* to a crisis meeting at your firm about low-cost competition. So the Risk Society accentuates the divide between winners and losers, and it is the individual customer – not the citizen or the worker – who is able to exercise most power.'

Mosaic and Risk Societies

Risk	Mosaic
Consumerism	Post-materialism
Shareholder value	Stakeholder value
Volatile income	Citizen's income
2-car household	2-bike household
Superstores	Corner shops
Personal computing	Network computing
Go for it	Get a life
Working harder	Working smarter
Economic growth	Sustainable development
Self-reliance	Mutuality
Workaholism	Search for balance
GDP	ISEW

Source: Henley Centre for Forecasting

The simpler solution

Growing numbers of people are resolving the dilemmas of today, quietly but quite radically. They are downshifting. The 1990s version of an age-old human desire to live a healthy, balanced life, in today's work-obsessed climate downshifting has come to the fore as a form of workplace rebellion.

People are already doing it in their thousands – by choosing to switch to less stressful jobs, work part-time or from home, or negotiate new working arrangements with current bosses. They see downshifting as an answer to the problems of stress, overwork and relationship breakdown which, as we have seen, plague so many of our lives. They see it as a way of regaining control, of finding a better balance between work on the one hand and home, family, friends and leisure time on the other.

The beauty of adopting downshifting as a way of life is that it is a fairly elastic notion, capable of adaptation to a variety of needs depending on an individual's circumstances and level of enthusiasm. It is possible to be a part-time downshifter, for example, or a serial downshifter 'between intensive periods of work' as well as a full-time practitioner.

Downshifting has become a media obsession in late-1990s Britain as the trend begins to take hold. In the US, downshifting and its forerunner 'voluntary simplicity' have been big news for a decade. Indeed, like so many other lifestyle trends, it has come to Britain as a transatlantic export. So what has been the American experience? What does it reveal about what may be in store for us?

The new American dream

In the US, the word downshifting is already common parlance. Between one in 20 and one in four Americans are believed to have opted for a simpler, more balanced lifestyle in the past ten years or so. The trend is aired and analysed in a variety of media forms from mass entertainment to specialist newspapers. Several best-selling downshifting guidebooks and literally dozens of simple living newsletters with titles such as *The Penny Pincher* and *The Tightwad Gazette*, cater to converts. Oprah Winfrey regularly features downshifting gurus on her television show. And the movement has even been the subject of adverse commentary in the *Wall Street Journal*, which in 1995 solemnly warned that the frugal behaviour of downshifters could potentially undermine the great American economy.

In the US business world, people are talking of the 'exit strategies' deployed by those stressed-out workers who are preparing to downshift, or are in an early phase of the process. Employers are looking on with growing concern as huge numbers of talented and successful professionals, many of them in secure jobs, are seeking their own personal exit from the rat race. According to Inferential Focus, a respected New York trends analysis company, 'the desire to take flight from current employment predicaments has become pandemic'. Daniel Yankelovich, a leading public opinion analyst, has also thrown his hat firmly into the ring. 'It's going to be *the* political issue of the future,' he told *Esquire* magazine in the spring of 1996.

The term downshifting was first coined in 1994 by Gerald Celente, director of the Trends Research Institute based in Rheinbeck, New York. Two years later Celente, who correctly predicted the 1987 Stock Market crash and the demise of the Soviet Union, estimates that 5 per cent of Americans are living a simpler life and that 15 per cent are likely to do so by the end of the century. He refers to the trend, rhapsodically, as 'a new Renaissance philosophy' which resonates right across the modern world. 'Western societies right now are very miserable places,' he says. 'People are very empty and they are looking for much deeper passions in life than those provided through material accumulation or through vicarious association with status symbols and people who represent them. Voluntary simplicity is very much a bottom-up movement. The politicians just don't get it, they will be the last to get it.'

America, of course, has had a strong simple living tradition from the days when the Puritans first landed in the New World. Its thread is traceable through the frugal-living Quakers to the nineteenth century Transcendentalists Henry Thoreau and Ralph Waldo Emerson who preached that a simple lifestyle could bring people closer to both Nature and God. Today it lives on, in most extreme form, in the plain, self-reliant lifestyles of the Amish communities of Pennsylvania, who spurn even the motor car.

But the peculiar circumstances of the late 1980s and early 1990s are driving unprecedented numbers out of the traditional workplace and making simple living converts out of millions. Many, of course, have been involuntarily downshifted by losing their jobs. More than three million workers employed by America's top 500 companies lost their jobs between 1980 and 1990 alone. But the embattled worker is also fighting back. Surveys show that up to half of adult Americans are now prepared to sacrifice some of their earnings and possessions in return for more time with family and friends and to themselves. Many young and middle-aged employees, over-worked and chronically insecure, are choosing to jump before being pushed. Home-working and part-time employment is booming, as is the number of professionals hedging their bets by offering consultancy services to several employers at once.

James Portwood, Professor of Human Resource Administration at Temple University, Philadelphia, has coined his own term for the droves of downshifting professionals. 'I call them MUMPS, Mature Under-Motivated Professionals,' he says. 'Most of these people would say they have done it by choice. But I don't think they would have done it *unless* the world of work had changed so substantially. Work used to be partly entertainment and to have a tremendous social value for people. It used to be like going down to the club to meet friends. Now it's more like being in a war. You don't want to get too close to somebody in the office because tomorrow they might be dead. The world of work has shifted so far in favour of the "hire 'em, fire 'em" style of employer that the risks to many workers of staying with a company have soared while the benefits have plummeted.'

His analysis is shared by many American economists and political commentators. Professor Juliet Schor, a Harvard University economist and author of the best-selling book *The Overworked American* believes slaving away at work in pursuit of more money and possessions has become a social disease. 'It is not surprising that downshifting has taken root in America because America was the first consumerist nation and, along with Japan, remains the foremost consumerist society today,' she says. Schor's own polling research suggests that one in four Americans made the decision between 1990 and 1995 to earn less to achieve a more balanced life. And it is a trend, she believes, which will take hold across Western consumer nations – and particularly in Britain.

To a large extent, Britain is subject to the same lifestyle trends as the US, says Schor. First, downshifting is beginning among highly-educated middle-class people who are over-worked and over-stressed. Second, Britain has experienced growing stress levels among people still in jobs after large-scale redundancies in their workplace. Third, Britain's inability to continue to compete with the world's biggest economic powers is producing a society receptive to a more simplistic lifestyle for large numbers of people.

Downshifting here and now

What meaning does downshifting hold in 1990s Britain? Are we turning to it for the same reasons as in America? Ian Christie, an associate director at the Henley Centre for forecasting, defines it as follows: 'It's taking a deliberate decision to opt out of the culture of consumerism and the career rat race. It's about cutting back on purchasing, reducing working hours, and perhaps bailing out of conventional work in search of greater quality of life and control over one's work.'

Professor Ray Pahl, one of Britain's foremost sociologists, has been studying our work practices, our attitudes to work and its role in our lives for the last three decades. He sums up the key elements of downshifting in these terms: 'Conventionally, it is a conscious attempt to live life at a quieter pace in order to spend more time away from employment. On the one hand, it is a response to greedy and thoughtless institutions, and on the other a pull to a more attractive activity than simply maintaining one's identity at the world of work.'

Moving house to cut mortgage payments or buying a home outright, perhaps in an area where house prices are lower, often goes hand in hand with downshifting, but not necessarily. You don't have to escape to the countryside to escape the treadmill of full-time conventional careers. Some people downshift serially, pulling out of the rat race in the summer maybe to pursue a sport or to travel, and then working hard the rest of the year.

Although the phrases *downshifting* and *voluntary simplicity* are sometimes used interchangeably and may share some common elements, the two phenomena are quite distinct. Voluntary simplicity is longer-established and rooted firmly in the environmental movement. Its advocates are likely to be avowedly anti-consumerist, and to practice self-sufficiency in as many areas of life as possible. Many of its practitioners never joined the rat race or aspired to the material trappings that so often go with it – but have always lived the simple life. Downshifting is a more recent and much more mainstream phenomenon, an expression of the gathering revolt against the 'long hours' culture and aggressive corporatism of the 1980s, and the relentless waves of redundancies that followed.

Pahl contends that modern society's obsession with work, and our culture of working excessively long hours is something of a historical accident: 'Historically, most people have *always* realised that employment is the least interesting thing they do. It's what they do to get money. The Industrial Revolution changed the way we thought about work, turning it into employment. It became more central – unless you happened to be a woman. It was made illegal for Mr and *Mrs* Smith to run a business together. The establishment of joint stock companies in the early eighteenth century excluded women.

'So downshifting now has three elements. It can mean men becoming more and more like women in terms of having employment as just one form of work that they do. It could mean a geographical notion, moving away from the city to the country, or it could mean consciously taking a lower-paid position.' Pahl believes that downshifting is a real and potentially important contemporary British phenomenon.

People often confuse downshifting with *downsizing*, which is easily done as the two phenomena can be two sides of the same coin. Downsizing, however, is what employers do when sales, workloads and orders for goods or services are too low to justify the current staff numbers. It is a euphemism for making people redundant, often involving a wholesale clear-out of staff at all levels of the organisation.

Doing and dreaming: how the media woke up to downshifting

The British public were introduced to the concept of downshifting in the mid-1990s. At least that was when newspapers noticed the phenomenon and began to run articles about it and interviews with people who were doing it. 'Go Forth and Simplify' was the heading on a *Sunday Times* article in the summer of 1995. But it was a debate staged at Oxford University on 15 February 1996 that fully ignited press interest. Duane Elgin, the leading American exponent of voluntary simplicity was one of the principal speakers. During the debate, he predicted that the American reaction against its work-obsessed, earn-and-spend culture was about to be repeated in Britain.

The media were intrigued by the idea of a distinct and growing band of people who no longer sought to 'have it all', and who claimed to gain more from spending less. Many more feature articles followed. Meanwhile, continental Europe was also getting to grips with this interesting new phenomenon. In the French media particularly, enthusiasm for what will almost inevitably become known before long as '*le downshifting*' was becoming noticeable. The main feature of the popular Paris-based news magazine *L'Express* on 27 June was 'Changer de Vie' (Change Your Life), with a front page picture of a sunlit desert island, its empty beaches fringed with palm trees, under an azure sky.

Popular modern literature is also reflecting the urge to downshift. One best-selling example is *The Horse Whisperer*, a book about the family traumas of a New York magazine editor who abandons her high-powered job for the Rocky Mountains.

The real evidence for the downshifting trend

There was a major omission in all the media mania about downshifting through 1996. Hard facts about the prevalence of downshifting practice and aspirations were rather thin on the ground. Undoubtedly, the issue had struck a chord among stressed-out journalists, hardly a representative sample of the British population.

Nonetheless, they exploited the anecdotal evidence to the full. What was missing from the debate and coverage of it in the newspapers was any real proof of the spread of downshifting in the UK, and attitudes towards the values underpinning it. The Henley Centre for Forecasting can now fill that gap.

In a survey of 2000 adults, the Centre found that 6 per cent of those in work said that they had voluntarily taken steps to reduce their income in the previous two years, and 6 per cent reported that they planned to do so over the following year. So if we add those percentages together, one sees that 12 per cent of those in work – in other words, about one in eight – said that they had either taken one of the crucial steps associated with downshifting or were at least thinking of doing so.

Much higher proportions reported that they were cutting back on spending, despite evidence of an economic upturn, and were anxiously seeking more balance in their lives. In the following chapters, we look at exactly who are the downshifters both here and in America, and what they might mean for Britain's social and economic future.

CHAPTER SEVEN

The New American Dreamers

Stop the Nineties, I want to get off.
Faith Popcorn, American trendcaster, 1991

The exact scale of downshifting in the US remains unclear. But it is almost certainly there to stay. A growing mass of polling data provides an unequivocal picture of deep nationwide discontent with stressful, money-driven lifestyles. What's more, it appears that many US citizens, perhaps a majority, are prepared to try to rein back their spending in pursuit of a more balanced, meaningful life.

So what about those who have gone ahead and made the change? What kind of jobs did they leave behind? What kind of people are they?

In 1991 Faith Popcorn, a leading American corporate market researcher, predicted that Cashing Out – her phrase for downshifting – would be one of the top ten lifestyle trends of the 1990s and beyond. The likeliest converts, she predicted, would be mainly high-achievers and big-earners, desperate to slow their racing heartbeats and swap twentieth floor glass cages for a desk at home or a new job in the country. 'It's not about copping out, or dropping out or selling out,' she wrote. 'It's cashing in the career chips you've stacked up all these years and going somewhere else to work at something you want to do, the way you want to do it.' Five years on, her predictions appear to come close to the mark.

The simple living pioneers

Probably the most comprehensive picture to date of the 1990s simple living movement in America was provided by a 1995 survey commissioned by the Maryland-based Merck Family Fund, and overseen by

50

Professor Juliet Schor. Of the 800 people interviewed by telephone, 28 per cent said they had consciously made changes in their lives – other than normal retirement – which meant making less money. A third of these were in their thirties and they included more women (32 per cent) than men (23.5 per cent). The most common changes were cutting work hours, taking a lower-paid job, or giving up work to stay at home.

The survey suggests that Americans are reacting in their tens of millions to the peculiar stresses of the 1990s. The typical American downshifter identified by the poll is well-educated and both younger and more likely to have children than the general population. In the Merck focus groups, downshifters described their new lifestyles in glowing terms:

- '*I left a job making three times the money I'm making now; but by the same token, I've got more time with my family, less stress. I've just had a little boy, I want to watch him grow up.*' Indianapolis man.
- '*It's been a sacrifice . . . our pay was cut in half . . . but I think it's the best choice because you're with your children and they're in a loving environment.*' Dallas woman who left her job.
- '*As I started climbing the corporate ladder, I really decided that I was hating it more and more and I was bringing more and more work home . . . I was already hiring people to clean my clothes, watch my kid and clean my house. I changed careers and got paid less. I sold the car and bought a '65 Falcon – and I'm much happier. I'm working two blocks from home and doing something I really enjoy.*' Los Angeles woman.

An overwhelming 81 per cent of the downshifters interviewed said they now led happier lives. But there were some sacrifices involved. Fifty-one per cent admitted to missing the extra money they had given up and a further 9 per cent were unhappy with their new circumstances.

Professor Schor herself confirms that downshifters such as those her survey identified are no 'drop-outs' in the ordinary sense of the word. More often than not, she says, they are high-achieving, high salaried professionals such as doctors, lawyers, teachers and administrators. 'What is so interesting is that this is a very mainstream trend. It isn't just about people who are dropping out of society. It often involves highly-skilled people who still want very much to contribute, but from outside the rat race.'

The US Government has not yet analysed the stampede to simpler lifestyles and there are no official statistics breaking down those involved by gender, age and class. What does emerge clearly from information such as the Merck survey and from personal testimonies in simple living newsletters and mainstream media articles is that American downshifters:

- come from all classes and ages although the most popular age groups are the thirties and forties
- are more likely to be women than men, but only by 6–4 margin
- tend to be highly educated and liberal in their politics. Teachers, doctors, lawyers and administrators are all prime candidates
- come from all income brackets. The Merck research revealed down-shifters right across the income spectrum, from $100,000 a year to $10,000
- tend in their previous life to have worked long hours and suffered high stress levels
- tend to continue working, although often supplement or substitute paid employment with voluntary or community activities
- tend to have strong support networks. Community halls, churches, cafes and living rooms are providing the setting for thousands of voluntary simplicity study and self-help groups
- live across the USA. The Pacific Northwest, especially Seattle, probably boasts the highest concentration. But every state has its converts. Alaska and, surprisingly, Washington DC, seat of the US government, come out top of one national mailing list of 25,000 downshifters

Drawing a new road map

People closely involved with the American simple living movement have differing theories about what is motivating 1990s converts and whether the majority will stick with simpler lifestyles or find it impossible not to jump back on to the treadmill.

For Professor Schor it all boils down to time versus money. Most downshifters, she argues, are economic refugees who may want to upshift in the future given half a chance. Her views are shared by the American establishment which hopes and believes that downshifting will prove to be a transient phenomenon, easily snuffed out by economic upturn. Other trendsetters and watchers believe motivations for choosing a simpler life run much deeper, often because it has proved true for themselves.

In Seattle, which has evolved into the epicentre of the national downshifters' network, you will find many adherents of the latter view. Foremost among them are Joe Dominguez and Vicki Robin whose personal finance bestseller *Your Money or Your Life* is credited with transforming the lives of tens of thousands of grateful fellow citizens. They now run the New Road Map Foundation, a resource centre for downshifters and environmentalists, with a 25,000-strong supporters list, through which they tap into the movement's zeitgeist.

They regularly broadcast their message on America's prime-time TV and radio chatshows and agree with Juliet Schor that downshifters come from all backgrounds and income groups. They disagree, however, that most are temporary rat race refugees who will jump back on the treadmill when the opportunity arises. They point out that many people on low incomes or middle class couples who have overstretched themselves have used their book purely to get themselves out of debt, but then find themselves becoming simple living converts. 'They start out without any plans for a simpler lifestyle as such but then they get hooked,' says Vicki. 'They love it, they feel liberated from the maw of materialism and they never go back.'

Still in Seattle, former college administrator Cecile Andrews, another downshifter-turned-guru, has as much first-hand knowledge of what makes people turn to simple living as any other living American. Highly educated, with a doctorate from Stanford University, she followed a traditional teaching career path before ditching her job in 1993, aged 51. She now spends her time running simplicity workshops and study circles, where small groups of people discuss practical ways to make their lives simpler, then go home and act on it. Since she opened her first group in 1992, 300 have started up in Seattle alone, with another 3,000 flourishing across America using her how-to-do-it booklet as inspiration.

Cecile Andrews' group meetings are based on Swedish models where study circles, she says, 'have a long history of transforming the lives of individuals and the country'. Each involves anywhere between six and 20 people from the same neighbourhood, meeting in each other's homes for a minimum of eight weeks. Some then dissolve, but most take on new converts and keep going. Several of the early Seattle ones have now been running for four years. 'The circles emphasise the practical and the positive,' says Andrews, who exudes a calm confidence. 'I always tell people to focus on the little things they can do to change their lives, not to scare themselves with the big picture. It's an evolutionary approach, you don't just change overnight. Each participant tells personal stories of how they are progressing with simplifying their lives and each week, before they go home, everybody talks about one practical change they are going to make that week. Then the next week they talk about how it went. Everybody encourages everybody else.'

In her personal experience, a remarkable 95–98 per cent of down-shifters have college degrees and a majority are aged 35 to 55. They are also widely read, more than averagely concerned about the environment, generally liberal in their politics and are what she calls 'high and middle achievers' – doctors, lawyers, teachers, junior administrators and clerks, downsized company managers, and so on. These people, she says, are so busy working they are achingly lonely and they worry deeply about community break-up and growing inequality in American society.

'The people who come to the workshops are people who have had a certain philosophy all their lives. They have been supposed to be getting ahead, having a good career and making money and all that is supposed to have made them happy, but it hasn't. It is once they've been through all that that people start to make changes. It's a mind-changing movement.' In her booklet she describes how many attendees come gradually to reject mass consumerism. 'A lot of people discover they never liked shopping or consuming much anyway. It was like being hypnotised, following the directions of some evil genie. We're like kids in a candy store, eating everything we can until not only does nothing taste good, but we get sick and begin a search for something more nourishing.'

Are downshifters opting out of mainstream society? Yes and no, she says. 'These are high-achieving people who want to live their lives fully and make a difference, but they also want to simplify their lives and maybe grow their own vegetables and so on.' She adds the important point that many downshifters, by pursuing portfolio lifestyles, are actually more secure financially than many mainstream workers. 'I have all these friends who used to have traditional careers and are now earning a living from two or three jobs. They may work part-time in a traditional job and then help run a newsletter and maybe make some extra money from a hobby like knitting or weaving and these people are actually much more secure than those in permanent, full-time jobs.'

Voluntary simplicity: a way of life

Whatever the majority's motives, a small sub-set of American down-shifters are driven first and foremost by ecological concerns. Adherents of voluntary simplicity in its purest sense, they choose to spend and consume less in order to conserve the Earth's natural resources. For them, living frugally is not the means to an end, but the end itself.

The slightly unwieldy term 'voluntary simplicity' was coined in 1936 by Richard Gregg, a British disciple of Mahatma Gandhi. He defined it as 'singleness of purpose, sincerity and honesty within, as well as avoidance of exterior clutter, of many possessions irrelevant to the chief purpose of life'. Duane Elgin's seminal book *Voluntary Simplicity* expands the concept further. 'The objective is not dogmatically to live with less,' he writes, 'but is a more demanding intention of living with balance in order to find a life of greater purpose, fulfilment and satisfaction.'

America's voluntary simplicity disciples take Elgin's words at face value. They are community-minded green consumers who earn just enough to meet their needs. According to Elgin, they tend to be very self-reliant – teaching themselves basic carpentry and plumbing skills and so on. They also tend to work with only a small number of other people, to eat a mainly vegetarian diet, to have few clothes and possessions, to recycle religiously and to be political consumers – boycotting companies they believe are unethical. Many are also highly spiritual, although not necessarily religious. In 1977 Elgin conducted a national survey of simplicity adherents to which 620 people responded. Of these, 88 per cent were involved in 'inner growth' activities, with meditation top of the list.

Elgin, a former business consultant who, in the early 1970s sat on an influential US Presidential-Congressional Commission on the American Future, is no woolly-headed idealist. For the past few years, his fluent, enthusiastic lectures on voluntary simplicity have been igniting meetings across the country. 'Voluntary simplicity: I call it downshifting out of the rat race and upshifting into the human race,' he laughs.

Elgin is anxious to lay to rest several 'myths' about the voluntary simplicity movement, which he believes now embraces several million people. Firstly, it is categorically *not* another 'back to the land' movement like that of the late 1960s and early 1970s, but is 'about making the most of wherever you are'. Secondly it does not mean living in poverty. And thirdly it is not a movement which has great ideals but will inevitably run out of steam for lack of skilled leadership because, he argues, there are many talented people among its ranks.

It's here to stay

Academics and trendwatchers disagree over how many downshifters fit into the voluntary simplicity category. At present it is clearly a small minority. Many people who practise it say they feel like isolated islands amid the huge sea of American consumerism. Yet as Vicki Robin and Cecile Andrews point out, many Americans driven to downshift by rat race pressures are finding they also enjoy simpler, green living for its own sake. America's rediscovery of its simple living roots is beginning to foster a new ecological awareness in the world's most profligate nation.

Of those tens of millions of Americans who fit the downshifting category, some will have lived the simple life for decades; many others will have been forced into it by losing their jobs; more still have been encouraged to join in as the snowball effect takes hold, encouraged by the vast array of inspirational DIY books on offer. Nearly every American family now has a story of someone they know who has moved from city to town or town to country, who has cut back their hours or switched to a less stressful job. City couples are starting again running bed and breakfast businesses in the country. Successful lawyers are learning to farm. Tens of thousands of professionals, especially women, are setting up as home-based consultants. All are jumping on to a rolling bandwagon. Quite where this new American odyssey will lead is uncertain, but one thing's for sure. Coca-Cola and McDonald's, Bloomingdales and Macy's should all be looking nervously over their shoulders.

CHAPTER EIGHT

The British Way of Downshifting

We headed the procession when it took what we see now to be the wrong turning, down into the deep bog of greedy industrialism, where money and machines are of more importance than men and women. It is for us to find the way out again, into the sunlight.
J.B. Priestley, *English Journey*, 1934

Many people in Britain yearn for a simpler life, indeed they spend years wishing their lives were radically different. Fewer in Britain than America have actually taken the plunge so far, but the potential for many more to follow suit and jump off the treadmill is huge. Thousands of people opt out of conventional career paths at some point in their lives to earn their living in a more satisfying way. Two-thirds of craftspeople working in Britain used to pursue other careers, for example.

Before 1996, the word 'downshifting' was virtually unknown, and the size of any British movement that was comparable with voluntary simplicity in the United States was unclear. Research carried out in 1996 by the Henley Centre for Forecasting provides the first hard evidence that downshifting *is* a significant, emerging trend. It also reveals that many more people may be preparing to cut down on their spending and consumption in search of a better life.

The survey was undertaken early in 1996 when the recovery from the economic recession of the early 1990s was accelerating fast. One might reasonably assume that consumer spending would follow a similar recovery curve. In fact, the Henley Centre for Forecasting survey showed that most people were still tightening their belts.

Only 16 per cent of the sample said they had not cut back or postponed purchases, and that proportion was even lower for men in full-time employment or self-employment. One-third of the sample overall had not taken a holiday over the previous year, and slightly more were eating fewer meals out at restaurants (43 per cent). One-quarter said they had made fewer trips out, and a similar proportion had cut back on visits to pubs. Interestingly, the proportions reporting cutbacks were even more common among men in full-time employment and among the self-employed. So much for the longevity of the 'economic miracle' proclaimed by Nigel Lawson when he was Margaret Thatcher's Chancellor of the Exchequer in the mid to late 1980s.

So why were so many people cutting back at a time when the feel-good factor was meant to be working its magic? The Henley Centre suggests that the sluggish housing market coupled with job insecurity were major factors. However, the survey replies indicate strongly that some people were making a positive decision to rein in their spending to reduce debt, to build up savings and so increase their sense of control over future uncertainties.

Four in ten would like to work part-time

In order to assess the resonance of the downshifting message, the researchers asked their sample for their attitudes towards jobs, income and lifestyle. They were asked about going part-time, opting to take a lower-paid job to reduce stress and gain more free time, having more time off work instead of pay increases. As many as 42 per cent of those in full-time work said they would choose to work part-time *if* they felt they could afford to do so. One-quarter agreed with the statement: 'I would be willing to take a lower-paid job if it meant less stress and more free time.' Even more (28 per cent), said they would rather have more time off in future than more money.

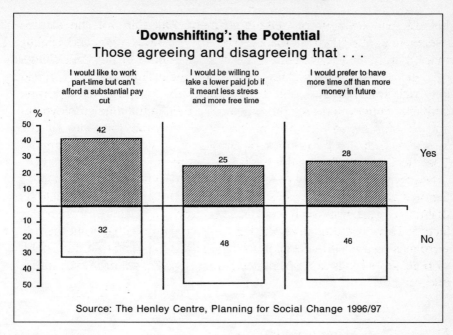

'Downshifting': the Potential
Those agreeing and disagreeing that . . .

Source: The Henley Centre, Planning for Social Change 1996/97

People seemed a little more hesitant when they were asked more specific questions about swapping pay for extra time for themselves or for more job security. Some 17 per cent would accept a 10 per cent pay cut in return for three extra days leave a year and three hours off the working week; 16 per cent would do so in order to work more at home and spend less time commuting; 26 per cent for greater job security.

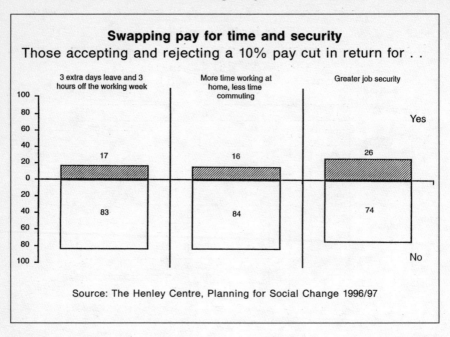

Swapping pay for time and security
Those accepting and rejecting a 10% pay cut in return for . .

Source: The Henley Centre, Planning for Social Change 1996/97

But the potential number prepared to make these kinds of trade-offs appears to be much higher, when a more general and fundamental question is asked: is it all worth it? People were asked whether they agreed or not with the statement: 'Dedicating yourself to your job isn't worth all the sacrifices you have to make.' Some 19 per cent agreed strongly, and a further 31 per cent agreed slightly, so half agreed to some extent with the idea that wholehearted devotion to paid work was not worth all the accompanying sacrifices. The proportions were even higher for those with children under five years. Only 19 per cent did not agree with the statement. The finding is very much in tune with Mori's estimate that one in five people consider themselves 'post-materialists' – people who think there is more to life than making money and who aspire to a better *quality* of life.

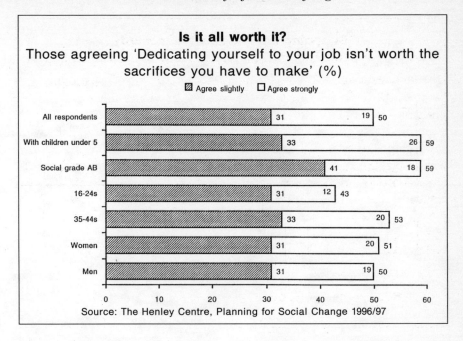

Is it all worth it?

Those agreeing 'Dedicating yourself to your job isn't worth the sacrifices you have to make' (%)

🔲 Agree slightly   ☐ Agree strongly

All respondents	31	19	50
With children under 5	33	26	59
Social grade AB	41	18	59
16-24s	31	12	43
35-44s	33	20	53
Women	31	20	51
Men	31	19	50

Source: The Henley Centre, Planning for Social Change 1996/97

Again when people were asked about the relationship between earning money and the quality of life, they were very much in two minds. Most people (55 per cent) agreed with the notion that they needed 'more money from work to keep up the quality of my life', although 18 per cent disagreed. But when asked whether they endorsed the statement: 'Earning more money does not increase the quality of my life', the proportions agreeing and disagreeing were exactly the same (40 per cent). The proportion agreeing rose a few points beyond that level in the highest earning AB socio-economic group and among people with pre-school children.

Essex man gives way to ethics man

We conclude from this research that the single-minded pursuit of a job and of material success is troubling large numbers of people in Britain. They feel the long hours work culture is eating up their lives, leaving them precious little time or energy for family or leisure. Many Britons feel that success at work and in the earnings league tables has been won at too high a cost to their private lives. They cannot be shrugged off as marginal concerns. Clearly, these kinds of doubts about the way work dominates so many of our lives and puts our health and well-being at such risk, are penetrating the hearts and minds of mainstream modern Britain.

The Henley Centre's research tends to confirm a common trend to emerge anecdotally – there is a huge *enthusiasm* for downshifting, but people are finding it very hard to actually bite the bullet and put its principles and philosophy into *practice*. Those likely to downshift most easily are those in the highest earning income brackets, particularly with some capital or savings to call upon. That is not to say that young people will always find it more difficult – much depends on their upbringing, their attitudes and their motivation. Indeed, the younger you are the less likely it is that you have got yourself into debt, and saddled yourself with big mortgages in the same way that many older people have.

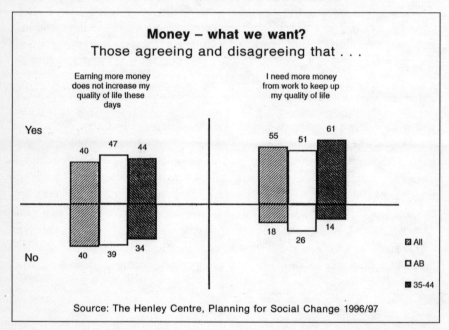

Money – what we want?
Those agreeing and disagreeing that . . .

Source: The Henley Centre, Planning for Social Change 1996/97

So the chances are that if you are still in your twenties and have not accumulated too much material and consumerist baggage, you too could successfully and swiftly downshift without too much angst.

So what clues does the report give us about downshifters in Britain? What kind of people are they likely to be? Many of them will be middle-class people who feel betrayed by the broken promises of the 1980s, or believe the rewards of traditional employment are now too few to justify the increasing effort.

Downshifters will flourish when they can make their own support networks and successfully lobby politicians to make such networks easily accessible, so that they don't feel isolated. 'More people need to become expert in self-help, and in effective time-management if simpler living is to become mainstream,' says Ian Christie. 'Children need to be taught the lessons of 'flow', so they too can find out how to become absorbed creatively in topics and activities that interest them. It should be on the curriculum. If we don't learn the techniques when we are young, it's so much harder, though by no means impossible, later. There are whole areas of downshifting philosophy which reach down to the way we bring up children. The immediate focus should be on providing useful practical guides, more information in the media generally.'

Downshifting is shaping up to be one of the most interesting social trends of the 1990s, the Henley Centre for Forecasting believes. 'The conditions are there today for downshifting to flourish, simply because the stakes have been raised so high in environmental and economic terms,' concludes Ian Christie. 'Probably for the first time in industrial history, we are now at a point where business-as-usual simply doesn't look like an option. I think the conditions are now in place for what might be a reaction against unfettered business-as-usual-industrialisation, that could become a major movement.'

CHAPTER NINE

Real Lives – Downshifters Tell Their Stories

You see things and say: 'Why?'; but I dream things that never were and say: 'Why not?'
George Bernard Shaw (1856–1950)

1: THE POST-MODERN ROMANTICS

Daniel Butler, 32, and Bel Crewe, 31. He was a business magazine journalist, she was a charity fundraiser. They now own and run a 13-acre smallholding on a remote hillside in mid-Wales. They have a two-year-old son, Jack.

From their sixteenth century farmhouse a few miles south of Rhayader, Dan Butler and his partner Bel have the most glorious panoramic views south towards the foothills of the Cambrian mountains, uninterrupted by buildings or roads. It's one of the few places in Britain where the only background sounds come from the birds and the elements. What they see from the windows at the front of the house has barely changed in hundreds of years. Outside the great glens of Scotland, this is the most isolated and under-populated part of Britain.

This is home for two rat race refugees who left London in December 1993 in search of a simpler, more rational and more enjoyable life. They bought the four-bedroom house, high above the Wye valley, along with 13 acres of pasture, woodland, duck-pond, pigsties and stone barns. It set them back £100,000, the same price that Dan got for his two-bedroomed flat in Camden, north London. For him, it was a childhood dream coming true. 'I always wanted to be self-sufficient, and read all the John Seymour books about it when I was growing up,' recalls Dan. The son of eminent Oxford academics David and Marilyn Butler, Dan spent his twenties working as a lobbyist and as a journalist for the Haymarket stable of business magazines, after graduating from Cambridge University in history.

In May 1991, amid a prolonged staff dispute with the management over union recognition, Dan was offered redundancy. He accepted without hesitation. 'It was the best thing I ever did,' he recalls. He met Bel in his late twenties just three days after he left London to stay in a borrowed cottage in Oxfordshire, to raise ferrets, to freelance and to work out what on earth he would do next. Not so long afterwards, Bel became pregnant. Dan decided this was the perfect opportunity to make his dream come true – to yield to the twin temptations of cheap property and romantic visions of rural idylls. In short, to head for the Welsh hills. Bel had yet to be 100 per cent convinced.

A former charity fundraiser with a degree in art history, Bel was in the early stages of pregnancy and feeling pretty awful when they began scouring Wales for a smallholding. Estate agents eyed the couple warily and routinely questioned them about their intentions: 'What are you going to do to make a living? There's not much round here apart from forestry and agriculture, you know.'

What Bel remembers more than anything about this time was the misery of being sick out of the car window as they inspected properties for sale, or bursting into floods of tears at the sheer disappointment of what they encountered at the end of various fruitless searches. 'There was one place we saw in the middle of nowhere. It had no phone, electricity, or kitchen. The nearest shop was ten miles away. Dan thought it was romantic, but it was actually hideous and I cried for an hour. What I'd had in mind was Exmoor or Somerset, or somewhere by the sea.'

Eventually, they rolled up at Tan-y-Cefn. Each of them was seduced by the spectacular views and its sheer peacefulness. They decided their search was over, bought the place and moved in. It rained solidly for the next three months.

Undeterred, they began to make themselves a new life, quite unlike the old one. Bel took charge of fruit and vegetable growing, using whatever books, magazines and newspaper articles came to hand to find out what, where and how to plant. 'I knew nothing. It was all trial and error,' she says. 'I find the vegetable and fruit growing absorbing – especially if it works and they come up.' Now her staple produce includes seven different types of potato. More exotic delicacies such as asparagus, sugar snap peas, mangetout, chillies, melons, and lettuce-leaf basil have also cropped successfully. She grows everything from seed. It's virtually all organic. The experience has changed her outlook, especially as it has meant their son Jack is getting a far more nutritious diet than he would have got in London. 'I've become more aware of environmental and conservation issues through growing our food. It makes you more respectful of what's around you, more thoughtful. It just makes such a difference, knowing exactly where it's come from and and what it contains. It's so much healthier, and that's important to both of us.'

Dan reared two Tamworth pigs, and bought in turkeys, ducks, geese and chickens. The pigs were slaughtered and the bacon eaten over the course of the first two years.

The couple reckon they are about 90 per cent self-sufficient in the summer months, less so during winter even though they freeze what they don't eat fresh from the soil. They don't even have to grow some of their free foods – like wild mushrooms – they just walk up the hill and pick them. But Bel and Dan don't simply exploit the land for themselves. They're careful to improve it and put something back too. 'We have an acre or two of conifers, which we're planning to cut down and replace with some native hardwoods,' says Dan. 'We're laying and planting new hedgerows as well, using hazel, hawthorn, honeysuckle and dog rose which will attract more birds and other wildlife.' The growing areas benefit from huge volumes of home-produced manure – pig dung and grass clippings, mainly.

Neither was earning very much in London. Two years after settling in Wales, their joint income is lower still. But so too are their monthly outgoings, principally on their mortgage, down from a combined £70,000 loan on their respective flats to £50,000. Self-sufficiency for much of the year means they don't need as much money as they did in London. Instead of automatically buying something they need, as they used to do, they will probably have a go at making it. Dan has acquired a cordless drill and has already made an outdoor table, and cold frames for the vegetables. Bel had trouble finding fresh pasta locally, so she makes her own.

As a business and economics journalist, Dan used to spend hours every day on all sorts of activities *associated* with work, but not actually working – like commuting, business lunches, chatting to colleagues by the photocopier. It took up several hours a day, all of them non-productive. Now, he writes articles and books about environmental issues and wildlife. The difference is that he does it when he wants and needs to, not necessarily every day. 'You don't have all the time-consuming distractions from the business of working here, so when I'm working to earn money, that's *precisely* what I'm doing.'

Inside the house, the tools of their transformed lifestyle are the computer and the fax-modem, the most high-tech possessions they own. These gadgets plug them into the outside world, and are the essentials for Dan's writing. For Bel, in particular, the technology is a lifeline to family and friends. 'It only costs a few pence to e-mail people, so I use that more than the phone these days – it's so much cheaper,' says Bel. 'I even persuaded my sister to go on e-mail so we can keep in touch better. It is isolated here. When we first came, I felt like we'd retired. It would be nice to have more people to visit locally.' Like Dan, Bel writes, but for her own satisfaction, not for money. 'I write to get my brain cells moving. I keep three diaries – a gardening one, one for mushrooming and for observing nature and one for everyday stuff. I would love to write stories too. I feel the need to do something else, to have another project, another skill.'

Dan thought he had earned about £25,000 and spent £26,000 during their first year on the smallholding. In fact he was earning £9,000 and spending £10,000. In 1995, his earnings rose to about £15,000. 'For us, the important thing is that our quality of life has risen immeasurably. You cannot put a price on the view across the hills that we have here, being able to see rare birds of prey such as red kites, peregrine falcons and goshawks wheeling around the sky.'

They have been fortunate in having loans and moral support from their parents in the early days to help ends meet. Some friends from their London days have not been so enthusiastic. 'The general reaction was that we must have been barking mad,' recalls Dan. 'My brother has made some very sniffy comments, and there are some friends for whom the life we lead would be hell on earth.' Bel adds: 'My friends in London are extremely reluctant to come out here for a weekend. For most, the journey is too long. At first it was all a bit too wild when people came here and they sometimes sat in embarrassed giggles, shivering. But we're a bit more organised now we've got the guest room painted and decorated.'

There is a downside of course. It's called winter, and in this part of Wales it can stretch to almost half the year round. 'The days are so short, and the weather so bad you can't get out and do very much. We tend to watch a lot of TV,' says Dan. 'We've been snowed in a few times, but I rather liked that. I was rather lonely in London, but here I've been happier than I ever dared to hope. It's been much harder for Bel, she's had quite a tough time.'

Her lowest point came when she developed complications during her labour with Jack. She endured an agonising one-hour ambulance journey from the cottage hospital at Llandrindod Wells to the general hospital at Hereford where she underwent an even more agonising forceps delivery. It took her over a year to recover. She remains philosophical about the experience: 'I could have had just as bad a time had I been living in Muswell Hill. Who knows?'

Their lives are dictated by the seasons, the weather and local culture, now, rather than the clock, as it once was. Dan explains: 'If you go into a local shop here, then chances are you have to wait while the old lady in front of you has her chat with the assistant, and then tries to find the right change to pay. If that happened in London, she'd probably get stabbed or something. Here, it just doesn't matter – it's normal.'

Bel thinks it unlikely that she would ever return to London. But she, more than Dan, often feels isolated and misses seeing people day to day. 'It's only recently that I have felt at home here – I've just been asked, and agreed, to become the secretary of the local children's playgroup charity, which is the height of acceptance! I subscribe to the *Smallholder* magazine, I belong to the Rare Breeds Trust. It would be nice to know more people here, to be able to drop in on more people.

'It really can be awful here in the winter, very wet and dark. I get terribly bored. It gets dark at 4 p.m. and you find yourself watching Oprah Winfrey, because there's nothing else to do. You get a bit stir crazy, and maybe Jack does too. Basically I'm living out someone else's dream here. I was the reluctant partner, coming here. I can imagine moving slightly closer to London perhaps, and living somewhere with a nicer climate. I'd never want to give up the gardening and the growing. Dan would stay here or somewhere like it for ever, whereas I feel more ambiguous about the future. You have to have a lot of energy to do what we have done. I am not sure whether the life we lead is sustainable, indefinately.'

Dan, however, can imagine living somewhere even wilder, where the skies are even wider for indulging his passion of flying his hawks Bob and Gwen. 'I am obsessional about flying hawks. It's what I love doing.' His partner draws the line at the idea of going somewhere even more remote. 'Dan knows that if he goes to Scotland, it's going to be a very lonely drive,' she says, firmly.

Dan's downshifting tip

'If you are thinking of moving somewhere isolated and doing self-sufficiency to a greater or lesser degree, get to know your neighbours before you buy a property, however far away they are. You can save yourself a lot of trouble that way by establishing where are the local rights of way, finding out the history of planning applications that might affect you. Our neighbours want to open a caravan park next to us, but we're hoping it won't happen.'

Bel's downshifting tip

'Sometimes it's better to throw yourself in at the deep end, when you're considering a drastic change of lifestyle. If you think about it too much, you might not do it. The complications might seem much bigger than they really are. If in doubt just ask around, talk to people, and there's a lot you can pick up from magazines and the local paper.'

2: THE YUPPIE CONVERT

Paul Bellack, 41, gave up his job as a property dealer two years ago. He now devotes his time to self-development courses and voluntary work and is training as a counsellor.

When Paul Bellack, a high-flying property dealer and archetypal yuppie, walked into his boss's office at Sun Life of Canada, in December 1994, and said he wanted to quit, the reaction was predictable. 'He completely flipped,' he recalls 18 months later with a boyish grin. 'He sent me straight off to see the head of personnel and told him to persuade me to stay, they even offered me a four-month sabbatical. But they could have waved half a million pounds at me and I wouldn't have budged – I wanted a new life, outside the rat race.'

When Paul left Sun Life's London office, the insurance company had just taken over a major rival, Confederation Life, and he had been asked to run the combined property portfolios, worth £800 million. After 19 years working his way up the organisation through loyalty and hard work, he was being offered a major promotion at a time when many of his colleagues were losing their jobs. Had he stayed, his staff would have doubled in size and his annual salary risen from £65,000 to £95,000. Instead, he chose to walk out without a penny. 'A lot of colleagues thought I was just going through a hippy phase and would snap out of it and come back after a few months,' he says, ensconced in an elegant pink chair in his small mews house in West London's exclusive Holland Park. 'How wrong they were!'

After spending several months touring India and New Zealand with a backpack, Paul has settled down to a life of self-development and voluntary work, plus the occasional property consultancy. Over the past few years, he and a business partner have also bought and rented out several properties, which nets Paul about £50,000 a year.

Most of his days are now spent training as a counsellor, attending yoga, photography and practical philosophy classes, and meditating. As a volunteer with the British Trust for Conservation Volunteers he has also learned the art of planting trees in nearby Holland Park. His former high maintenance lifestyle has vanished with his job. He has sold his car and now cycles everywhere. After years of dining in expensive, fashionable restaurants he has discovered the joys of cooking and now rarely eats out. His one-bedroom house, in a quiet backwater, is beautifully decorated, but minimalist and he has given away many of his expensive clothes. Recycling, down to the last envelope, has become 'a real passion'. 'If I went back into my office now and saw all the waste – of money and paper and everything, I would be horrified. The important things in my life now are consuming as little as possible, helping other people and self-development,' he says, with no trace of irony.

As his new life develops, Paul hopes to devote more of his skills and time to help causes he believes in. Already, he is scouting for suitable new properties for the Out of This World chain of co-operative supermarkets. And he is also helping friends to develop a financial framework for a job-creating, fair trade project in Mali, West Africa, which would export tree products to Britain. 'I don't want a full-time job, I want to do lots of different things,' he explains. 'If I pursue the counselling course, for example, I can see myself counselling for maybe ten hours a week and really enjoying it – but not taking it up as a new career. At the moment I am looking around at what's available, sticking my toe in the water and seeing what grabs me!'

So what has brought about this extraordinary change from archetypal Eighties yuppie to dedicated downshifter? 'I spent nineteen years with

Sun Life,' he says, 'working my way up from a twenty-year-old general dogsbody to commercial and property investments fund manager. I would buy and sell properties worth £20–30 million a year. I was never stressed by the work, I loved it, but I felt I was not working to my optimum. I always felt there was a gap in my life – a spiritual or life growth gap – but for years I pushed it to one side.'

Two events, he says, finally brought this dissatisfaction to the fore. In May 1994, Sun Life sent him on a week-long leadership course run by industrial psychologists on the outskirts of Niagara Falls, Canada. 'I spent five days looking inwards, away from the pressures of work, and I loved it. It gave me space to think about what I really wanted to do.' At the end of the course he was asked to write down five personal or business goals which he thought were achievable within the next year and was told the list would be sent back to him in six months time. Top of the list was 'to make up my mind, once and for all, about my future with Sun Life'.

Back in England, he forgot about the course as the work routine took over, until a friend persuaded him to enrol on a yoga course on the Greek island of Skyros. 'I did yoga, movement into dance, body healing and writing courses and loved them all. It was a real spiritual awakening for me, and it made me realise there was a lot more to life than the company,' he recalls.

Paul returned to work deeply unsettled and a few months later received the list of priorities he had written for himself in Canada. It provided the final spur and he decided that morning to leave the company. 'It really gave me a feeling of power, to make such a major decision about my life and show that I was in charge of my own destiny at a time when other people were being laid off all around me because of the merger. If I had been made redundant instead and given a £150,000 payoff, I think I would have been a completely different person today.'

The reaction from friends and colleagues to his dramatic change of course has been mixed. His former partner at Sun Life was deeply shocked when Paul chose to leave the company, but has come to terms with his decision over time, and they remain friends. Paul's Austrian-born father, a former senior manager at the Smith & Nephew pharmaceuticals company, and his British mother, who live in Sussex, have also, to his surprise and delight, been very supportive. 'My parents were very proud of my career at Sun Life, so I was worried about telling them I was going to leave, especially my father who has always been a great believer in hard work. But they have been very positive about it, and when they see me they always comment on how much more relaxed and happy I am.'

His girlfriend, a New Zealander whom he met during his last few months at Sun Life, is also very happy with his new lifestyle. But among friends and former colleagues, the reaction is mixed. 'Some people still think I'll outgrow my "hippy phase" and go back,' he says. 'Others are desperate for me to go back because it threatens their own idea of themselves and their pursuit of career. But a lot of people admire what I have done and are envious of what I have the time to do.'

Although Paul's current annual income is still more than three times the national average, he does not believe his affluence contradicts his new, downshifted lifestyle. 'I do definitely count myself as a downshifter – although I don't like the word, it's too negative – because my energies are going in different directions to before,' he says earnestly. 'I know I was in a privileged position when I made my decision because I don't have a wife and family to support, and my business is still bringing me a good income. But I *have* given up a lot of things – my car, holidays in five-star hotels and so on, and I can imagine myself going much further down this path. I can see myself ending up on a small farm somewhere, living a very simple life. I could go out and earn a lot of money, maybe half a million pounds for a year's work, but I'm not interested.'

He does, he confesses, miss the 'comradeship and buzz' of the fast-track world he inhabited for so long, but describes the loss as 'insignificant compared to the enormous benefits. Downshifting, he believes, is now 'a real subtle trend' among an increasingly insecure and disenchanted yuppie class. And what of his own future? 'At the moment I don't see myself back in the rat race, ever. I have a whole fresh lease of life. I feel happier and have more energy than ever before and I'm confident I'm on the right path.'

Paul's downshifting tip
'I would absolutely recommend it, although it is much easier for those without families. But people should think carefully first – and take it step by step.'

3: THE ACTIVE CITIZENS

John and June Berry, 57 and 54, live in Birmingham with two of their four children. He gave up his senior management job in information technology to bring up their young daughter while June began a career late in life as a community worker.

John Berry sits in his blooming, perfectly-tended summer garden in an inner-city Birmingham suburb talking passionately about the 'greed-driven' corporate culture gripping Britain. Every half an hour or so, he goes to check on his nine-year-old daughter Christine, who has a throat infection. John has done most of the child-rearing since she was four and is obviously expert at it. He also knows a good deal about the corporate culture he now reviles, having spent a distinguished 27-year career at Boots, culminating in a £70,000 post as retail information technology manager.

'Traditionally in companies there were always issues like customer care and business ethics which many employees believed in,' he says. 'But in the late Eighties there was a clear move in industry, which Boots typified, towards decision-making which was far less concerned about people and far more interested in profit and personal reward for those at the top. For me, it became a much less satisfying environment to live in.'

John had always stood out among his fellow managers at Boots' headquarters in Nottingham. When his four children were young, he always left the office first to get home before their bedtime, and was the only one to acknowledge his Labour Party membership among his peers. But in the late 1980s, dismayed at the company's direction, he began to think seriously of leaving his job.

The final spur, however, came in early 1991 when his wife June was offered a job by the Methodist church as a community development worker in a largely Muslim area of Birmingham. June had spent 25 years mainly as a housewife, although, since the mid 1980s she had taught English for a few hours a week to Asian adults at a Nottingham further education college, and at adult evening classes at local schools. The new job offered much wider horizons, finding out how the Church could support the local community and how to build bridges with the mosques: 'When the children got older I had wanted to do something more fulfilling and worthwhile, but it was quite difficult to pitch myself into a full-time job because John's was so all-consuming,' she recalls. 'I was really quite unhappy for a few years, so when this job came along I really wanted it although it was poorly-paid and away from Nottingham.'

Christine was then four, and it would have been out of the question for June to take the job with John in full-time employment. So he took the plunge and told his employers he wanted to leave. 'They were horrified,' he recalls. 'My managing director persuaded me to work part-time and I did that for a while, travelling quite often to Nottingham. But before long my dissatisfactions with the company and increasing commitment to the family took over and I said "No." I retired in December 1992.'

Today, ironically, he is as busy as ever. But most of his work now is voluntary and unpaid. As part of her job, June now chairs a community business, Apna Style (Apna translates as 'our own' in Urdu) which manufactures traditional Muslim schoolwear for Birmingham pupils. Demand is high, and the project has the enthusiastic backing of Birmingham council's Labour leader and its director of education.

John has gradually become as involved as his wife in Apna Style and now does the company's accounts, marketing and administration. He is also chairman of the Out of This World organic, co-operative foodstores, based in Newcastle, Nottingham and Bristol; serves on the board of Traidcraft, Britain's leading fair trade company; and is vice-president of the board of EAN International, an international standards body which allocates product barcodes worldwide. But this time he is giving his expertise for free.

The Berrys still live in a five-bedroomed house, to accommodate their large family, but their income has dropped dramatically to around £30,000 a year. This is based mainly on his pension and her salary. They now have less expensive holidays and eat out less, but both are adamant that they have not radically changed their lifestyle. 'Although John was earning a huge salary at Boots we didn't have the lifestyle associated with it,' says June. 'I've never been a person who needed a lot of material things, in fact having so much money was almost an embarrassment to me.'

The Berrys still have a share in a cottage in Snowdonia where they escape for weekend breaks. And they are anxious to point out that they have not 'downshifted' in the sense of working less hard or depriving themselves of previous luxuries. Rather they are living an equally busy but more community-based life. 'Downshifting in terms of saying, "look, there is a different, less selfish way of life we can all pursue," is definitely what we are all about,' says John.

Both parents say they are happier, but admit that their children, Mark, 26, Neil, 24, Christine and Ruth, a 21-year-old adopted daughter, all had serious problems adjusting to the move. 'Leaving Nottingham was a very negative experience for the children, especially as none of us really likes Birmingham,' June confesses. 'I've benefited because I am doing something really fulfilling, but none of them have really made friends here.'

On the other hand, his children were very supportive of John's reasons for leaving Boots at the height of his career. 'Ideologically, all of us were right behind mum and dad,' says Mark, who is studying for a science masters degree. 'The salary shift was obviously quite dramatic, but we had always lived quite a simple life. When I was studying for "A" levels, there were eight of us in the class and six of them had their own cars. It was rather strange for me because I knew my dad's salary was higher than their fathers', but I thought it was obscene that they had cars at that age.'

In fact, when it came to the crunch, it was John himself who found it hard to give up the security of a big salary and a lucrative pension at 65. His company pension was geared to retiring at 60, and to retire before 55 meant losing a lot of money. 'Making the change was much harder for me than I thought it would be,' he says. 'I found the decision to leave Boots, and potentially not earn any income for the rest of my life quite difficult.'

Working part-time and phasing himself out of Boots helped to ease the change. But both John and June believe they are now too involved in work and community activities and haven't yet got the balance of their new life right. 'June says I keep doing all these things because I miss the buzz of the business world, but I don't think that's true,' he protests with a smile. 'It's more that I want to be useful and work with organisations I believe in – and I find it difficult to say no!'

June, who was working a 50-hour week, has now gone 'part-time', working around 35 hours a week with Mondays off. 'I realised what was happening one suppertime, when Christine shouted at us to stop talking about work the whole time.'

John and June's downshifting tip
'The big changes in life are not finely based on calculation but are acts of faith.'

4: THE LIBERATED MANDARIN

Petra Laidlaw dedicated her life to a 'fast-track' career in the Civil Service, in classic textbook style. She ran the private offices of three Cabinet ministers. Several other postings took her to the heart of national policy-making. At the age of 45 and earning £60,000 a year, she had gone far and looked as though she would go further, but opted to take voluntary redundancy.

It took Petra Laidlaw only a short while to conceive and plan an early exit from a high-powered career in the Civil Service, but a full decade to implement it. As far as most colleagues were concerned, here was an independent and capable career woman who had the talent and the application to make it pretty well to the top of her profession, and make a success of it until she retired. They were right. She had those qualities in abundance, and indeed rose to the ranks of senior management, still an uncommon achievement for women in the Civil Service. But by her mid-thirties, Petra was questioning whether she really wanted to give up all the best years of her life to hard graft, however exciting and rewarding. 'I thought about the fifteen years I had already done, and then reflected that I still had another twenty-five years to go. It seemed an awful lot. It occurred to me that I could get to the age of sixty and not have done anything else with my life.'

She resolved privately to set herself a new goal and drew up a strategy to achieve it: to save and invest enough money to leave work at 50 and to start exploring the rich potential of life beyond the office. Her goal was simple enough, but one which few consider achievable, if they consider the idea at all – namely to secure for herself a life of leisure while still young and healthy enough to enjoy it.

'I always enjoyed my work right up to the end,' recalls Petra. 'It was fascinating work. I always got a buzz from sorting out political crises, or achieving impossible tasks against impossible deadlines!' For most of her career she was working 60 to 70 hours a week, and by the end was running a division of over 70 staff. 'I don't think I would have been regarded as particularly workaholic. The Civil Service I joined was notorious for its long hours culture, and for many years I was happy enough to go along with it. But, probably around the time I was deciding not to work past fifty, I saw the light about working smarter instead of harder, and tried hard to keep my own hours and those of people working for me within reasonable bounds. I was no longer prepared to take work home with me or work at weekends. I tried to do my bit about spreading the word that long hours are bad for everyone's health – including the organisation's – and that shorter hours are a sign of efficiency and virtue.

'But even then I had precious little time to myself. All my weekends were spent doing the weekly shopping, seeing to domestic correspondence and trying to keep up with my closest friends. Even then it was hard to see them more than once or twice a year. Once I had done all that, there was no time to relax and do anything else I wanted to do.'

So, she sat down to work out the minimum sum of money she needed to save if she was going to be able to live on the income from it. 'For a minimum income of say £10,000 a year, I needed to save up a capital sum of £200,000. I reckoned that if I set aside a fair part of my salary every month and invested it in a way that would produce growth, I could build up that sort of sum over ten to fifteen years. So I made that my target and stuck to it. And saving a high part of my salary made me used to living all along on a lower income than the salary suggests – a good preparation for when I stopped work.'

Petra did all this with very little advice from others. 'I spoke once or twice to financial advisers, but in the end did my own financial planning. I prefer to make my own mistakes rather than have others making them for me. It's also cheaper. You can pay out an awful lot to all the intermediaries wanting to take a cut along the line.' And she kept the plan away from her managers at work: 'It would have been very unwise to reveal anything other than 100 per cent commitment.'

So how was it that such an eminently bright, capable and independent woman decided to cut short at her prime such a fascinating career at the heart of British politics and government with plenty of money and status?

Well, to understand that you need to know a little more about her personality and about the changing culture of Britain's Civil Service. Petra graduated from Reading University in the early 1970s in Italian and Linguistics. Her first job was teaching at a special school for severely mentally handicapped children. She decided to do a Post-Graduate Certificate in Education, part-time at the South Bank Polytechnic, London. After a year, she and her fellow students were told that their qualification would not, after all, be recognised by the Department of Education. 'So, I thought, to hell with this, I'll do something else, and if I can't beat them I'll join them.'

She applied for the 'fast-stream' of the Civil Service training, got accepted and 'drifted in'. Petra felt at ease with her new colleagues, the surprising informality of the Whitehall environment and its co-operative ethos. 'I would never have wanted to work in an environment where backstabbing for personal advancement was the rule. People do not generally tend to go into the Civil Service for personal glory – there is little to be had. The pleasure comes from contributing something, however anonymously, to our national life and doing the job honestly and well. At the Department of Education and Science (now called the Department for Education and Employment) in her early career, she helped to develop policy on bullying and truancy and worked on a major survey of the nation's school building stock.

Later on, she was closely involved in the original thinking on the radical school reforms of the late 1980s and early 1990s, the development of the national curriculum and the creation of OFSTED. She was private secretary to Norman St John Stevas (now Lord St John of Fawsley), when he was Leader of the House of Commons. More recently, she was Principal Private Secretary to John Patten when he was Education Secretary, and to Gillian Shepherd when she succeeded him.

Petra looks back wistfully at the job she had in the mid to late 1970s, dealing with medium to long-term expenditure plans. 'With the discovery of North Sea oil, all the talk was about educating people for all the leisure we would be enjoying by the 1990s. It seems hopelessly naive now. But at the time, everyone was envisaging that with our new-found national wealth and computers to take away all the drudgery, we would all be working something like a thirty hour week, and enjoying an egalitarian affluence. What happened to the dream? The competitive side of human nature stepped in. Those with jobs ended up working longer and longer hours, and enjoying a generous slice of the growth in national income. But while we worked forty, fifty, and sixty hours, others could get no work at all – and missed out accordingly on the growth in national wealth.

'Perhaps one of the failings of the 1970s was the belief that somehow, with a bit of central planning and a bit of good luck, the bounty that was coming to us would be spread evenly. One of the positive things to come out of the Thatcher years was the gradual recognition that these things could never come to everyone on a plate. Unless those of us in work actively decided to do less – fewer hours over a whole career span or full hours over a shorter career span – there would never be a chance of everyone getting as much work as they wanted and taking their share of the growing affluence. The dream was only ever going to come about, if all of us individually were prepared to put something into it, and perhaps make some sacrifices to give others a chance.

Although she likes to think that by opting for redundancy at 45 she opened up opportunities for other people, Petra would be the last to say she was acting altruistically. When the offer came, she was still some way off her target of £200,000 by age 50, but the redundancy money would make it up. She calculated that she could square the circle financially, and went for it. 'I was just lucky that my circumstances fitted. I was not bringing up children and my mortgage was much lower than someone who had bought their house later on would have been.' A lot of people she worked with wanted to take redundancy, but it was not so easy for those who had not made financial plans well in advance.

Petra will never forget the day she left Whitehall for the last time: 'It was a glorious sunny day. I walked home and my soul was singing. For several days afterwards I just walked around London – a city I am probably unusual in loving. Everything looked so good, buildings that I had not seen, old details that I had never noticed, old alleyways into little gardens I did not know existed. I just went where my feet took me – no maps – all round the East End, the West End, north London and Docklands. I just wanted to go where my fancy took me. It was a metaphor for what was happening in my life. The sense of freedom was phenomenal.'

Her family had mixed reactions. 'My mother, inevitably, was anxious about my security, but a sister who is quite a bit older than me and is dying to give up work was very envious. Friends, especially those who did not know me so well wondered what had come over me, but I think they all saw that it was right for me once it had sunk in.' So what is her new life like? What does she do with her new-found freedom? Well, she is researching her own family's history, trawling through piles of letters, postcards and other documents, and turning up some exotic ancestors. She will write it all up, though probably just for her family not for publication.

She does occasional consultancy jobs, puts several hours a week into financial management and planning; swims twice a week at the local municipal pool, walks virtually everywhere without rushing; enjoys seeing her friends, and spending much more time with her partner John and her cat Melvin.

Petra lives modestly, but comfortably. She paid her mortgage off out of her redundancy money and reckons that simply not going to work is saving her thousands of pounds a year. 'I used to spend well over £100 a month on home-to-work transport, and another £100 on my cleaning lady, who was anyway due to return to Sweden when I gave up work. On top of that I must have spent something like £500 a year on clothes for work and several hundred on entertainment at work for my staff, the occasional business lunch, and so on.'

In addition, she finds that being able to do things in her own time comes cheaper. 'Instead of madly stocking up on everything in sight when I go to the supermarket, I just buy what I need when I need it. Going to the theatre, the cinema or the gym at the times they call off-peak – which is when I want to go anyway – is much cheaper. And I don't feel the same need to splash out and crash out on exotic holiday destinations. All in all I need much less money now than when I was working.'

For some people, the career or the full-time job will always be so absorbing and stimulating that it is an end in itself. For others, like Petra, it may start off that way and then become simply a means to an end. Petra Laidlaw's story illuminates several truths about our attitudes to paid work, the huge and sometimes excessive sacrifices the work culture extracts from us, and about the imbalance work has wrought upon our lives. In particular, it helps to nail one popular canard: namely that women are keener than men to opt out of the rat race simply because they want to spend more quality time with their children. Petra has no children. She has struck out simply so as to get more out of life. She had no particular project or alternative career in mind when she left her job. 'Certainly, I was taking a great leap in the dark, but for me that feeling, that very uncertainty was one of the attractions, part of the great pleasure of it all.'

Petra's downshifting tip

'Know yourself! And know the environment you work in. If you don't see yourself working there until you are sixty or more, plan ahead. Saving anything at all when you first start work and your income is low may seem impossible. But just reflect: anyone putting away a couple of hundred pounds a month in growth investments from when you start work ought to be able to retire in their mid-forties. Work smart, think smart and you'll be in command of your own destiny.'

5: THE WOODLANDER

Bill Robinson, 48, was a British Telecom manager, and is now charcoal burner and conservationist. He lives with his wife, a childminder, and their two teenage children just outside his native Truro in Cornwall.

Beneath the billowing green canopies of oak trees in Idless Wood, a mile or two north of Truro, Cornwall, lies a hidden world of foxes and badgers, wrens and chiff-chaffs. Go walking in these ancient woods on a dry day and you might spot wisps of pungent smoke drifting up from a clearing off the main track, near an Iron Age hillfort. When it's wet, you're more likely to hear the whirring of a chainsaw and the muffled thud of logs encrusted with moss and lichen being hurled into a trailer. For as well as being a haven for wildlife and country walkers, this woodland is also Bill Robinson's workshop.

Bill joined British Telecom straight from school as an engineer and over three decades worked his way up the organisation. He ended up running the company's business line installation and maintenance operation for Cornwall. Privatisation in the 1980s had triggered wave after wave of cost-cutting, streamlining and job-shedding, as BT faced growing competition in a global market. So by the time Bill was at the peak of his managerial responsibility, in charge of about 30 employees across the county, the pressure on him to perform was relentless.

'I enjoyed it all, but by the end it had become a rat race,' he recalls over breakfast at his home one wet May morning. 'Budgets were being reduced, but all the time you were expected to make improvements.' Bill had to travel a great deal for business meetings to Plymouth, Exeter and Bristol. This was fine while BT put him up overnight in a comfortable hotel, with a good dinner and a drink with his colleagues at the end of a hard day. But these perks were cut and soon he was having to travel to these meetings and back in a day. 'I was getting up at 6 a.m., and driving up to two hundred miles on a day trip. I was getting home later and later, after the children had gone to bed, so it wasn't good for family life.' In the late 1980s, he was asked to train to be a customer care tutor. He had to go away on courses more and more. 'I enjoyed it, but it was taking me away from my basic job, which caused a bit of friction.'

One day in 1994, with another round of job losses in the offing, Bill's senior manager took him aside on one of his regular trips to Plymouth and asked: 'Bill have you thought about redundancy?' He had. BT's redundancy packages had become more attractive with every round. At the same time, Bill's enthusiasm for the corporate life was waning fast, and he yearned for a new and less stressful life. He began to wonder whether the woodland on his doorstep which he had loved to roam from childhood might provide him with a more interesting source of income.

'I was listening to an item about charcoal burning on the BBC's early morning farming programme and thought maybe I could try that. I found a charcoal burner called Mark Ventham near Plymouth and he showed me how to make charcoal. I bought my first kiln from him.

'I had always had a good rapport with the Forestry Commission, which owns this wood so I went to see Ben Jones, the local beat forester. I told him about what I had in mind. He said: "Well, I've got some trees on the old Iron Age fort site that need some sympathetic thinning." That was it. I decided I would leave BT.'

Within a few days, Bill was the proud owner of 3,000 standing oak, birch, beech, hazel and holly. He swapped his briefcase for a chainsaw, and spent two days soaking wet from the rain learning how to use it. A grant of £1,400 from the Devon and Cornwall Training and Enterprise Council helped pay for courses and new machinery. He paid over £400 to the Forestry Commission for the right to cut down the selected trees on the neglected, overgrown ancient site. He kept the timber he had felled to turn into logs for firewood and charcoal, in his kiln set up a few hundred yards away from the fort site.

The proprietor of the newly-formed Cornish Coppice Company struck his first deal at Mallet's hardware store in Truro. It was selling imported charcoal. Bill went in one day and persuaded the owner to take a bag of his. 'When I went back the following week the bag had sold and he asked me for more. Luckily my first summer's trading coincided with some wonderful weather, which meant that people were having plenty of barbecues. I sold virtually everything I made.'

Now in his late 40s, Bill loves his new life. He has cleared the overgrown woods growing on the Iron Age site. Now the sunlight can penetrate, there's an abundance of new life amongst the remaining younger trees: rowan and birch saplings have appeared as have honeysuckle and bilberry, wrens, jays and butterflies. Now he is thinning out another site at Idless and thinking of getting a second kiln. 'At BT, I was just another manager whereas now people are much more interested in me and what I'm doing.' He was earning £28,000 a year when he left BT, and working 50 to 60 hours a week. 'I probably work as hard, and I'm not earning so much money as before. Kay and I still have to take out dollops of redundancy money to live on every few weeks. But the difference is I'm enjoying my work, it's closer to home and it fits better into family life.'

When he burns charcoal, for example, the process takes 24–30 hours. For safety reasons, Bill has to watch over it the whole time. 'I have to stick a tent up, the family brings a meal up to me and it's actually quite pleasant all sitting round the kiln. If I was at home, I'd probably be sat in front of the TV.

'What I like is the flexibility. If I don't have a customer to supply that day, I can go off walking. I've got more time for the community – I'm a school governor and I'm on the parish council.' But how has the switch affected his family? Do they enjoy having a woodland entrepreneur amongst them, where once they had a besuited manager? 'My daughter Rachel, who's nineteen, is an outdoor type, very practical and has always been interested and supportive. She hasn't got regular work at the moment so she's helping me with the logs and charcoal. In fact, we're thinking of doing a course together on weedkiller spraying.'

His son Chester, 15, is more sceptical about what his father has done. 'He was the least happy about the situation, because he regards money and status as very important. He'd like us to go abroad for holidays, instead of staying in this country on the rare occasion when we actually take a holiday. Chester liked me as a manager. I say to him: "Look I'm the managing director of a company," and he says, rather cuttingly: "Yes, and you're the only employee."'

But Bill's wife, Kay, is pleased with the way life has turned out. Perhaps it helped that she switched jobs at the same time as he. She gave up working as a school lunches superviser, and became a registered childminder. Over lunch at their modest, cosy home, on the edge of the wood, she said: 'I did have some doubts at the start. If he hadn't got something lined up when he left BT I don't think it would have worked out so well.'

For the Robinsons, opting for a simpler lifestyle wasn't the financial gamble it has been for some. They don't have a mortgage, for instance. Perhaps because they have always been careful with money, they are hard pushed to think of material sacrifices they have had to make. Bill says: 'We don't go to the pub so much these days, and we've cancelled a daily paper. I find I don't need to spend like I used to – on lunches out with colleagues, for instance. I don't need so many new clothes – I wear my old suit trousers up in the woods!'

What about the downside? 'I miss the company of my colleagues at BT and talking over the kind of everyday work decisions that I now have to make on my own. But overall I'm happier now.'

Bill's downshifting tip
'Make sure you have something to do after you leave your current job, and enough money to live on. Don't take on too many things at the start. Lastly, don't get blinkered. Keep your mind open to change, be flexible. You may enjoy your new work, but who knows? Something else might crop up in a couple of years that might suit you better, and you might like more. It hasn't happened to me yet – but I don't rule it out.'

6: FREEDOM IN FREELANCING

Denise Moll, 57, set up a secretarial business from home when she was made redundant after spending most of her adult life in conventional employment.

Denise Moll lives alone, has no television set, rarely eats out and buys all her clothes from charity shops. She survives on around £6,000 a year. Yet this is far from a hard luck story. Her life, she insists, has never been better.

Since taking redundancy four years ago from the Ockenden Venture, a refugee charity based in Woking, Denise has worked from her small but cosy one-bedroom flat in the Surrey village of West Byfleet. She now spends much of the daytime walking with neighbours along nearby Basingstoke canal, practising yoga and meditation or doing unpaid voluntary work. In the evenings, she types book manuscripts for clients or works in her capacity as membership secretary for several voluntary groups, including the Lifestyle Movement which advocates simple, non-consumerist ways of living.

'All my life I worked for other people,' she says with feeling, explaining her decision to go freelance. 'Yes, I have had some anxious moments wondering how ends are going to meet, but they have somehow, and I am so much happier and have so much more time for myself and other people.'

After graduating from secretarial college in the 1950s, Denise worked in London for an advertising agency, a firm of architects and a PR company before moving to the United States in 1961. There she worked for several years as an administrator for an Episcopal church, developing a strong interest in charitable work. Back in England, she again moved from job to job before being appointed personal secretary to the Secretary of the Church Commissioners in the late Seventies. From there, she moved to the Ockenden Venture in 1981.

Originally employed by the charity as personal assistant to Joyce Pearce, its founder and driving force, Denise found herself run off her feet by her energetic and inspirational boss. She was also housed by the charity, often sharing a home with refugee children. At one stage, she spent 18 months running a household of four teenage Vietnamese and Polish refugees. Although she loved her job, it was very involving and sometimes highly stressful. 'I did literally whatever had to be done, and it often changed from day to day. It was almost my entire life.'

In 1985, however, Denise's world was turned upside-down by Ms Pearce's death. The charity, shaken by its founder's loss, went through several turbulent years and heavy job losses. Denise hung on, spending a few years administering various projects and finding UK sponsors for refugee children in Macau.

But by late 1992 it became apparent that there was no real job left for her. 'One of the directors who was friendly towards me took me aside and said they needed to make me redundant,' she recalls. 'I said fine. I had been there twelve years and enjoyed it, but a lot of people had lost their jobs and it was an enormous relief to leave in the end. I left in November with £1,600 – enough to buy a computer and a fax!'

Two months later, aged 54, Denise was happily ensconced in a new flat, working from home. What had persuaded her to take such a leap in the dark? 'Well, I was always quite dissatisfied at work, particularly in later years, but I didn't really know why. Then I went to stay with a friend on the Isle of Wight who is a self-employed carer of elderly people, shortly before I left the Ockenden Venture, and she was obviously so much more relaxed than me, spending lots of time walking her dog and so on, that I suddenly thought, why don't I do it?'

Denise is emphatic that she herself has not fallen into semi-retirement. In fact, she says, she will probably work till she is older now than she would have in more conventional employment: 'During my [former] working life, I often resented the time spent on the job. I always had other needs, spiritual needs you could call them, which weren't fulfilled. But I was quite surprised that I felt so happy and so free when I was alone, and working for myself. I find it quite hard to think of work these days, I just think of life.'

Denise had much less money to begin with than many downshifters. At the Ockenden Venture she earned £6,500 a year, but now earns a little less, although her income fluctuates quite dramatically from month to month. After losing her job she bought her 'one luxury', a much-loved navy blue Nissan, with a few thousand pounds in lifetime savings. But in every other area of life she has cut back – without, she insists, any serious hardship. 'The amazing thing is that I thought living in this much poorer way would be very restricting, but it's not, it's liberating. I've found that I can actually manage with a lot less and I don't want more, in fact I'm still giving things away!'

Denise, who has never married, confesses to being 'an inveterate shopper' when she was younger, but now considers make-up and expensive clothes 'a waste of time'. She almost never eats out, preferring to cook or visit friends in the evening. She does miss paying regular visits to the theatre and cinema which she can now rarely afford, but considers the loss a minor discomfort compared to the benefits of her new existence.

Denise also points out that she could probably earn significantly more should she choose to. She often works in the evenings, leaving her days mostly free for other activities. Abandoning full-time employment has also allowed her to develop her philanthropic activities, many of which were inspired by her contact with Joyce Pearce. She sits on the National Peace Council's Northern Ireland working party which tries to promote peaceful solutions to the conflict. And, as a member of Through Heart to Peace, a British women's group, she pays regular visits to sister organisations in Bosnia and Croatia, trying to find ways to help heal the divide between the different ethnic groups. A third group, the International Council of Wise Women of Great Britain, through whom she has made many friends, has also become one of the mainstays of her income by appointing her its membership secretary.

Denise describes herself as a non-political downshifter and as spiritual rather than religious. She believes the steps she has taken to work part-time and simplify her life will eventually become commonplace. 'I think people will come to it in their own way. There will be a lot more leisure time and part-time working, and people will be thrown more on their own resources.'

When she herself took the step, her friends were very encouraging, although her sister, to whom she is very close, feared that she would not be able to cope with such a huge change, or with less money. 'A year later she said, I was totally wrong, you're so much happier and more relaxed,' recalls Denise with a smile. 'When I was working for other people I would rate my happiness at five out of ten, now it's nine or ten. My personality has changed, I'm much more outgoing and less prone to anxiety or depression. My whole quality of life has been transformed.'

Denise's downshifting tip
'Follow your inner impulses and don't be afraid to live off less. It can be very liberating!'

7: CITY SHIFTER

Karen Field, 32, was a television commercial production assistant, and is now a self-employed aromatherapist. She lives in west London with her husband, an advertising executive.

Karen Field trained as an actress and dancer, and later worked as a production assistant in an advertising agency making television commercials. To outsiders she lived a glamorous, exciting life. But she found her work was so stressful that it was taking over her life. She remembers dashing off at lunchtimes in taxi cabs to have acupuncture or shiatsu to try and snatch a few moments of peace and relaxation before plunging herself into the whirlwind of work once again: 'All I remember was lying there all stiff thinking, "Oh, my God, in half an hour I've got to get back." Emotionally, I was really down and my health wasn't good. I was having problems going to the loo, and basically I think all of it was stress-related.'

Now Karen is a self-employed aromatherapist. In just a couple of years she has been transformed from a rather thin, driven and anxious person to a contented, confident and outgoing woman who exudes health, well-being and *joie de vivre*. It wasn't an easy journey, but it was one she knew had to be made. Falling in love helped, of course, as it often does.

Some people go through their working lives never managing to combine what they are good at with what they really enjoy doing, simply settling for one thing or the other. It has taken Karen a decade to achieve that combination, and she has done it by taking a few risks, adopting a flexible attitude and above all by knowing when, and when not, to compromise on her goals.

Like thousands of other little girls, she wanted to be a ballet dancer as a child and was taught classical ballet at the Arts Education School in Hertfordshire. She went on to drama school in London. 'I spent a year trying to get my Equity card. I really liked performing, but hated what went with it. So much could hinge on your appearance – you might perform well at an audition, but sometimes that would not be good enough unless you looked exactly like the character they were trying to cast. I decided it wasn't for me, and then I thought – what the hell am I going to do now?'

On the advice of her father, she did a secretarial training course and soon landed a job as a secretary with WCRS advertising agency in Drury Lane, London. 'It was an exciting, energetic place with its own wine bar sunk behind the reception area. I found it very seductive, full of young, trendy and creative types of people. It was the mid-1980s, and felt very much in tune with the times. I worked with a group of account executives who were making television commercials for Carling Black Label, Sharwoods, BMW, among others. There was a real buzz about the place, a sense of fast-lane living, adrenalin and deadlines. I felt like I was performing again. It was really good fun.'

A natural organiser, Karen was promoted to the job of personal assistant to a senior director, a powerful woman who became a mentor figure and encouraged her to take on more responsibility. It was around this time that she started going out with Dominic, one of the young executives. Her boss was head of the department that Dominic worked in, so to avoid a potential conflict of interests she decided another job move would be a good idea. With four years experience as a senior PA, she joined another advertising agency, Leagas Delaney, again as personal assistant to a senior director, but she didn't feel sufficiently challenged in her new job.

'I felt quite flat, and I was on the point of leaving so I went to chat to Tim Delaney, whose company it was. He said: "Look we don't want you to leave." It just so happened that they wanted someone to work in the television department as a trainee producer, which is something every secretary in an advertising department wants to do, but it is a closed shop. I had to take a bit of a pay cut, from £18,000 to £16,000, but in career terms it was a big break.'

Suddenly, Karen was pitched into the front-line of the world of multi-million pound budgets and corporate clients. She was now part of a team, directly responsible for handling the logistics of TV commercial production for household name corporate clients. She worked on a commercial for Adidas starring the tennis player Stefan Edberg. David Lynch directed one in Los Angeles. 'It was very exciting to start with – risk-taking, ground-breaking, trendy, artistic advertising. The agency didn't do run of the mill stuff. You wouldn't see them doing, say, a commercial for Jif.'

She found herself working harder and longer hours. 'I would start at 9 a.m. and things would be reasonably under control until about 10 a.m. It would tend to get rather manic after that because often there would be several productions going on at once, and not enough staff to deal with the work that had to be done. So, for example, you would get various account directors running out of meetings saying, "Look, this has got to go on air tonight." So I would have to drop everything, get down to the editing suite, and make the changes to the film they wanted.

'Sometimes with radio commercials, you would have to play the commercial down the telephone line to a client for approval just a few hours before it was due to go out on air. At first I believed each one of these last-minute panic jobs was a 'one-off', but soon I found I was doing it virtually every day. Then when I got home exhausted, the phone would ring and it would be work. There were periods when I must have been working sixty-hour weeks. It was completely manic.

'You see, I am an organised person, yet I was required to work in chaos. Again, I didn't feel in control of anything, and yet work was taking over my life. At the same time, budgets were getting smaller, and you were expected to do more with less. What finished me off was the idea of being solely responsible for a budget of perhaps £100,000. What I wanted was a better quality of life, more time. Emotionally, I was down.

'By this time I was engaged to Dominic. He didn't like what was going on, and he encouraged me to take back control over my life that I had lost. I realised I needed to make a shift. I was interested in alternative lifestyles and complementary health so I started looking around.'

She found a course that appealed in aromatherapy. 'It was a nine-month course, and you got to study all sorts of things in depth, like nutrition, clinical medicine and counselling. I managed to get a career development loan from my bank to cover the cost of the course, about £2,500 to £3,000. The advantage of that was that you don't have to pay anything back until you start earning money. I used the money to buy a couch, books, essential oils.'

Almost every student on her course was at a turning point in their lives, either through redundancy, divorce or grown-up children leaving home. Karen, by now, felt a changed person and was making new friends. 'I had been a real nightclubber, a party person but that sort of lifestyle just fell by the wayside, as did some of the people I socialised with. Some could not comprehend why I went in for aromatherapy, "touching people . . . eurghh!" was a typical reaction.'

At this time in 1995, she and Dominic were renting a cheapish flat in Chiswick, west London, and saving up to buy a house in the nearby suburb of Ealing. Money was tight. The couple married in June. Karen set up in practice almost immediately from the spare room at her new home, but had to supplement her income by temping initially. The aromatherapy business picked up, and now she particularly enjoys visiting a small private hospital each week where she gives massages to heart patients recovering from coronary artery by-pass operations. 'It's so rewarding – a lot of the patients feel they have been given a second chance, so they are looking at life in a new way. Many are from abroad, from different cultures and they often bring the whole family.'

Karen now feels she has found her niche and restored balance to her life. 'I used to be thin and quite manic. I used to smoke and drink a lot of black coffee, eat out at the drop of a hat and spend lots of money on designer clothes. When I was working on those commercials, I was burning out. Now life is very different, but it's better. I have to be more careful about money now – on a good week I earn £250, sometimes it's only £100. But I feel I am back in control. I eat properly now. I am lucky enough to have a husband who has supported and encouraged me at every stage – it would not have been possible to do what I have done without him.'

And what about the future? 'I can't envisage being an employee again, not unless I really had to. Ideally I would move to California, because there the holistic movement and personal development philosophy are more advanced than in Britain. That's something we might do over the next five to ten years. What I would really like is to be able to offer a range of treatments, such as counselling, so that I can help more people take control of their lives. That would be tremendously satisfying. For me, it's important to keep learning.'

> **Karen's downshifting tip**
> 'Be patient and give yourself a break while you are in the process of change. Allow yourself between six months and a year to adjust. Make sure you have support from something in your life that remains constant, whether it's going to the gym, or a relationship.'

8: A GRAND UNION

Frank and Rosalie O'Nions, 61 and 54, are footloose and fancy-free as they look forward to their Third Age. They have swapped lucrative careers and an affluent lifestyle to live on a canal boat near Rugby.

Frank and Rosalie O'Nions lived in a cottage worth over £100,000 in the picturesque Sussex village of Buxted. The nearest town, Tunbridge Wells, is the epitome of affluent southern commuter-belt living. They ran two cars to maintain their separate businesses, took expensive annual holidays, and between them earned £45–£50,000 a year.

Their new home lies within a mile of the lorry-filled M1, a stone's throw beyond the small Northamptonshire village of Crick. It is 19 metres long, by two metres high and wide, boasts the name 'Pail o' Water', and lies at the heart of England's canal network. They have been there since 1994.

'Most of our friends thought we were completely mad, giving up such a life to move on to a narrowboat in the Midlands, but as time goes by they have resigned themselves to it,' says Frank, a youthful 61-year-old. 'On the other hand, we have had tremendous support from our four grown-up children who all thought it was great.'

For 20 years, Frank was a successful self-employed contractor who installed refrigeration systems for the major supermarket chains. Rosalie, for her part, was a popular designer of upmarket knitwear, with customers such as Liberty's, Scotch House and Gucci in New York. Both independent, highly motivated people, they greatly enjoyed their work.

But by the early 1990s, new stresses were creeping in. Rosalie, who paid her home-based knitters decent wages, was finding her range increasingly undercut at the trade fairs where she exhibited her designer knitwear by imports from the developing world. And Frank found the powerful supermarket chains ever more demanding. 'I would drive 30,000 miles a year which was wearing me out and at the same time the wages were going down and the hours they expected you to put in were increasing,' he recalls. 'I would do long contracts somewhere like Glasgow and only get home every other weekend. At the same time, wages for a skilled engineer had dropped to £12 an hour – the same level as ten to twelve years ago.'

The couple, who say they have never been very interested in possessions, were also becoming increasingly disenchanted with the south. 'I know it sounds silly,' Frank apologises, 'but I started feeling really uncomfortable in the south-east, when half the country couldn't possibly afford to live there. On my travels, I felt I was seeing two different Englands. It began to feel quite immoral.'

Having made up their minds to move, the O'Nions put their cottage on the market in August 1994. 'We thought it would take a couple of years to sell and we would think about where to go next,' recalls Frank. 'Instead we had an offer immediately and had six weeks to move out!' That weekend, while visiting their son in London, they made a trip to Camden Lock on the Thames canal. 'There were lots of boats moored along the canalside and Rosie just turned to me and said, "That's it, we'll live on a narrowboat," and I said, "Fine!" ' says Frank. 'I spent fifteen years in the merchant navy as a young man and I've always loved the water, I just didn't think it would be Rosie's cup of tea.'

Their home is moored among holiday narrowboats alongside a quiet stretch of the Leicestershire arm of the Grand Union Canal. Painted dark green and decorated with jaunty bright flower patterns, it cost the O'Nions £31,000 to buy and do up.

Inside the boat, there is one double bedroom, a sitting-room/cabin with sofa seats that turn into another bed, a kitchen, separate dining-room/study and shower. Like many households, the walls are covered with black and white family photos, there is a TV and video in the sitting-room, and even a mobile phone. Central heating is supplied by bottled Calor gas. On the downside, they point out, there is no bath, washing machine or armchairs and the waste storage unit beneath the boat has to be emptied out into a holding tank every two weeks.

For the first few months after moving, Frank completed a few refrigeration contracts, but he has now discovered a new talent – for making wooden painted puppet theatres and puppets. 'I was always a great one for woodwork and I had kept my antique woodworking equipment, lathe and bench, and so on. I just experimented with a few children's toys and the theatres really took off,' he says. He started touring craft fairs in the summer of 1995 and the orders are now pouring in. Rosalie still designs knitwear but has reduced her former output by 75 per cent and now sells only at the same craft fairs as her husband. They both have storage space in converted barns rented from an inn owner and Frank often pays his rent in kind, by doing repairs on the holiday moorings.

The interest on the money they had left over from selling their cottage, plus Frank's pension which began at 60, brings them a basic income of around £7,000 a year. This they expect to supplement, with their craft sales, to around £15,000. 'We are actually working longer hours now, but we are much happier,' says Frank. 'We work when we like – including evenings or weekends – or, if we have the urge, we can just take off and go locking for a week. We could probably earn much more if we wanted to – but we don't.'

Frank and Rosalie O'Nions are at the greener, more radical end of the downshifting spectrum. Frank read American guru Duane Elgin's seminal work, *Voluntary Simplicity*, five years ago and was deeply moved by it. 'He put into words, a lot of the feelings I had about consumerism eating up the world's resources and so on. He answered a lot of the questions I had been asking myself about how we should live.'

What do they miss? Very little, they say, although both confess to a fondness for designer clothes (Frank's collection of £250 Nino Cerruti suits still hang, unused, in a cupboard on the boat). 'We are both quite vain,' laughs Rosalie, 'but unfortunately, there's no place for them in narrowboat life.' She says she also really misses having a good bath – but the lack of a washing machine is no problem. A neighbour in Crick lends hers.

For Frank, getting used to life without his previous business was much harder than making do with less. It took him a year before he invited the local refrigeration installation firm in Rugby to come and clear out his equipment. Meanwhile he was made a lucrative offer to head a refrigeration company's installation team for Marks & Spencer stores. 'I was sorely tempted, but I decided, no, I have made my decision to stop,' he says.

The O'Nions' income is now around the national average and they still drink wine in the open air every evening and take occasional holidays in France. But they are achieving their aim, they say, of living more simply and happily than they did before.

'I have reached that stage of life when I feel I have to make some form of payback to society for what I have taken out,' explains Frank. 'For me that means living in a consciously green way. We recycle a lot and only use natural materials for our products. But we are not out here wearing hairshirts.'

They are both emphatic that voluntary simplicity does not mean pursuing an extreme 1970s-style 'good life', as illustrated in the TV series of that name. Rather, they believe they are in the vanguard of a much more realistic movement towards cutting down by degrees on possessions and spending.

'The *Good Life* ethos was all about self-sufficiency,' says Frank. 'I think it was a programme born out of the oil shortages, about a dream world where people could dig up their gardens, plant vegetables and go it alone. Nobody can do that.'

'We are not doing this to opt out, in fact the opposite,' adds Rosalie. 'We believe other people should follow suit.'

After 35 years spent living in Sussex, the O'Nions have no regrets. Their four adult children (both were married once before) are very supportive, although they lead very different lives. One is a hospital accountant, another works in the media office of Camden Council, London, a third is an administrator at a performing arts college, and the fourth has followed his father's footsteps into refrigeration engineering. 'I don't think any of them is concerned to get to the top of the tree to make lots of money. They are all much more concerned with people. On the other hand, none is likely to do what we have done in the near future.' Many of their former friends in Sussex, however, find it hard to come to terms with the O'Nions' radical change of lifestyle – or the reasons for it. 'We don't see a lot of them any more, but that's life,' shrugs Rosalie.

Frank and Rosalie's downshifting tip
'Don't worry about trying something new. Be adventurous. You will adjust after a few months, and you're likely to end up much happier.'

9: SIMPLE LIFE PIONEERS
Euan McPhee and Nona Wright, both 49, and their daughter Catriona, eight, are preparing to move to Cornwall in pursuit of a simple, ecological lifestyle since Euan took voluntary redundancy after a long academic career.

On the surface, Euan McPhee and Nona Wright are the embodiment of British suburban living. Like millions of other families, they and their eight-year-old daughter Catriona live in a semi-detached house with a small garden in a pleasant residential area of a middle-sized English town. Canadian-born Nona is a librarian, Euan a further education lecturer, one of the first in Britain to teach ecology.

But the couple have always shared a strong streak of self-sufficiency and an environmental awareness which marked them out from neighbours in their former home in south London, and now in Guildford, Surrey. They do not own a car, and only bought a TV set three years ago when Catriona was old enough to feel left out at school without one. They grow some of their own vegetables, and a vine yields enough grapes to make four bottles of wine a year. Euan – who stood unsuccessfully as a Green candidate in the 1989 elections for the European Parliament – also brews his own beer.

So when, like tens of thousands of other families, they were suddenly confronted first with mounting job insecurity, then with the spectre of mid-life redundancy, their response was not the typical one. Euan, who was fighting to keep his job at a local FE college, chose to take voluntary redundancy in 1995 'before I was pushed'. He and Nona decided to sell their house, cash in their endowment policies and buy a plot of land in Cornwall where they hope to create a 1990s version of the *Good Life*.

'We don't want to be like Tom and Barbara,' says Euan, 'trying to live outside society. I still feel I have a lot to contribute, but my ambition has moved away from the traditional career ladder towards wanting to see what kind of simpler, greener life we can achieve in the community we move to.'

The family plan is to be as self-sufficient as possible, keeping a few chickens, 'one or two goats' and planting extensive vegetable and herb gardens. The cottage and six acre plot of land they have in mind lies just outside the village of St Day, near Redruth, in the heart of Cornish tin mining country. There are a few run-down outhouses on the land which Euan hopes to rent out cheaply to local craftsmen. Nona, who currently has a part-time job helping to run an organic produce home delivery service in Guildford wants to start one up in Cornwall once they are established. She has also recently completed two years training as a counsellor, and hopes to use her book-keeping skills to do some home accounting in the neighbourhood. 'Within a few months, we will have no money coming in. We are trusting to our instincts that we are doing the right thing,' she says.

Euan and Nona are well acquainted with the concept of downshifting. Together they edit *Living Green*, the newsletter of the 24-year-old Life Style Movement which has a 500-strong membership nationwide. The movement's motto, 'Live Simply, That All May Simply Live', sums up its world view as one in which selfish Western consumerist lifestyles are threatening the planet's future and draining the Third World's land and labour resources. This is a view with which Euan and Nona whole-heartedly concur. Even so, they did not make their decision to embrace the simple life lightly.

Nona has spent the last eight years since her daughter's birth working in part-time librarian jobs and applying for literally dozens of full-time posts in a dwindling market. 'Technology and the restructuring of public library services seems to have left no niche for me. I have been putting my hand to all kinds of different things for a few years now, so I am probably more mentally prepared for the future than Euan is.'

Her husband, since taking redundancy, has worked as a part-time lecturer at the University of Greenwich while he and Nona mulled over the family's future. 'I have spent all my life in academia – first in research and then in further and higher education and my ultimate ambition was always to become head of department in a university,' he explains. 'When I first took the redundancy, I applied for quite a few jobs and then there was a period of mourning when I realised I wouldn't reach that level after all. After that came the excitement when I realised that circumstances had allowed us to try and lead the kind of simpler, more spiritual life we were always striving towards. We are both much happier. I feel my life has been re-routed – in both meanings of the word!'

Their new life, he cheerfully admits, will not be all plain sailing. With the proceeds from selling their home, and his £20,000 redundancy payment, they will have enough to buy the cottage and grounds outright with some to spare. But he expects their annual income to drop from £28,000 to around £10,000. They are also determined not to buy a car, which will restrict their freedom of movement, although the village school will be only a mile-long cycle ride away for Catriona. The family's two-yearly trips to Nona's family in Canada, where her mother and four married brothers and sisters live, will also be impossible to maintain.

But his daughter's future is Euan's biggest concern about embarking on a new life. 'At first she was upset about leaving her friends, but she is coming round. She especially likes the idea of more land and more animals,' laughs Euan, a gentle, grey-bearded man. 'But I am worried about providing for her future college education. Like every parent, I want Catriona to achieve her best potential. Not having any financial assets will be a disadvantage, but I believe the benefits for her from moving to Cornwall are more important.'

What's more, both Euan and Nona firmly believe that the market forces shaping Britain's economy will work increasingly in favour of people opting, like them, for part-time, short-term or community-based work. With further education colleges shedding staff nationwide, Euan believes it will not be difficult to find one or two days lecturing work a week to supplement their income. And Nona, who hopes to use her book-keeping skills to do home accounting for her future Cornish neigh-bours, points out that statistics show that only 55 per cent of the population is now in permanent, full-time employment. They both strongly believe that they are in the vanguard of a significant new movement in Britain towards a less work-obsessed, less consumerist society.

'It is very encouraging that we are not alone in trying to simplify our lives and consume less, exciting to be part of a broader movement,' says Euan. 'There is now such a great gulf in Britain between those who are working and those who are not that it is very unhealthy for society. There are enormous stresses on people both in and out of work. I personally consider downshifting a valuable contribution towards a more equitable, more balanced society.'

Nona agrees, but admits to finding the prospect of such a radical change daunting. 'I'm not worried about having less, we just need enough money to live on,' she says, 'but the prospect of not having the regular pay cheque coming in, not knowing quite how it will all work out, I do find quite daunting.' On the other hand, she says, at least she and Euan are choosing their own downshifting course. 'We are better prepared psychologically than most people because we chose to do this. Many of the professional people we know in Guildford are reaching fifty and being told by their company that they are no longer wanted. They have no choice about living more simply.'

Euan's downshifting tip
'Take it slowly when you make such a big decision about your future and don't overstretch your resources, by trying to live in too big a house for your new income, for example. Trying part-time work is always a good halfway house. Also invest in a good computer (we just have) and use the Internet to keep in touch with the wider world.'

10: DOWNSHIFTING ENTREPRENEURS

Andrew James, 48, and Sophie Chalmers, 33. He lost his job as a marketing manager in 1991 and her television research contract ended soon afterwards. They ploughed their life savings into a new business providing advice and support for professionals working from home, and nearly lost everything. They sold their comfortable London home and bought an old mill set in a secluded valley in south Wales. Their joint income has sunk from £65,000 to £30,000 over five years.

'Men are such boring old farts,' exclaims Andrew James over lunch at the family home near Chepstow. He is musing on the psychology of plunging into self-employment from the relative security of mainstream jobs, and pointing out that women are often the more adventurous sex. 'Women tend to be so much more creative and imaginative in selecting new business ventures, whether it's cake-making or marketing organic meat. But men tend to carry so much baggage with them when they leave their old jobs and often just go on doing what they did before, but as consultants, working for themselves using their old contacts.'

Andrew should know. He speaks from bitter experience after losing his job in 1991 as a marketing manager. It soon dawned on him that he was not only ill-prepared but completely unsuited for work as an independent consultant.

Now he and his wife Sophie make their living by helping others steer their way through the minefields of working independently from home. They are downshifting entrepreneurs, for want of a better description, and so are many of their customers. It sounds like a contradiction in terms, but let's examine what this couple has done, where they are now and where they hope they are going.

They have opted out of traditional ways of working, and established a socially-useful business that chimes with the changing shape of a service-led economy and the new corps of independent 'knowledge' workers. They work together as a team, blurring the edges between home, work, and family life that help provide definition and structure to most people's lives.

Like most good ideas, their subscription-only magazine *Home Run*, edited by Sophie, published by Andrew, was conceived out of personal experience and a gut feeling that it would plug a gap in the market. Along with countless others trying to launch themselves into self-employment, Andrew came unstuck at a pretty early stage. 'I hadn't had any training or experience of how to charge for my time, for instance, and quickly became disillusioned. I realised I was too much of a perfectionist to be any good as a consultant.'

At this time, Sophie, whose contract as television researcher had ended soon after her husband's redundancy, was combining freelance typing at their home in London with caring for their baby son Caspian. Change was very much in the air: 'A cousin set up in business marketing ski pole stop-watches, but he hadn't a clue at the start,' recalls Sophie. 'To find someone to make the product for him, he looked in the *Yellow Pages*, and went to the first person he found. He launched at the wrong time of year. At each stage, something went wrong, in the great tradition of British amateurism.' The experience led them to resurrect an idea Andrew had some months earlier, to launch a newsletter for home workers. 'Suddenly, here was the person I could envisage reading the magazine, picking up tips about how to make your new business work and avoid some of the pitfalls,' says Sophie.

On a wing and a prayer in July 1992, they sent out a mailshot to 15,000 potential clients, using £8,000 of their savings. Only 50 took out subscriptions and sent cheques. 'We should have written off the £8,000 and returned the cheques, but we were too stupid. We sent out the newsletter and had two very tough years when it was just haemorrhaging money like mad.'

The business was on the brink of collapse, having absorbed all £22,000 of their savings, and there was nothing to pay their mort-gage. By happy coincidence, an article about *Home Run* appeared in the *Daily Telegraph* in 1994. The piece renewed interest and brought more subscriptions in the nick of time. Soon the business moved into profit for the first time. Their daughter Saskia was born. They sold their London house, put everything into storage and started house-hunting in rural south Wales, close to a cottage they used to rent for short breaks near Chepstow. They took out a reduced mortgage and bought Cribau Mill together with 20 acres of pasture, grazed by neighbouring farmers' cows and sheep.

Here they compile and despatch their magazine to 2,000 subscribers ten times a year. Their target is to achieve 10,000 subscriptions. Andrew takes charge of the computer technology, and the technical side of the business. Sophie edits and shares the administrative responsibilities. 'We work as a team. I do the first run of the magazine and then he pulls to pieces what I've written,' says Sophie. 'As editor, I have the last word.' They recently took on an assistant for the business so that Sophie no longer had to work a seven-day week, and there is a nanny to care for the two children during the day.

Long gone are the 'perks' of their old lifestyle, the company car, the Bupa health cover, the monthly salary cheque, the sick pay. Their joint income has fallen to £30,000 compared to about £65,000. The perks of their downshifted life are less tangible, but worth a great deal more – at least to them. Andrew got on the phone one day to a public relations contact in London, who asked him: 'What's going on in the country, then?' Andrew replied: 'Well, the sheep are bleating.' 'Yes.' 'The hunt's just gone past.' 'Uhuh . . . .' '. . . and I'm looking at the flowers in the garden.' 'Oh shut up, that's enough,' replied the jaded PR man.

Sophie continues on the theme of advantages of their new life: 'We have lunch with the children. You can open the front door and let them run out and play, knowing they'll be safe. They will go to a lovely state school in the village two miles away when they're old enough (Caspian is now 5 and Saskia is 3). We have a much more relaxing time with our friends than we did in London when we would gabble our news over dinner to each other. Here friends come up for a weekend, and we've got to know them better. There's more time to talk.'

Andrew and Sophie were never ones for flashy clothes or fast cars in London. Travelling to Nepal, Africa, Australia and France was their luxury. 'We used to have two expensive holidays a year, now we have one short inexpensive holiday every two years. We don't need holidays now because we are where we want to be.'

They work hard and play hard. Instead of watching TV, she relaxes by doing tapestry and writing a novel: 'My outlook has changed. Our work and income begins and ends with us. If we don't get the money we don't pay the mortgage. On the other hand, we are in control. We are NOT going to be made redundant. The hard work we have put in is finally being rewarded.

'It is idyllic. Emotionally, I am happier in the country. I am a real country bumpkin. I love going out running and falling over badgers going out for their evening snout around. It's so fresh, clean and quiet here. When I go to London I feel so sorry for my friends living with all that congestion and filth. The nearest thing I have seen to a traffic jam here is three cars at a junction on Remembrance Sunday. It wouldn't suit everyone of course, perhaps if you're used to having a corner shop handy or nipping out to Peter Jones. Having children is a bonus out here, because you meet other people through your children and their playgroups. We've stopped eating out at restaurants – we go for dinner to other people's houses.'

It wouldn't suit every couple to work and live together 24 hours a day.

These two manage it by being extremely good friends and giving each other time off. 'We're equals, although when we started, it was very much Andrew running the show and I was the unpaid secretary. I learned my editing skills as we went along, and Andrew was generous in giving me space to grow, and give me the leading role in the business.'

How does Andrew reflect on the changes of the past few years? 'I enjoy work, but I was not a company man. Going abroad, chairing conferences and preparing strategies I found enjoyable, but I could not abide drawing up endless budgets. I also found that while I was great at having ideas, I was not so good at implementing them. What makes this business work is that Sophie is a doer, whereas I am a waffler. I much prefer to hide away in an ivory tower and plot. If left to my own devices, I would spend most of my time working out some new program on the computer, instead of doing the business.'

It's a common problem, becoming so transfixed on the tools you use to do business, that you overlook the winning of the new customers. This is one of the single most important causes of failure – lack of new business. 'Once people have a computer at home they ring us up and say: "Right, what do I do now?" It's like a commuter saying: "Well, I have my car for commuting. Give me a list of jobs that commuters do." There is a notion that somehow other people will be thrilled to give them work.

'What I do not miss about my former life is office politics, commuting, inflexibility of working times, compulsory drinks in the pub, especially when someone is leaving, being asked at two hours notice to make an impromptu speech at the company Christmas Party, and the company Christmas Party.' He would, however, welcome a shorter commuting trip – that is why they are converting the old mill 20 yards from their house into offices so they can physically separate working and home life.

Ask Sophie what she misses and she replies: 'Friends.' For Andrew, the list is rather longer: 'I miss the feeling that I can go away on holiday and not have to worry about anything. I miss the feeling of security that I can do a sickie. I miss international travel, going off meeting my peers in The Hague.'

They are not keen on the word 'downshifting'. 'It sounds so negative – as though you are taking a cut in income without gaining anything,' says Sophie. 'We look at it as swapping salary for sanity. If you look at it that way, you are *upshifting*. You are taking a deliberate decision to switch off, and get a life.'

101

> **Sophie's downshifting tip**
> 'If you have a dream, make it happen. Work out what it takes, step by step, to make it work, then do it. The bad times come good in the end if you believe in what you're doing and you stick with it.'
>
> **Andrew's downshifting tip**
> 'If you're a couple, you need to share the vision for changing your life. The other partner has to be supportive. It won't work if, say, the wife is still expecting a clothes allowance and resents her husband being around the house during the day, or keeps asking: "When are you going to get a proper job?"'

11: THE TEMPORARY DOWNSHIFTER

Alison Hogan, 41, was earning a high salary as a public relations consultant. A self-confessed workaholic, Alison knew that her commitment to her work was damaging her health. She considered resigning. Instead, she was allowed a six months unpaid sabbatical. It gave her the complete break she needed, and her employers the chance to retain a highly valued member of staff.

Like many people who are tempted by the idea of abandoning secure, well-paid employment, Alison Hogan has a consuming passion worlds apart from the demands of her job. For her, it's sailing, and owning a quarter share in a yacht.

In 1996, Alison was granted an unpaid six months sabbatical by her fellow partners in the financial public relations company where she works in London. She was single, aged 41, well-paid but worn out by the long hours she spent doing her job. The breathing space enabled her not only to sail in the West Indies, but also to study for her yachtmaster's qualification, to go on a creative writing course on the Greek island of Skyros, and to take her parents to Ireland on a holiday. It also gave her the time to resolve a long-standing dilemma: did she really want to stay in a job that demanded so much of her?

'I got a real buzz from my work, and a great deal of satisfaction, but I didn't know whether I wanted to spend the rest of my life going from one stressful project to another. No one else in the company had taken a sabbatical before but the senior partner was sympathetic when I raised the idea. He knew I would have resigned otherwise. I was so desperate to have some real quality time for myself, but hadn't the discipline to carve that time out against the pressures of the job.

'My working day started by 8.30 a.m., and I would rarely get away before 7 p.m., often later. At weekends we were on call, so even if I was sailing, I would have my mobile phone on and get the Sunday newspapers to see if any of our clients had been written about. If so, I would follow up with the client and journalists. I was a classic workaholic. Being single it was easy to keep on working in the evening and to volunteer for weekend meetings.

'Just before my sabbatical started I was having an exceptionally busy time – one of our corporate clients was the subject of a take-over bid. My shoulders used to ache so much with the tension I had to have physiotherapy.'

The debate within the Board was not primarily about whether Alison should be given the sabbatical. The issue was whether she should be paid in her absence. 'In the end, it was decided the company wasn't big enough to set a precedent of paid sabbaticals. I had savings and had assumed that I would live off that money during those six months, anyway.'

Five months have now passed. She's a lot fitter than she was, thanks to her efforts in the gym with her personal trainer, and her tendency to walk places instead of driving everywhere. Her time off also prompted her to consult a firm of 'executive mentors' about how she might overcome her workaholism, work more rationally and feel more in control. 'The woman I saw told me I had to become firmer about establishing my priorities and sticking to them, setting aside time for myself, family friends and community, which I'm determined to do.'

So what has she decided to do about her job? 'I'm going back, but I'm determined to work more sensibly and learn to say "No" more often. If necessary I am prepared to earn less money. I'm sure it won't be easy to break the habit of a lifetime, but I have so valued my six months, I believe I have learned some important lessons.'

While working, Alison did not have the time nor the energy to invest in a serious relationship for some time. Now she is seeing a fellow sailing enthusiast, a headhunter in the City, who has two teenage children from an earlier relationship. 'He's only ever seen me laid back and relaxed, so he wants to try to make sure I get the balance right when I go back to my job too.'

How does she reflect on her few months of freedom, and does she feel that she has made the right decision? 'If I had been ten years older, I doubt whether I would have gone back, but I'm still relatively young and I still feel there is a career in me. My taking a sabbatical has certainly struck a sympathetic chord amongst some of my colleagues who work equally hard. Our work is hugely rewarding but can take its toll. I am anxious to see whether it is possible to retain the momentum of the business, whilst getting more balance into our lives.'

Alison's answer to prolonged stress overload was to make a *temporary* downshift. It worked out well, and she knows how lucky she is to have had a sabbatical and to work with colleagues who recognise the value of such a break. Sabbaticals are rarely given by British employers. The break gave her the time she needed to recharge her batteries, gave her the space to re-think how she works, and the opportunity to keep her job. The break enabled her business partnership to keep a highly skilled and valued member of the team, and to welcome her back refreshed and re-motivated.

Alison's downshifting tip
'The more people talk about career breaks and sabbaticals and explore the possibilities with their employers, the more awareness will spread of their benefits for individuals and organisations.'

Downshifting back to the future

If the Welsh hills are not remote enough for you to get away from the miseries of modern life, you could consider turning back the clock a few thousand years and becoming a hunter-gatherer. Michael Fomenko, 66, has lived wild in the tropical rainforests in northern Queensland, Australia, ever since he abandoned city life in Sydney, 40 years ago. He uses a bow and arrow to hunt bats and wild pigs. He gathers berries, fishes from rocks in the Pacific, sleeps in a cave and cooks his food on an open fire. He enjoys good health.

Nicknamed Tarzan, by local Aborigines, Fomenko's family fled Stalinist Russia and settled in Australia in 1939. The boy became a brilliant athlete and only just missed being selected for Australia's 1956 Olympic team. Soon after he turned his back on modern life and headed north. 'When I came to the Great Barrier Reef, and then saw the jungle I thought it the most beautiful place in the world,' the *Daily Mail* (11/7/96) reported him as saying. 'There's plenty of food for me, oysters, fish, lobster, wild pigs. But I know there are dangers – lightning or crocodiles and sharks.'

One of his worst experiences was being captured by the police, and being taken to undergo psychiatric tests in Brisbane in the mid 1960s. They found that he was suffering from nothing more than an aversion to modern life, declared him sane and returned him to the jungle.

PART THREE

PREPARING FOR CHANGE

I ought, therefore I can.

Immanuel Kant (1724–1804), German philosopher

CHAPTER TEN

Could It Be You?

It is very tempting for people exhausted by long working hours and stress to seize on the idea of downshifting, as if it were *the* key to happiness for the rest of their lives. Rebalancing your life and changing down a gear can indeed prove to be a life-transforming experience. But it is important not to romanticise the concept unduly, nor to rush into a new and simpler life too hastily. You may love it for a few weeks, treat it like an extended holiday, and then suddenly find yourself getting rat race withdrawal symptoms. That could land you in an altogether new quagmire, since it takes much longer to accelerate to cruising or sprinting speed if you've just pulled up to look at the view, or because you are suddenly bored by running.

It is crucial to talk through and plan for the financial, practical and emotional realities before you make any decision. After that, it is a good idea to sit on it for several weeks, even months if you can, until you are 100 per cent ready and eager to take a sideways leap on to a different track altogether.

The first five steps

Step 1: *Look before leaping*
If one day it hits you like a revelation that you need a change, the first thing to do is to discuss it with those closest to you. If you're single, you don't have to convince anyone else to go along with you, but for couples and families it is obviously essential that the whole household is involved in any decision. The subject should be broached diplomatically, and well ahead of any irrevocably dramatic gesture at the workplace. It is no good

coming home one day and announcing: 'Guess what? I've packed it all in, and I feel *wonderful*,' because you may not get the sympathetic hearing you might expect. Indeed, tempers may flare, and saucepans and valuable items of china may be hurled through the air.

If one partner is keen to downshift, and the other not, then the sooner you know the better, so you can get on and thrash out the issue openly. Now is the time to resolve such conflicts – not after you have sold the house, uprooted the children from their schools, and bought that job lot of 25 goats and a barn conversion in west Wales. Talk about it now. A constructive way to start the conversation might be to think about the sort of life you want to be living in 10 to 15 years time. You must both be persuaded that it is likely to work, or can be made to work, before making any irrevocable moves. And don't be impatient. Getting used to the idea and talking it over from all the angles may take months rather than weeks.

Step 2: *Find out what you really want from life*
If you think you want to explore the idea further, start listing your dissatisfactions with your present life. If it is hard to put into words, try answering the following eleven questions as a starting point. If you answer yes to all or most of the questions, then a simpler, more sustainable and rational life may well be what you are yearning for. Finally ask yourself the larger question: How would you spend your time if you knew that you only had a year to live? It may seem like a rather melodramatic question, but it is a wonderful way of concentrating the mind on what you really want from life.

Are You A Closet Downshifter?

---

1 Do you constantly wish you could spend
more time with your partner/family/
friends?   YES ❏ NO ❏

2 Do you feel you never have any/enough
time for yourself, to spend on hobbies,
gardening and leisure or just to relax?   YES ❏ NO ❏

3 Do you feel that your work is taking so
much out of you that you don't have
time to enjoy the money you earn,
spend it or invest it prudently?   YES ❏ NO ❏

4 Do you believe your pattern of work is
giving you health or stress problems? YES ☐ NO ☐

5 Are you chronically or permanently
tired? YES ☐ NO ☐

6 Do you dread going into work in the
mornings? YES ☐ NO ☐

7 Do you feel your work doesn't truly
reflect your values? YES ☐ NO ☐

8 Are you unhappy with the contribution
you're making to society? YES ☐ NO ☐

9 Do you think you would be happier if
your career changed direction
completely? YES ☐ NO ☐

10 Do you have so many commitments
that other people – cleaner, nanny,
babysitter, gardener – are impinging
too much into your personal life? YES ☐ NO ☐

11 Do you spend much of your time
fantasising about your next holiday
and then collapse when you get there? YES ☐ NO ☐

Your answers may well be ambivalent. It may be, for example, that you believe your job is indeed leaving you exhausted and stressed-out with too little time for your family, but that nevertheless the work you do reflects your personal values and is helping you contribute to society. This is the kind of dilemma which currently faces millions of busy working people, particularly parents of young children. If this sounds like you, the next step is another paper exercise.

Work out all the possible ways of making your present life easier and more enjoyable, such as:

- asking your boss if you can sometimes work from home
- getting more help around the house
- taking more frequent breaks

If you think these changes could improve the quality of your life then take them up with your partner or manager, or both, and try and make them happen. You can always come back to the idea of more radical change later if those steps don't achieve what you had hoped.

Perhaps you should start talking about sabbaticals in your place of work, or flexi-time, or different ways of getting the job done and see how many other people are interested. Nothing will change unless people talk about change.

On the other hand, if you are convinced you cannot juggle your present life to make it more bearable, think hard about what other employment options you would rather pursue. Then ask yourself the following questions:

- Which matters most to you, job satisfaction or income?
- Would the new job option you favour give you as much fulfillment and income as the present one?
- Would the preferred alternative *really* give you more free time and reduce your stress levels, or might you end up still working long hours and having new anxieties to cope with? Would you really end up with the kind of balanced life you are aiming for?

This kind of exercise may make you appreciate your job more fully, whatever the day-to-day irritations and pressures. You may realise that the advantages of sticking with it outweigh the disadvantages, especially if you have a sympathetic boss and senior colleagues who agree to take you seriously.

Step 3: *Weigh up the pros and cons*
If you decide as an individual, couple or family, that change is the only way to achieve a more balanced lifestyle, then test your gut feelings against a practical list of pros and cons. This will mark the first step from fantasising about downshifting into making it a realisable proposition. Your list should cover job satisfaction, home and personal life, earning power, emotional stresses and reactions from the outside world.

Take one of the authors of this book as an example. Early in 1996, Polly decided to consider applying for voluntary redundancy from *The Observer*, where she was Whitehall correspondent. She and her husband talked about whether she should leave her job to go freelance and work from home. Here is the list of pros and cons they drew up:

Pros

✓ A better home life with proper weekends together. [Polly used to work every Friday evening and Saturday. Allan, her husband, worked Monday to Friday.]

✓ Reduced stress levels and better health. As a freelance, I can better control my work levels.

✓ More time and energy to enjoy seeing my family and friends.

✓ More time to get fit through exercise.

✓ New work opportunities. The chance to diversify after seven years on one national newspaper, into working for other newspapers and magazines, researching new projects and writing books.

✓ Big redundancy cheque in the bank to help ease the transition to freelancing and provide a safety net for the future.

✓ More flexibility for the future. If we start a family or decide to work abroad it will be much easier because I will no longer be tied to a single employer.

Cons

✗ Loss of status and a guaranteed writing platform.

✗ Sharp drop in regular income. Annual salary likely to drop by £20,000 a year.

✗ Loss of job security and benefits such as paid holidays, sickness and maternity leave.

✗ Loss of camaraderie in the workplace, and the daily opportunity to spark ideas off other people.

✗ Coping with negative reactions from colleagues and others that I have somehow 'copped out' because I'm not immediately joining another media organisation full-time.

✗ Having to cut back on luxuries and expensive holidays because of a drop in income.

When Polly and Allan looked at the list it was immediately apparent that the pros were all about life-enhancement and an exciting, if slightly scary new future, while the cons were all about coping with the loss of long-held status and job security. Although the latter were by no means irrelevant, they were far outweighed by the lure of a much better quality of life.

Step 4: *Think positively*
So you have decided that the pros outweigh the cons and you want to

change the direction of your life. But is it practical for you to do so, as an individual, a couple or family? Before you start thinking about what form this change is going to take, it is essential to evaluate all the risks and to make sure that the odds are on your side. You need to think about how much money you can afford to live on; what kind of essentials and luxuries you cannot do without and how much they cost; whether you are prepared to move homes to save money, and so on. All these practical aspects of your new life must be worked out in detail before you act. In the next chapter we discuss how to work out your personal finance, employment and housing needs for a down-shifter's lifestyle. But for now, let's assume you have sorted out all the practicalities to your satisfaction, and concentrate on the big picture.

The psychology of downshifting is enormously important. Switching to a less hectic, more balanced lifestyle brings great rewards, but there are also risks. Ask yourself the following questions:

- Will this affect my close relationships for better or worse?
- Are those closest to me supportive or hostile?
- Will I be able to curtail my spending habits and live off less money?
- Will my colleagues make snide remarks to my face or behind my back if I leave for a way of life that has no status or security?
- Do I care if they do?
- How will this new lifestyle develop?
- Where might I/we be in three or five years time?

Change is rarely easy for anyone. Many people go to great lengths to avoid it, but it has a habit of lurking in your subconscious until you decide to confront it. Prepare yourself for mental swings ranging from euphoria through doubt to possible depression if you decide to make a big change. Such mood changes are especially likely in the first few weeks or months as you adjust to a new life.

If you adjust your lifestyle a step at a time you will probably find the transition much more smooth and sustained than going all out from day one. It may take time to discover where you want to concentrate your energy and creativity, so don't rush it. Above all, remember that this is not about opting out of society, in fact you may end up contributing more to the general good than you did before – even if your consumer spending power goes down. Remember, you are not an oddity – there are likely to be millions of other potential downshifters like you out there thinking much the same thoughts.

Step 5: *Test the waters*

Once you have thought through the pros and cons and worked out a rough idea of how much money you think you need to live on, and how you might earn it, spend some time in transition. This gives you a chance to see how you like living on less without committing yourself to it. So carry on with your present job (or jobs) but spend a few months living and spending in a much more conscious way. Write down your daily expenditure so you can see just where the money's going. Then try and cut back spending in the areas you have already identified for making savings. Many of the half a million Americans who have bought a copy of *Your Money or Your Life* found they could slash their expenditure by 15–20 per cent within a year just by keeping a closer eye on their everyday spending. See how much, or how little, you miss the little luxuries.

Meanwhile, think consciously about the amount of time you spend at work and getting to and from work compared with hours spent at home or on hobbies, exercise or community activities. How much do you resent not having enough time for the latter? How would you adjust your time every day to get a better balance? After six months or so, you should have a good idea whether your budget plans will work and how strongly you really want a different lifestyle. Working out how you would best like to divide up your time will also help you to decide on future employment. Compare how much time each month you would ideally spend on a paid job with the monthly income you think you could get by on. Then calculate whether the working life you had in mind would provide enough income to make your new lifestyle work. You may be planning to go part-time, or spend a period of time re-training, and you need to make sure that you can finance the change without difficulty. Remember, many people who decide to downshift are cushioned by a few thousand pounds in savings or a redundancy cheque. This is not essential. But it is certainly prudent, if possible, to build up a safety net to help carry you through the first six months or so.

The men and women we interviewed in Chapter 9 of this book seemed pretty well equally content with their downshifted lifestyle, and genuinely appeared to have few significant regrets. But it seems reasonable to assume that men and women experience quite different pressures, and ask themselves different questions when pondering whether to forsake a traditional career path in favour of a simpler, more flexible lifestyle. Let us now examine some of these issues and see what practical advice we can offer.

CHAPTER ELEVEN

The Gender Agenda

You always wanted a lover,
I always wanted a job . . .
Pet Shop Boys with Dusty Springfield, *What Have I Done to Deserve*
This?, 1987

What men need to consider

Even in these enlightened times of sexual equality, the New Man, political
correctness and much talk of the 'sharing, caring Nineties', most people
would agree that men experience life differently from women. They
worry and take pleasure and work differently to women. Their sense of
identity is more likely to be derived from their work. That means their
attitudes to downshifting might be completely different as well.

This competitive male world, however, has been with us for a great
deal longer than Thatcherism. In fact there is considerable evidence that
work, or at least the need to conform to corporate ideals, was far more
central to the male psyche and sense of identity a generation before the
so-called 'greedy '80s'.

In their study of managers in industry in the 1960s sociologists Ray and
Jan Pahl explored why it was that this group worked so hard. They
concluded:

'For them life is a hierarchy and success means moving up in it . . .
very often it is the fear of falling rather than positive aspiration to
climb which pushes these men on. Those who had an experience of
downward social mobility in their family history were the most
determined to have a successful career. They work, then, because
they are trapped in a competitive society; above all they don't want
to fall. The men were not, however, usually prepared to admit that

117

they were driven on for selfish, materialist reasons. They would talk of 'challenge', responsibility, as well as family commitments.' (From: *Managers and their Wives*, Penguin 1971).

Yet many of the wives felt the sacrifices their husbands were making, allegedly for the family, were not worth making. What *they* wanted was to see more of their husbands.

Another study published nearly 20 years later, detected a shift in male managers' attitudes to work. They were less likely to put work first than those of the previous generation. 'Managers of all ages seemed concerned to improve the quality of their personal lifestyles outside rather than within work . . . they have consciously reduced their psychological dependence on employment.' (From: *Reluctant Managers*, 1989.) R. Scase and R. Goffee

Nonetheless, many men are *still* brought up to be breadwinners, protectors, go-getters, physically demonstrative in their interactions, active more than passive. More British men work over 48 hours a week than any other males in European Union countries. Until the 1980s, men's working hours had been steadily going down, but in the 1990s they have risen significantly. Now, three-quarters of men work more than 40 hours a week, and 16 per cent work more than 50 hours a week, according to a report *The Family Friendly Workplace* from the recruitment consultants Austin Knight. Two-thirds would like to shorten their hours. Presenteeism, where people make sure they stay at their desks or workplaces until after the boss has gone, has become a prevailing feature of today's workplace.

New men on the march

But there are signs that men are rebelling in order to re-balance their lives. Throughout the 1980s, and beyond, the expansion of part-time working was associated almost exclusively with women returning to the labour market after having children. Now more men seem to be opting for it, as more employers appreciate that switching to more family-friendly practices can increase productivity. The educational charity New Ways to Work campaigns for a change in culture so that people with domestic commitments are treated no differently from those in full-time employment. It carried out research on men who work part-time (or flexibly) for more than 100 public, private and voluntary sector organisations. While once such practices, such as redundancy, may have been stigmatised, they are now being actively sought by many men as an important key to building more stable and fulfilling relationships between men, their families and the outside world. The study *Balanced Lives: Changing Work Patterns for Men* (1995) finds men not only involved in child-care and the care of older relatives, but also contributing to the life of their communities.

America's leading advocate of 'communitarianism', Amatai Etzioni, among others, has pinpointed the 'parenting deficit' as a prime cause of community breakdown. In his book *The Spirit of Community*, he argues that the revival of communities is unlikely to take place unless there is comprehensive re-alignment of the energies of men and women with children.

Charles Monkcom, co-ordinator of New Ways to Work, feels these changes are emerging: 'Downshifting has been going on for years, but it is now affecting a new group, male executives in large organisations, who in the past have tended to put work before home life. I think there was a fundamental deal between organisations and men, one that was implied rather than spoken, a psychological contract, where the employers said: "You give us your time, your energy and your effort, and we will reward you with money and status." The idea that people stayed in their jobs for perhaps twenty years was considered OK.

'Now people starting off in work know that it is most unlikely that they will still be in those jobs for that long. We have a great deal of unemployment, and the truth is if you are over forty-five, and male, it is probable that you won't get another job if you are made redundant, so that implied deal, that contract, is disappearing.'

Locked out of family life

On top of all that confusion, consider the male backlash against the advent of the Child Support Agency. It mobilised huge numbers of men, who for one reason or another, had separated from their wives and partners. Many complained that the agency was placing upon them quite unfair financial burdens that did not take full account of all the circumstances. Some were furious that they had been reduced to virtual penury by the maintenance payments the CSA required them to hand over to ex-spouses who were living far more comfortable lifestyles than they. In some cases, men were barred by ex-partners from seeing their children. This simply added insult to injury, they felt.

'Many men felt they were being completely disenfranchised,' says Charles Monkcom. 'They felt shut out of family life, and having what they saw as fewer rights and entitlements over their children. They weren't getting any sort of deal any longer from their work, their marriages or from their children.'

Monkcom believes that downshifting, whether we like it or not, is a realistic prospect for large numbers, so we had better get used to the idea. 'Global competition is working against Western Europe. It seems likely that Western Europe will have a decreasing proportion of the world's wealth.

'If there is decreasing wealth and job opportunities, then it may be that everyone has to expect to have about five per cent chipped off their annual income – or work even harder just to stand still.'

The gains made by feminism in the 1970s and '80s in the workplace, the home, in politics and in popular ideology and culture were long overdue. No one can argue with any credibility that women should not have the same opportunities as men, the same access to education, to career advancement, to personal development. Women have achieved much in those directions, but they still have a great fight on their hands to translate theoretical victories into practice. But where has this left men? Arguably, men are now even more confused than women about their role, their legitimate concerns, their responsibilities and ambitions.

Possible pitfalls

- **Coping with loss or diminution of status.**
  As the traditional breadwinners (particularly those over 40) men may be more resistant than women to the idea of giving up the kudos and security of a high-status or mainstream job.

- **Adjusting to a different working environment, possibly self-employed working part-time or just working a 35-hour week rather than a 50-hour week.**
  The idea of spending more time working from home or outside a traditional office may not seem like an attractive option. The colleagues that you have become accustomed to having around you all the time may no longer be there when you want to talk to someone about a problem or chat about the football on TV the previous night.

- **Concern about providing for children on a smaller income.**
  Society still regards men as the traditional family breadwinners. Men will tend to worry about earning enough for family holidays, school fees, and so on, more than their partners. However, with job insecurity now so widespread, it can often be a safer bet to switch to something different that you know you will enjoy and will be good at. Even if the income is likely to be lower, you will be positively transformed into a more relaxed and productive individual if you *believe* there is more of a long-term future in your chosen alternative.

- **Change is risky, but nothing that is worth having is without risk.**
  The point is that if you believe that the steps you are considering are broadly going to take you in the right direction and that the alternative employment option is exerting a strong pull over you, heart and soul, then does status really matter that much? Or does independence of mind and spirit matter more than any negative feedback you might get from your peers. Anyone who leaves a place of work is unsettling the unique equilibrium of that particular group. Subtle, and not so subtle pressure may be placed upon those who might be seen to be threatening the cohesiveness of the group, by looking beyond it.

The question for you is whether to *yield* to that pressure or *resist* it. Only you can decide.

What women need to consider

> *Don't you know that it's different for girls?*
> Joe Jackson, singer and song-writer, 1979

Many women now in their thirties, forties and fifties grew up believing that 'having it all' was a legitimate, indeed entirely rational, aspiration. They were inspired by practical life management manuals such as *Superwoman* by Shirley Conran, and their dreams were nourished by magazines such as *Cosmopolitan*. Many came to believe that it was quite feasible, desirable even, to combine parenthood with a demanding career, and still have the energy to be a passionate lover too. Some exceptional women manage to combine these roles, or at least persuade the rest of us that they do. But many more have tried and failed to live up to this ideal of modern womanhood. The dilemmas presented to women by their multiple roles are probably as agonising now as they ever have been.

The disenchantment and confusion caused by the failure of the feminist dream is explored by the writer and broadcaster Ros Coward in her book *Our Treacherous Hearts* (1992). In a series of interviews she carried out with women about their lives and aspirations, she found a great longing in many to give up traditional paid employment. As one single mother put it: 'Who wouldn't choose to stay at home, even on the social, if the only choice is some shitty job being bossed around by some awful man?' Lack of recognition in a male-dominated working environment was a frequent complaint that made women feel that their careers were not worth the candle.

A woman film editor for BBC News with two young children, often worked long and unsocial hours. The competitive ethos sickened her. She cut her hours to 30 a week, and felt enormously relieved: 'When the news has been edited no one outside can tell who did what bit. One bit of work looks very much like another and it's meant to . . . So how do people get recognised as being good? Well, guess what, they parade their personalities! You get men staggering around with large stacks of tapes, saying, "Phew! That was a hard edit," and wiping their brows. I don't want to be judged on my personality. I want to do a good piece of work and be judged on that – only it doesn't happen like that.'

Moreover, Coward was startled to find that many women felt uncomfortable about having money over and above immediate needs, and the specific advantages they could see it brought the family. One, whose husband earned £100,000 a year preferred to live off her earnings as an archivist: 'He spends his money on family things, like cars and holidays. But day to day I support myself. I usually travel by bus and find it hard to be extravagant.'

Beyond Superwoman

The kind of attitudes Coward encountered and described may help to explain a number of things – the strong representation of women in environmental and anti-consumerist movements, and evidence that the stereotypical 'high-powered career woman and mother' is not quite the role model it once was.

Although male managers are twice as likely to be made redundant as their female counterparts, women managers are three times more likely to resign of their own accord, a survey by the Institute of Management found in 1994. Maybe women see the writing on the wall earlier than men do and they are engineering their way out of stressful, demanding work in male-dominated environments, or reducing their dependence on them before they burn out. But that could be because women are more flexible than men in balancing work and home life, and less addicted to status and the power of the peer group.

A questionnaire survey in 1995 conducted by Coutts Career Consultants in London to 500 clients who had quit their jobs, found that women found new jobs nine weeks earlier on average than men. In a bigger survey on people made redundant across Europe, involving 10,300 interviewees, women again bounced back into employment significantly earlier than men. 'This could be a sign of women's greater adaptability to changes in circumstances,' says Adrian Ramskill, Coutts' Career Operations Director. 'Maybe women are just better than men at picking themselves up and starting all over again.'

Certainly, women have always been more nomadic in terms of their employment patterns, moving in and out of jobs and self-employment, according to their circumstances. They tend to be more accustomed than men to flexibility in employment, mainly because of the breaks they take for having and raising children. In turn, they are more likely to accept insecurity in employment as a fact of life. We are not arguing that women should give up interesting well-paid jobs that they enjoy any more than we are urging women with young children to seek jobs that they neither want nor need. The only people who should make those decisions are the women themselves.

The point is that the old feminist battles have become largely obsolete. The argument now is no longer about *whether* women should pursue career or motherhood or both. It is about *how* they can best combine whichever roles suit them. Economic trends are now calling the tune and it is one women should listen to. Four out of five new jobs likely to be created by the turn of the century will go to women. Many, if not most, will be part-time. That suits most women who currently work part-time – the majority of them do not want full-time jobs. It could also favour those men and women, whether singly or in couples, who are thinking of slowing the pace of their lives and downshifting.

Our own instincts and experience of talking to the downshifters in Chapter 9 suggested to us that women may well find that they can make a smoother transition between the one-dimensional world of fast-track career and the multi-dimensional, downshifted world, than their male friends and partners.

Possible pitfalls

- **Awareness of hostility and resentment.**
  Women may encounter hostility or concerns from colleagues that they are letting the side down in one way or another. 'So you couldn't stand the heat,' others might say in a superior fashion. Of course, this may be partly true, but it is still hurtful. You may also be accused of putting home life before your career and thus, by implication, putting back the cause of independent womanhood. As we near the new millennium this is a very outdated view. Flexible working patterns, home computers and so on are making the modern workplace far less essential to a fulfilling work life than it once was.

- **Uncertainty – am I ready for this yet?**
  You will almost certainly have some doubts about whether you are doing the right thing in switching careers and lifestyle. This is likely to be especially true of women with young children who intend to stop working or to work instead from home and are worried, maybe even resentful, about reducing the pace of their careers. If the pressure for change is coming from your partner, you must work out whether you really want to leave your job or are being pushed. You should not go any further unless that question has been resolved.

- **Concern about losing workplace contact.**
  Fear of loneliness and isolation is another potential turn-off for women considering more independent employment options. Women choosing to work part-time or from home may feel cut off from the workplace camaraderie. This is often offset, however, by having more quality time with partner, friends and family. Shifting from full-time to part-time or self-employment can bring new friends and networks. Just being aware of the potential danger of isolation will encourage you to foster those new connections.

- **Loss of financial security.**
  If you are a single woman contemplating downshifting then you only

have your own circumstances, obligations and desires to consider. If you have children, then naturally they will be major factors in the equations you have to calculate, if not *the* major factor, as will any elderly dependents you may have. If this is broadly your situation, then clearly your finances and your financial security will be uppermost in your mind. But your own personality and adaptability, in particular your willingness to take risks, will also play a crucial part in your decisions. If you are still equivocating, then there are only two pieces of advice we can offer, at this stage:

1: Bear in mind that if you are happy, the people around you are more likely to be happy too. Children take their cue from their parents in all sorts of ways, and your own parents or elderly dependents are likely to have peace of mind if you have too. It stands to reason.

2: Read the rest of this book. We are going to attempt to show you how we turn the theory into practice, how to turn mere survival back into living.

Persuade your partner – or salvage your sanity!

If you have a partner who does not share your interest in downshifting, don't despair, for there are several options open to you. Maybe the biggest obstacle is one of communication and perception. Maybe they simply don't know that there are alternatives to the status quo. Perhaps they are too busy to concern themselves with anything other than the work they currently have in hand. The first step is to start talking to your partner about alternatives. Realise that if there is any downshifting to be done, you will be the one who has to engineer the changes that lead to it.

You could reach a compromise – the variations on the downshifting theme are almost limitless as we have tried to demonstrate. You could downshift, and your partner could carry on regardless. You could both downshift, and re-negotiate your personal and working relationships along lines that you both find more attractive and sustainable. This too is not an altogether failsafe strategy. In the end, an unavoidable truth may stare you both in the face. You may have to make a rather fundamental, life-changing choice. You may have to decide what or who is more important to you – your spouse or your sanity?

PART FOUR

FROM HERE TO SIMPLICITY: THE ESSENTIAL GUIDE TO PUTTING IDEAS INTO PRACTICE

CHAPTER TWELVE

You and Your Money

I find all this money a considerable burden.
John Paul Getty Jnr

Whether we keep our money in a teapot or a bank vault, the way we spend it reveals as much about ourselves to the outside world as the way we earn it. Our cheque book stubs, credit card statements and welfare payment books can tell the story of our lives far more succinctly and accurately than the edited highlights we choose to record in our diaries. Inevitably, the more money you have, the easier it should be to decide that you can get by on less or strike out in a new direction that makes a lower income more likely. Downshifting is not impossible without a few thousand pounds stashed away, but it is certainly more difficult and will probably take longer. We are acutely aware that a positive decision to simplify life, and accept the principle of living on less money, can never be a general prescription, while there are so many millions in Britain and the world living in poverty, or on the brink of it. We do not underestimate the genuine difficulties many people have in making ends meet. But at the same time, it is worth pointing out that some of the downshifters we interviewed for this book had modest incomes before they decided to change gear. Most people can incorporate some downshifting philosophy into their lives, if they wish to do so, without having to embrace the whole package.

Make good your bad habits

When you make the decision to downshift, whether now or in the future, partly or wholly, your attitude towards the way money is earned and spent is likely to undergo a transformation. If you have fallen into bad financial habits, and your use of money is more like sado-masochist abuse, the first point to understand is that you can change if you want to. The key question is one of motivation. If you seriously want more time to enjoy life, to study, to spend more quality time with friends and family, to learn new skills then you will probably find a way to make it happen. Having committed yourself to this goal, you now need a plan for achieving it. This plan should increase your financial independence, liberate you from bulimic 'earn it and spend it' binge living and make you feel altogether happier and more in control.

Cheques and balances: how much are you worth?

Here we show you how to give yourself and your family, if you have one, a financial health check. Whatever ails you, there is no cure or prognosis without a diagnosis. It will not require you to make wall-charts that you have to fill in every day, not will it involve a great deal of paperwork. Much of what we are recommending is simple common sense. Our main purpose is to inspire and provoke new ways of thinking about money, not to start a cult that has its own jargon, slogans and mantras. What we are recommending is not self-denial and hair shirts, but self-discovery and silk shirts (if you conclude your life would not be complete without silk shirts). Remember, over a lifetime, a great deal of money is likely to pass through your hands. Someone starting out in an average job now, earning £17,000 a year for 40 years, will earn nearly £700,000 by the time he or she retires. 'Where does it all go?' we ask ourselves. Now is the time to translate that rhetorical question into one that you can answer.

The 5-step financial health check

Step 1

Make a list of your assets. Record the main items, such as house, car and furniture, household appliances, computer equipment, jewellery, ward-robe contents, etc. Next to each heading write down your estimate of what they would be worth gross if you tried to sell them. Then do the same for any savings and investments that you have, including pensions. Do not build into any equation an expected legacy or windfall. For the moment, we are interested only in your present financial circumstances, and so should you be. Record the current value if you were to 'cash in' these investments now.

Step 2

On a new sheet of paper make a list of your liabilities, all your debts from your outstanding mortgage to the money you owe, including interest, on loans from credit card companies, bank overdraft, the £100 you borrowed from your friend last month to stop your bank balance going into the red again, and so on.

Step 3

Add up your assets and your liabilities. Subtract your liabilities from your assets. The end figure is your net worth. If you have more than you owe, the figure will be positive. If you owe more than you have, yours will be a negative net worth; this is not the most auspicious start to a newly-downshifted life, but don't panic.

Step 4

Now you need to compare your income with your outgoings. Make a note of your income for the past year from earnings (your wages or salary) and from 'unearned' sources such as interest on savings, and dividends from shares, etc. Use the net figure after tax and other deductions at source have been taken away. Write down this net income total.

Step 5

Now list and cost your outgoings. These are your spending over the same period, under the relevant headings: mortgage payments, rent, food, eating out, transport, telephone, clothes, fuel, car, holidays, and so on. Try to separate out which outgoings are work-related, so that you have headings that are wholly or mainly connected with your employment for items such as lunches, travel and clothes. Write down the total.

This health check will help you to decide whether you can afford to earn less. If you cannot work out the figures because you don't keep bills and receipts, then make estimates. Thereafter, start keeping those important pieces of paper so that you can make a more accurate assessment next time. If this exercise seems too tedious a chore to contemplate, then spread it over a few days. Don't feel you can get away with not doing it. If you conclude, after taking stock of your life, that it needs a change of pace and direction, you will find it hard to make progress unless you carry out a regular personal financial audit.

A matter of life or debt

Now you know where your finances stand, and exactly how good or hopeless you are at dealing with money. Leaving aside your mortgage for a moment, let us pause to consider the question of debt, but don't put the paper and pens away just yet. Some people are almost professional debtors, spending much of their lives avoiding their creditors or getting themselves into even worse trouble trying to pay off the money they already owe. If you have significant debts, several hundreds or thousands of pounds, and you don't already have a proper strategy for eliminating them, then get one. The longer you are saddled with these obligations, the longer it will take you to downshift – you cannot proceed while weighed down by these burdens. To lighten your load you have four options: cut your spending; increase your income; realise an asset; or raid your savings or investments. Combining several of these choices rather than just selecting one, will enable you to banish the debt much more quickly. Most people in employment are able to put some money into savings or investments on a regular basis. If you have both savings *and* non-mortgage debts, then consider why you have not used the former to pay off the latter. But just remember that the interest yielded by your savings is likely to be eaten up several times over by the interest you are paying on your debt. The best course for anyone in serious financial trouble is to get some debt counselling. Your nearest Citizen's Advice Bureau should be able to point you in the right direction.

What should be far easier than getting out of debt is making sure you don't get into debt in the first place. Simplifying your life means simplifying your finances. Credit cards are an invitation to debt, so cut up all those you can live without. Try to see whether you can get by with just one. Several credit card companies no longer charge an annual fee. Once you have cleared your credit card debts, then make sure you *always* pay off the outstanding amount before each monthly deadline. Then and only then will your credit card become a convenience instead of a burden.

How we use money to keep our treadmill turning

You can now pinpoint your exact position on the two financial axes of Assets and Liabilities, and Income and Spending. You have also written down what you actually do with your money, once you have earned it. Do not throw your notes away because what you have written down may be used in evidence against you; but only if you *choose* to interrogate yourself along the lines we are about to suggest. You are about to find out whether your spending is rational or whether perhaps it is simply propping up a lifestyle that is making you weary, depressed, empty and disillusioned. You are about to discover the difference between what you *actually* spend and what you *need* to spend if you decide that your priorities in life are changing. When we pursue conventional career paths we tend to spend our money so as to *comfort, compensate, conform* and *compete*. At the epicentre of our all spending urges lie these four 'Cs'. We often use money to prop up burdensome lifestyles that we strongly suspect are completely unsustainable, rather than to help to create new sustainable, liberating ones. It's easily done. We did it. Let's look at some examples of this spending behaviour that spans all these four 'Cs', and some which fit into just one category or another. Holidays and travel are a good example of a type of spending that gives you comfort, and compensation, and enables you to compete and conform to the rat race.

'I want a week in paradise and I want it now'

Holiday destinations, what you do when you get there, and the sort of accommodation you stay in reveal a great deal about you to the people you leave toiling away in the office, the factory or the shop. Like clothes, they are subject to fads and fashions. When you work very hard and very long hours, then you feel stressed. People and their demands crowd in on you, and eventually you want to escape. A few days in paradise are what's needed, well away from all the people you have to please day in and day out. Take one of us, Judy, as an example. In 1995, when she was working as a staff journalist on *The Observer* newspaper, she took three expensive holidays and enjoyed each enormously. She went to a health farm for a week to bliss out, de-stress and have her body pampered and pummelled; to the remote west coast of Scotland and the islands of Rhum and Eigg, to enjoy beautiful landscapes, walk, explore and just 'be'; and to a quiet corner of Majorca with her partner to do much the same thing, and to eat some good food that someone else had cooked. All perfect holidays. Cost? Getting on for £3,000 or about 10 per cent of her post-tax annual income. Judy likes to think that she went to these places simply because she really wanted the experiences; she suspects she went for comfort and compensation for the hard edges and disappointments she experienced all the rest of the year; and also because she, and her equally busy companion, left it all to the last minute, as usual, and couldn't think of anywhere else to go.

When the going gets tough, the tough go shopping

We need money and spend money in order to meet our basic physical, or subsistence needs: for food, light, warmth, hygiene and shelter. We spend money to conform to the expectations of our peers and to mark ourselves out from them, to define ourselves as members of a tribe, but also as individuals within that tribe. We also spend money to meet our own and others' emotional needs; to have fun and make up for the times when we have had too much fun working or playing.

We might as well stay with Judy, since she is in soul-baring mode. When she was in full-time employment, she reckons she spent about £100 a month, often more, let us say £1,500 a year on clothes, both to cheer herself up and to conform to the general expectation, especially applied to women, that one must look smart for the office and not wear the same clothes too often. (Within four months of taking redundancy she had spent only £35 in total on clothes.)

Judy's supermarket bills were inflated by the 'comfort and compensate' factor. There was a high proportion of ready-made meals, bought to save time on cooking and by the need to get round the store so quickly that she never looked at the prices. Food, general household spending, dry cleaning, and luxuries such as cut flowers (the cheer factor again) came to about £100 a week for herself and her companion, or about £5,200 a year of which her share was £2,600 a year. It has since fallen by half. We could assume that £1,000 of that was job-related comfort and compensation spending. Despite having copious quantities of convenience foods at home, the idea of actually heating them up was often just too exhausting to contemplate, so takeaways would sometimes be sent for, or impromptu restaurant jaunts made during weekday evenings. Annual cost? Probably about £750. Popping out for lunch with colleagues, say three times a week, and the occasional round of drinks on a Saturday night after the paper had gone to press would set her back about £30 a week, or over a 46-week working year about £1,380. Then there were tube fares for getting to and from the office Tuesday to Friday, and petrol and car parking money on Saturday. About £800 a year. She also used to have a cleaner coming once a week, because there never seemed to be any time to keep the house straight herself. The cost of that was £1,300. Now her cleaner just comes on alternate weeks, because Judy now has more time to clear up her own grubby trail of chaos that she leaves behind her. So that's another £650 kept in the kitty that would have been spent while in full-time conventional employment. Maybe we should at this point add up all these figures to find out how much Judy was spending simply to comfort, compensate, compete and conform in relation to her job. She makes it a grand total of £9,080. In other words, nearly one-third of her disposable income, just over 30 per cent, was spent on propping herself up at her work, just maintaining her position in the rat race – not improving it, not moving ahead, just surviving. Now pick up the pen and paper again, and work out what proportion of your spending is devoted to propping yourself up in your job, just keeping the treadmill turning. You may be every bit as aghast as Judy was, and as some of the downshifters we interviewed were after they carried out similar calculations.

Getting more from less: the four new 'Cs'

You've now worked out your annual rat race membership fee – the amount you spend just to perpetuate this one-dimensional, career-oriented, anxiety-inducing lifestyle. Naturally, the figure is likely to be a great deal higher if you take into account the type of house you live in and the kind of car you have, and all sorts of other expenditure that is peculiar to you and your life. We have not gone into all conceivable variation on the expenditure theme – only you can judge whether your house, your car, your hang-gliding lessons, and your top-of-the-range camcorder give satisfaction and good value.

However, you may well have concluded by now that too many of your spending habits reflect the needs that we have already ascribed to Comfort, Compensate, Conform and Compete. If so, what do you do? How can you develop a more rational, healthy and effective way of managing and spending money? Here's a suggestion: think about whether your spending patterns might change if you placed four new 'Cs' at the top of your list of priorities. What would they be? We suggest you try out Control, Challenge, Compatibility and Creativity.

Give yourself a break – take control

Let us explain what we mean. The people who feel fulfilled and generally content are often the ones who have a strong sense of having influence and *control* over their lives. They believe that they, not fate, shape their destiny and they consciously take responsibility for doing so. The way that they spend money expresses that feeling of control. These people usually have a good idea what they want from life. They have goals and plans for achieving those goals. Their spending is tailored to these and money is a means to these ends not an end in itself. Money, for this type of person is a tool rather than a comforter. If this person sounds like you and you discover you are motivated to do so, then you are likely to make a highly successful and enthusiastic downshifter! If you decide that your *goals* in life are changing, then your *behaviour* will change accordingly. So too will the way you think about money and the way you spend it. What's more you may decide that the way you earn your money needs a thorough re-think. If you are unhappy in your current job, try to pinpoint the source of that unhappiness. It's quite possible that the key problem is one of control, or the lack of it. If you are frustrated at not being able to do your job your way and that you are wasting your talents on an organisation that does not deserve you, self-employment could suit you perfectly. It is by no means a soft option. There is no one else to blame when it goes wrong, but win or lose it is all down to you.

The power of the consumer

We can also use money to *challenge* what we don't like about our lives and the world around us. As we have described earlier, the consumer is sovereign in Western cultures and that supremacy has brought about an excessive plundering of finite natural resources. But the flip side of the 'sovereign shopper' idea is that people can use their money to challenge business and commerce to clean up their act. You don't need to be a member of Friends of the Earth or Greenpeace to be a useful and active environmentalist, just someone who shops and spends money sensibly and sustainably. If you don't like the way battery hens are kept, don't buy their eggs; if you disapprove of exploitation of certain developing countries by oil companies, don't buy their products. If you make a connection between commercial cause and environmental effect, follow that connection through when you select the goods and services you are buying. Nothing concentrates a business executive's mind more effectively than an emerging or threatened consumer boycott, as Shell's U-turn over the deep sea disposal of the Brent Spar oil rig demonstrated. He or she has no option but to listen and do something to placate the angry consumer. The political power of the sovereign consumer is huge and usually underestimated, if contemplated at all. Use it!

Spending + believing: do they add up?

When you spend money to challenge the status quo it can make you feel influential, and rightly so. In turn, this helps you to feel more in control of life. Now let us examine the third 'C', to find out how much *compatibility* there is between your spending habits and your personal philosophy. Unless you are a monk, a saint or a hermit, there is likely to be some degree of mismatch between your use of money and your general outlook on life. Let us take the motor car to show you what we mean, because it is a classic example of our schizophrenic attitudes as citizens and consumers. People love their cars, find them indispensable, lavish money on their upkeep, and even – heaven help us – give them names. Often these are the same people who are careful to recycle all their bottles, jars and newspapers, seek out organic food, and in most other respects shun environmentally damaging behaviour. Of course very few people will be able to eliminate incompatible spending and consumption patterns for all sorts of good reasons. Realistically, the best you can aspire to achieve in dealing with this kind of inconsistency and mismatch is reduce it. Maybe, for example, we should aim to use the car only when there are no other viable alternatives. The more we use public transport, and walk or cycle to places, the easier it will become to do so because the pressure to improve provision and facilities will increase through simple people power.

Give your right brain a free rein

Finally, in order to feel that we can reduce our dependence on money to comfort and compensate, to conform and compete, we need to build more *creativity* into the way that we spend, save and invest it. We rely too much on advice from bank managers and other financial advisers when managing our money. Many of us are too busy earning to think enough about making our money work for us, through savings, investments, and pensions. Financial planning should never be an optional extra in anyone's life. Remember it's your money, and your future we're talking about. It is never too early to make plans for a comfortable, and enjoyable old age free from money worries. Thinking creatively about our finances means breaking out of our short-term 'here and now' mindsets, the unthinking rituals of earning and spending. Creative money management involves planning, foresight, intuition, checking out hunches, keeping in touch with new services and offers. It means trying to get some pleasure and satisfaction from our investments as well as maximising returns. Here are some tips for injecting some creative and lateral thinking into your money management:

- Too much money sits in bank or building society accounts earning paltry amounts of interest. That money could be earning its keep better elsewhere. Check in the weekend broadsheet personal finance sections each week to make sure you are getting the best rate of interest available. You may have more in your instant access accounts than you really need for emergencies. If so, consider putting part of that sum into a higher-earning account for three months, a year or five years.

- Try not to delegate too much financial management and planning to others. Your money can be badly invested, when you are too busy to keep track. Moreover, unless you are careful to avoid it, the money that you put into your savings, investments and pension funds may go into all sorts of undesirable trades such as tobacco manufacturing, arms trading or despoilation of rain forests.

- The whole business of investing money wisely so that we do not gain from others' misery and loss, now or in the future, is so vast that it properly belongs in another book. Fortunately, it has been written already. It is called *The Ethical Investor*, by Russell Sparkes, and we commend it to you. Regard it as your first ethical investment, if you have made no other – it will quite likely be the first of several that you decide to make. Ethical, or socially responsible, has become a fast-growing sector of the investment management field. The first ethical unit trust in Britain, Stewardship, was launched by the insurance company Friends Provident in 1984. Over the ensuing decade the value of its funds, and others that were set up in its wake, grew to more than £800m. The good news for those who incline to the down-shifting philosophy is that ethical investment is likely to match or out-perform other forms of investment.

- Make a will. Everyone over the age of 18 should make a will, down-shifters included. If you die intestate (you did not make a will), you are simply adding to the distress of loved ones that you leave behind. Not only will they have to sort out your affairs, they may also be denied part of your estate that you would have wanted them to receive. Instead, it might go to the tax man. Making a will eliminates the extra hassle relatives would otherwise experience, and ensures that they get what you would wish them to inherit.

Another important area to consider when you are thinking of down-shifting is your likely old age. Most private pensions are earnings related. How do you cope as a downshifter?

Pensions and retirement

Few people really understand how pensions work, know exactly what provision they have and what income they are likely to receive on and after retirement. If this sounds rather like you, then we suggest you research your current pension provision as a matter of urgency. Assess how well it matches your present and future needs and investigate some alternatives. The sooner you do this the better. Individuals need to save at least 10 per cent of their income over their lifetime in order to build up a pension equal to half their salary at retirement, according to the National Association of Pension Funds. Living better on less is a realistic, liberating proposition for large numbers of people. Living better on a pittance almost certainly isn't.

Downshifting is about making life better for *good*, not just for now. The time, effort and money you invest in a good pension while you are earning will be handsomely rewarded in your old age, and should save you a great deal of worry about making ends meet.

If you are now aged between 20 and 50, then by the time you retire, Britain's famous 'cradle-to-grave' welfare state is likely to look very different. Whichever political party is in power, the holes in our welfare 'safety net' are likely to be much larger. Do everything you can to protect yourself and your family from the risks of falling through it.

There follow some basic tips on retirement planning for those who are in full-time or part-time employment, those who are self-employed or thinking of working for themselves, and finally those who are not currently earning.

Pensions: *if you're employed*

Whether you plan to stay in a full-time job or switch to part-time employment, consider exactly what your present or would-be organisation is offering and contributing in the way of an *occupational* pension. If you have already changed employers a few times, find out exactly what you have waiting for you on retirement in the way of *preserved* pension rights. Does your present employer operate a scheme and are you in the scheme? If so, think about whether you are paying enough into it. Are you contracted in or out of SERPS, the State Earnings Related Pensions Scheme, essentially a top-up of your basic state pension. Can you afford to make some Additional Voluntary Contributions [AVCs] to your occupational pension? It might be very worthwhile to do so, especially if you plan to downshift in a year or a few years time and are currently earning more than you need to spend.

If you are in any doubt at all about the answers to these questions, telephone your employer's occupational pension scheme manager or adviser immediately to make an appointment and in the meantime jot down some more questions that spring to mind to ask him or her. If your employer does not operate its own scheme, it is possible that you pay into a personal or portable pension. Make sure you really understand what it is you are paying into, and what you can expect when you retire. Either way, whether you have an occupational pension or a personal pension scheme, find out what the consequences might be if you decide to go part-time, if this is a step you are considering. It may affect your decision about cutting the hours you work. If you are in employment and you have no current pension plan, do think very seriously about the benefits of getting one.

Perhaps you may decide to go self-employed in a year or two, to downshift *gradually*. In that case, buy into a pension that allows that sort of flexibility and doesn't penalise your freedom to manoeuvre in any way.

Pensions: *if you're self-employed*

Working for yourself is usually pretty hard work, and can take over your life just as easily as working for your former boss did. Planning your retirement usually comes pretty low in your list of priorities if it figures at all, but plan you must. You, more than your employed fellows, would probably benefit from seeking independent financial advice.

Don't just look in *Yellow Pages*, try to get a personal recommendation. An independent adviser will be able to tell you just how reliable and productive your current pension arrangements are, and point you in the direction of the right arrangements for you if they are inadequate or you have none.

There are various schemes on the market to suit your unpredictable earning patterns, so that at the end of each trading year, you may contribute a *lump sum* out of your 'profits' into the pension. Remember, you don't have to invest a fixed monthly sum to build up your pension, just like you might have done when you worked for your former single employer. You can vary these contributions, according to how well your one-person business is doing. Remember also that your pension contributions are tax-free, so it is an excellent way of saving.

In addition, the old 'belt and braces' approach may be appropriate: spreading the risks *and* the opportunities of making money for your old age is often a good idea. So do think about setting aside some of your self-employment earnings that you don't need for meeting monthly outgoings into a pension – and also of putting some into ordinary savings and investments too. One day you'll be glad that you did, even if it seems like a real pain now.

Pensions: *if you're unemployed*

If you are not earning now and dependent on State benefits, then the very mention of pension and retirement planning may seem like a cloud-cuckoo-land. Your immediate need is to get employment, of course, and maybe what you have read so far will help you get it. We hope so, because only once you are in work and earning money can you then contemplate *setting aside* money for when you are older.

If you are, or about to become, the non-earning spouse of someone who is in employment or in self-employment, persuade your other half to act on the above advice pronto! Your future may depend on it, together or separately, one way or another. If you have earned in the past check up on your own entitlement, perhaps from preserved pensions. You may be one of the fortunate people to whom divorce, separation and premature death of a spouse never happens. But these days, who can be certain, either way? Find out, just to be sure, what would be the position if you found yourself in any of these circumstances.

Do remember that pensions are not without their drawbacks. As a general rule, you may not withdraw any of your pension until retirement age. On retirement only a small amount may be drawn out in cash, the rest used to buy an annuity that provides regular income. Consider supplementing your pension provision with other investment schemes such as unit trusts and Personal Equity Plans (PEPs).

CHAPTER THIRTEEN

A New Way of Working

Next week there can't be any crisis. My schedule is already full.
Henry Kissinger, US diplomat

With our jobs no longer supplying guaranteed security and identity, Britain is ripe for a revolution in 'flexibilisation' of work. The aim? To help us as individuals to find a better balance between family, job and all our other commitments and activities.

In this chapter we help you to turn daydreaming about finding this nirvana of a balanced life into reality. We suggest ways of figuring out what kind of work would suit you best and lay out the alternatives open to full-time conventional employment. We hope you will be pleasantly surprised at the number of options which beckon from the world beyond the rat race treadmill.

Ten steps to making the break

Many people don't get past the stage of bellyaching about their employer, sitting at their desks daydreaming of escape. If, on the other hand, you are unhappy enough to seriously consider leaving your present job you will now be faced with a bewildering, but exciting choice of alternatives.

You will need to ask yourself whether you want to switch to another permanent, full-time job in the same field or a full-time job in another. Alternatively, you may prefer to try working part-time, re-training or working for yourself from home. Maybe you want to juggle some kind of career with being a mother or house-husband. Whichever course you think you might like to follow, it is essential that you think it through and plan ahead in great detail before making any moves. You may be

143

surprised to find that the course of action you thought was the most attractive, wouldn't work at all well for you in reality.

The first step to take is to carry out a paper exercise to help you work out what you really want to do and – just as important! – whether your particular skills are suited to fulfilling your goal. If not, you may need either to re-train or to modify your plans. The following simple ten-step exercise is designed to help you on your way.

Step 1: *goals*
Try and work out what you really want to do. Start by listing and ranking the things you dislike about your present job or employment. Then ask yourself honestly how far short your job falls from meeting your aspirations. You may come to the conclusion that changing your employer but staying in the same field would solve most of your problems. If so, then that is probably the best course of action – at least in the short term. If not, then more drastic action is called for.

Step 2: *identify your strong points*
Ask yourself what kind of work you would shine at. The answer probably lies, at least in part, in your past. Remember, your present job is not all you have ever done or the only skill you know. List all your achievements since starting school, not just academic, but hobbies, sports and community activities too. Look at the list and pick out the six achievements you felt best about. What was it in each activity that gave you a buzz? It could have been, for example, acting as part of a closely-knit group, or alternatively making a success of going it alone. It could have been working outdoors; a sense of danger or security; the adrenalin of physical activity; or the excitement of solving a problem or conducting some penetrating piece of analysis.

Step 3: *highlight key skills*
Go back over each of these episodes and highlight the key skills you used to achieve the result. Then do an audit of your current skills and specialist knowledge. How many marry up with your list of rewarding activities? Are there any gaps that a bit of training, on or off your job, could fill if necessary?

Step 4: *mix and match*
Review your two lists and see what themes keep recurring. Did the skills you used to apply, and which made you feel good, involve mainly data,

ideas, people or things? Were the activities carefully planned and structured or did they evolve as you went along? What kind of working pace did you feel most comfortable at and to what level of pressure do you best respond?

Tease out which skills from past and present give you most satisfaction of all to point you in the right direction for the kind of jobs which would be most suitable. Often it will turn out to be different from what you do now, or what you thought you wanted to do in the future.

Step 5: *highlight dislikes*
Do the same exercise as above for the six activities in your life which you have least enjoyed, isolating what it was about each which turned you off. Was it boredom, no time to think, dealing with people, working on your own, too much pressure or travel, or not using your hands or your brain? This will help you identify what *not* to do in the future so that you don't jump from the frying-pan into the fire.

Step 6: *get feedback*
We can all be self-deceiving. Ask two friends who have known you a long time what they think are your greatest strengths and weaknesses. Check this against your own list.

Step 7: *count up opportunities and pitfalls*
Note any opportunities in the offing which may help to smooth the way for you to change your working life. These could include a redundancy cheque, the fact that your children will soon be leaving home, or the possibility of linking up with friends who have similar goals, dreams and ideas. Then write down everything which might constrain your options and choices for the future. Do you have expensive school fees to pay or elderly relatives you may soon be caring for, and so on? But don't be too intimidated. Treat this as a list of hurdles to be crossed and accommodated, *not* a catalogue of excuses to do nothing.

Step 8: *budget ahead*
Take a good hard look at your cash flow. Whatever your next career, it is likely that you will take a cut in income, at least initially. So look back at the calculations you made after reading the last section on finance and work out what you need to survive, as opposed to how much it takes to maintain your current living standards. Then compare this figure with the kind of salary you will expect to earn by following the new career path of

your choice. You will quickly see whether it is financially viable in the immediate future or not.

When doing this, remember to calculate whether your new working life means that you will be saving on things such as commuting, business clothes and working lunches. If you will no longer be needing these expensive accessories your costs will go down significantly. What's more, if the aim is to switch to a less stressful way of working, you are also much less likely to need the expensive retail therapy such as frequent restaurant meals or weekends away to keep you going. But don't overdo the slash and burn. It is important to be able to enjoy simple pleasures and treats in life and if you end up permanently worried about making ends meet you will be just as stressed as you were in your high-pay high-anxiety job.

Step 9: *dream your impossible dreams*
Let go and write down everything you dream of doing – however way out or ambitious it may seem. See how many fit in at all with the lists you've prepared. Then eliminate the dreams to which your talents and likely earning power 'barring that lottery win!' are clearly unsuited and aim for those which are realistically achievable.

It may be, for example, that you've always wanted to try living abroad for a few years, but that is just not compatible with your family commitments and your employment options. On the other hand, you may also have always wanted to live in the country and if your skills are suited to working from home either through self-employment or tele-commuting, then this dream may be realisable sooner than you had dreamed possible. A good idea at this point is to imagine your ideal life in five years time – the work you're doing, where you're living, your family set-up, how you spend most of your time. This will help you with Step 10.

Step 10: *set aims and objectives*
Sort out your aims and objectives before you begin to actively explore new ways of working or prepare to hand in your notice. Your aims are the grand strategic visions for fulfilling your realistic dreams five years ahead and beyond. Your objectives are the stepping stones to get you there. They are tactical, measurable and you can set deadlines for them. Your aims may be:

- gain control of my life
- work fewer hours
- spend more time with my family
- move to the country

And your objectives may be:

- within a fortnight to draw up a *curriculum vitae* and send it to potential employers in the new field I'm interested in
- within three months prepare a detailed plan for my own home-based business
- within one month put the house on the market

What will work for me?

The guide above will help you identify what work you are likely to be good at. Many of you reading this and looking to downshift will already have a very clear idea of what it is you want to do. Others may be planning to carry on as normal while their partner downshifts. But what about those of you who don't have a clear vision? Well, as we said earlier, there are a whole range of options available, and a growing number of specialist handbooks on offer to help guide you. Below we take you through the new ways to work which are likely to become the mainstream employment patterns of the future. Remember, you are not alone! At a glance, the main options open to you are as follows:

Flexible working

1   full-time hours
2   part-time hours
3   job share
4   term time working
5   telecommuting

Self-employment

1   from home
2   in an office

Unpaid work

1   volunteering and community activity
2   homemaking

Flexible working 1: full-time hours

If what you are looking for is more control over when and how you work, but you don't fancy going it alone, then flexible working is probably the right path to follow. In 1995, around one in ten men and one in seven women in full-time jobs were working flexible hours. Many jobs are now advertised in newspapers with flexible hours of work which mean employees can negotiate to work during the day outside the standard hours of nine to five, or work evenings and/or weekends if it fits in better with their outside commitments. The good news for those of you who like the idea of flexitime is that the trend is ever upwards. More and more employers are becoming attracted to it as a way of keeping experienced skilled workers who have to juggle other commitments such as a young family.

Beware however any attempt by a present or future employer to make employing you on flexitime an excuse to reduce your job security and employee rights. It may be, for example, that a potential employer might offer you full-time flexible working to suit your need to work evenings rather than full days, but may try to deny you pension rights or full sickness cover. It is essential to check the fine print before signing any flexitime contract.

Flexible working 2: part-time hours

If you are looking to work less hard and can afford a reasonable cut in salary then part-time working could well be the answer. Traditionally, part-time employment usually meant a low skill, low-paid job such as cleaning or piecework. But increasingly, part-timers are becoming accepted in office jobs and in the professions, particularly in the form of job sharing.

While trade unions remain highly suspicious of part-time work because it often means few rights for the workers, many social commentators see it as a way for both men and women to create a better balance between employment and family. At the moment, many women face the following unpalatable choice: competing on men's terms and choosing not to have children; taking the risk of a career break to start a family; or trying to balance long working hours with child and home duties, an unequal struggle which all too often ends in exhaustion or divorce.

If you opted for part-time work you would be very far from alone.

Between 1987 and 1995 the number of women working part-time rose by 12 per cent to 5.2 million, while for men the number rose by 50 per cent to 1.2 million.

Of course, many of these people will have been forced to take part-time work after losing full-time jobs. Nevertheless, switching to working maybe 20 hours or even 30 hours a week after the endless drudgery of a full-time 48-weeks-a-year job is liberating and rewarding if done by choice. It can allow you to fit work around everything else in your life – family, friends, hobbies – instead of your job always coming first. With this better balance is likely to come greater peace of mind and a healthier, if more frugal, lifestyle. For all these reasons, part-time workers are often better workers. A 1996 survey by the Policy Studies Institute in London found employers only too happy to have part-timers on their books because they were highly productive and motivated, took few days off and had a low turnover rate.

If you're planning to take the plunge, however, do think through future expenses. If you were thinking of moving to a bigger home, for example, you may have to shelve your plans. And if you are likely to start a family in the near future, or to be caring for an elderly relative, you need to make sure your new income (perhaps plus savings) will cover the extra expenditure.

Flexible working 3: job share

Job sharing is another flexible friend which is finding favour with both employees and employers. It involves two people sharing one full-time job between them. They usually divide the working hours, pay, benefits and holiday entitlement down the middle. So, if you job-shared a solicitor's post, for example, you might end up working 20 hours a week on around £15,000 a year and be entitled to two weeks annual holiday and half a full-time employee's pension entitlement.

Job sharing is now an accepted way of easily introducing part-time working into traditional full-time occupations. One high profile example is the directorship of Anti-Slavery International, the world's oldest human rights group, which is now shared between two women. The joint appointment in 1996 of Zerbanoo Gifford and Barbara Rogers broke new ground as the first job share awarded for the top post of a major British voluntary organisation.

If you enjoy your present job but find the long hours or the pressure of work exhausting, why not suggest a job share to your boss? You might be surprised at how positive a reaction you get. Employers who don't want to lose talented staff are growing more amenable to being propositioned like this from below – and they may well prefer to offer you a job share than see you walk out.

If you are offered a job share with your present employer or elsewhere, however, do beware that you are not being asked to do more than half a job. Sharing a five-day-week job and salary does not mean that each of you should work three days worth of hours a week to catch up on any overlap and so on. Nor should you feel any pressure to work beyond your allotted hours. Otherwise, you'll be heading straight back towards square one.

For those looking to pursue an active career on a part-time basis *Job Sharing: A Practical Guide* by Pam Walton offers lots of detailed advice.

Flexible working 4: term time working

Term time working is an ingenious way of giving parents who would otherwise not be able to hold down a paid job the chance to do so. Initiated by enlightened employers, it gives workers with children the same conditions of service as full-time or part-time employees but allows them to take unpaid leave during school holidays. This is obviously an ideal arrangement if you are a single mother or father. Often single parents are put off getting a job by the cost of childcare which can often be so high that the family is better off on welfare benefits. Under a term time working arrangement, a parent can both earn a living and be the prime carer of his or her children.

Unfortunately, term time working has yet to catch on in a major way, but pressure is mounting on both politicians and employers to smooth the path for single parents looking to get back into work. At present most of the organisations pioneering term time working are in the public sector, with local authorities taking the lead. As a starting point, it might be worth contacting your local council to see whether they have jobs available on a term time basis, and whether they keep a register of local employers who do.

Flexible working 5: telecommuting

Telecommuting is perhaps the best publicised of the new ways of working. Made possible by the huge advances in information technology and the explosion in home-owned computers, it allows people to work at home some, or occasionally all, of the time. Telecommuters keep in touch with their managers and outside clients by telephone, fax, email and the Internet.

At present around 600,000 people in Britain telecommute at home for a single employer, but numbers are expected to rise steadily over the next 20 years or so. Another 700,000 or so people are freelance teleworkers, working via computer from home for several employers. Not only does telecommuting make sense for employees with expensive commuter journeys, but it makes sense for employers too. People often work more efficiently from home, especially in short bursts, than in the office where there are constant interruptions. And employees who are allowed the flexibility of working from home some of the time are likely to be happier and therefore more productive. It is important, however, to establish ground rules from the start. You may want the flexibility of working from home, but you must make sure that your employer is not going to baulk at paying for your phone and fax bills.

If you think telecommuting would suit you, why not raise it with your employer? For all you know, there may already be other people in the building who have negotiated just such an arrangement. Similarly, when applying for new jobs, sound out prospective employers. It may well be easier to establish such a working arrangement from day one rather than persuading your boss a few months down the line that you should spend part of your week working from home.

Self-employment – is it right for me?

All the above are, of course, variations on the theme of the traditional full-time job with one employer. But it may be that you are ready for something more radical. Perhaps it is not so much the long hours, the commuting or the stress that has got to you, but the fact that you are working for someone else. Maybe you would prefer to set your own agenda, be in control of your own working life, even, dare we say it, make your own mistakes. If so, then switching to self-employment may well be your best course of action.

In the past, small-scale self-employment was mainly limited to a fairly small range of jobs, such as running small shops or pubs, cleaning people's homes, plumbing and decorating, or freelancing as a typist. Until the last decade or so, most of us worked in traditional full-time jobs. But in recent years there has been an explosion of freelancing in many areas of employment. One is our own field, journalism; others are legal work, with more and more lawyers hiring out their skills as consultants; computer programming; and accountancy and book-keeping businesses where individuals can now comfortably work for a range of clients from home with the aid of computer and fax machine.

Charles Handy, in his best-selling book *The Age of Unreason*, points to the need to re-invent work through what he terms a 'portfolio' approach. A portfolio lifestyle, as defined by Handy, involves five kinds of work: (1) waged, with money paid for hours worked; (2) fee work, for results delivered; (3) homework, from looking after children to shopping, cleaning and washing the car; (4) gift work, done for free outside the home, for friends, charities and so on; and (5) study work such as learning a new language or training for a sport.

This kind of lifestyle, which aims for a balance between traditional work, i.e. a job, and the demands of home, community and study is easiest to assume if you are self-employed. People in one job can still aspire to a portfolio lifestyle, but all too often, the job eats up so much time that there is little left for anything else. The joy of self-employment is that, so long as enough money is coming in, you can balance your life to suit your own needs, not the company's.

Have I got what it takes? Asking this question is vital, as it is no good embarking on a life of self-employment in a fit of enthusiasm if going it alone doesn't suit your personality or skills. Most practical books on self-employment, otherwise known as starting a micro-business, agree on the necessary qualities you need to possess to be a successful entrepreneur. They include:

- a high degree of motivation and self-belief
- drive and determination
- a willingness to listen – and learn
- a very clear focus on what your goals are
- resilience, self-discipline and self-reliance
- effective time management
- good communication skills

If you've got all these in abundance, you've got the makings of a successful self-employed person. But it is as well, also, to consider the potential pitfalls of being your own boss. In *Go It Alone*, a book on self-employment by Richard Greensted, ten interviewees who went solo talk frankly about the pitfalls they encountered.

Their jobs were diverse (they included a literary agent, a marketing adviser, an interior designer and a surveyor) but they encountered many common problems. These included loneliness, a feeling of isolation from the outside world, frequent ups and downs as work poured in and then dried up, and sometimes serious problems with cash flow when clients paid up late.

Before you embark on self-employment it is vital that you think through how all these pitfalls, and any others you can think of, would affect you. Would you take it all in your stride? Or are you a real worrier who would find it impossible to switch off if you were going through a thin patch?

Remember also to take into account the concrete benefits you will lose when you are no longer employed by someone else. These include paid annual and public holidays, sickness pay, paid maternity leave, and employers' contributions to pensions. Added together these can be worth a lot to you as an employee – and should not be discarded lightly.

Self-employment 1: from home

Where do I work from? Once you have decided that being your own boss would indeed work for you, the next question is where to make your base. For many people the answer is blindingly obvious: home.

Working from home may sound to you like a backward step, inextricably linked in your mind with housework. Yet in fact home-working is likely to provide the biggest revolution in modern working lifestyles of them all. The Henley Centre for Forecasting estimates that 7 million full-time employees, 1.6 million part-timers and 1.3 million of the self-employed (based in offices and other workplaces) could all successfully work from home right now. No longer a cottage industry, the availability of relatively cheap fax machines and personal computers have allowed a huge range of professional, creative and business people to work from home.

For those seeking an independent approach to work and living in the 1990s, being based at home has many advantages. One of course is that it saves the costs of commuting which are often considerable. Another is that you can write off many work expenses, such as the use of one or more rooms as workplaces, or a percentage of your phone bill, against tax. Similarly if, as a self-employed person, you become VAT-registered, then you can also claim back 17.5 per cent VAT on desks, shelves, the cost of installing a business telephone line and many other expenses.

Once you have seriously decided to try home-working, it is sensible to appoint an accountant, if you don't already have one, to help you run through all the costs and rebates which may not have occurred to you. Alternatively, you could buy one of the many how-to-do-it books on setting up a business at home, or find a course on home-working – many local authorities run them for free. It is essential that you work out in great detail how much money you will need to cover your costs for the first 12 months, including overheads and living costs. Then work out how much money you have to make a day, a week or a month to break even. Is this realistic? If not, you may have to rely on savings or modify or delay your plans.

We ran through some of the lost financial benefits and potential pitfalls of working from home above. Before handing in your notice and telling your employer you are going it alone, it is also important that you think through the loss of all the crucial support systems which you take for granted as someone else's employee.

Your company or employer pays your telephone and fax bill, supplies your stationery and posts your letters. They also market and advertise the company's products or services. If you go it alone you will no longer only have to use your well-honed and proven skills as, say, a researcher, a computer programmer or a plumber. You will also have to wear several other professional hats. You will need to be able to sell your business to potential clients with confidence, to run your own book-keeping and accounts (unless you pay someone to do it), to organise your own office equipment and to do your own budgeting. If any or all of these are things which you hate doing or think you would be no good at, you must think carefully before going ahead.

The other crucial element to home-working is making sure that your work and family lives won't conflict. Many people believe working from home will give them much more time with their partners and family, only to find themselves locking the study door to get away from the children who are constantly interrupting their work.

To work successfully from home, you must draw clear boundaries between your work time and your home time. Statistics show that homeworkers are a startling 30–100 per cent more productive than their office counterparts, so working from home should indeed allow you to spend more time with the family. It's just a matter of shutting off from family life during those hours when you are working. One obvious way is to set yourself fairly rigid daily or weekly hours of work and stick to them. Also, keep one or two rooms for work only and make sure that family life (in the form of children's toys, for example) doesn't intrude into your workspace.

Finally, it is obviously vital to get the support of all those you live with before embarking on a home-based career. If your partner is based at home and is worried you will be under his or her feet, you've got a problem. Suddenly spending a lot more time at home can alter relationships and create unexpected tensions. Women, in particular, often find that when they take up home-based working their partner also expects them to run the household more or less single-handed on top. If these kind of problems emerge, it is crucial to sort them out early on. Even better to think and talk them through before you make the final decision to set up at home.

Having said all this, if it suits your personality and circumstances then working from home can be the ideal way of having all worlds. Both of us, as freelance journalists, are enthusiastic converts. We find that not only do we work faster and more efficiently, but we have saved considerably on commuting costs and the trappings of high-powered and high-salaried jobs. Most importantly we have greater control over our lives.

Self-employment 2: in an office

For those who find it impossible to work at home, surrounded by distractions such as children, or a sinkful of dirty dishes, they prefer to rent an office space to help them re-create the discipline of a nine-to-five working environment. The only major drawback to this solution, of course, is that it costs more money than working from home. But that is a calculation which you will make when working out your finances for your new working life.

Unpaid work 1: volunteering and community

Many of our interviewees in Chapter 9 had found new rewards and fulfillment in voluntary work for community or environmental groups after leaving full-time employment. All, without exception, preferred their new lives to their old. But it is important to plan for such major life changes, and to make sure you are suited to them and that you can afford them.

A 'portfolio' lifestyle, where you consciously include time for unpaid work, is probably the most rewarding you can achieve in modern society. Working for a voluntary group, for example, may solve a long-held need to contribute in a certain area, such as animal welfare, or may open up entirely new horizons for you.

Many charities pay volunteers' travelling costs and lunches. And they often provide a whole new world of contacts and friendships.

Unpaid work 2: homemaking

Similarly, switching to a job with fewer hours or less stress to allow you more time and energy for home life and children brings obvious rewards. Apart from the emotional benefits, it can allow you to spend less money on expensive childcare. But, again, it is essential both to think through such a move and to work out in advance whether you can afford it. It is no good swapping the stress of long hours and no time with the children for the stress of not having enough money to pay the bills. Neither is it any good choosing to spend more time at home out of a sense of duty when really you want to be in the office going flat out for your next promotion. Don't be pushed into making the wrong decision. As with all the employment options we have run through, the crucial point every time is to choose a new direction which will suit you and your family and bring you all a happier, more balanced life.

CHAPTER FOURTEEN

The Roof Over Your Head

Houses are built to live in and not to look on . . .
Francis Bacon (1561–1626), English politician, philosopher and essayist

Just as we use money and our jobs to comfort and compensate us, so we use our homes in much the same way. Who hasn't left the office dog-tired and depressed only to revive when we reach the safety and comfort of our own surroundings? As the outside world becomes more unfriendly, so more and more of us are retreating into our personal worlds based around home, family and friends. We may feel insecure and undermined at work, but at home we are in control. This shift in attitude is reflected in many areas – our growing enthusiasm for DIY home improvements, gardening, takeaways and home video viewing, to name but a few.

To be completely autonomous in our own homes, of course, we need to own them, hence one reason why so many of us are willing to take on mortgages. If we are subject to a landlord's bidding and whims, we lack control in the same way we lack control as employees. Owning an attractive, comfortable home makes a huge difference to our morale and well-being. Yet it can also bring stress and hardship to those who over-stretch themselves.

In order to own the homes we want many of us still take on mortgages which stretch our resources to the limit, despite the tough lessons of the late 1980s. This often means having to scrimp and save in other areas. The unnecessary financial stress can even end up straining personal relationships. Moving up the property ladder usually also goes hand in hand with spending more on furnishing and decorating. All too often, we end up using credit or loans to buy that gorgeous new sofa or wardrobe – and end up paying well over the odds in interest charges.

If you are looking to simplify your life, it is worth thinking hard about where you really want to live and what, to you, are the essential elements for an ideal home. Many of us would undoubtedly be able to lead freer, more spontaneous lives if our housing costs ate up a smaller slice of our salaries.

Wanted: the downshifter's dream home

If you have decided to downshift, or are considering doing so, then where you live is a vital part of the equation together with the employment you choose and the income you expect to earn.

When you first sit down to decide your future life, try and be open-minded about where you live, both in terms of location and size of property. Being flexible about your home may make a big difference to whether or not your plans to downshift will be viable. Of course, your decision will be governed by many considerations including the size of your family, where you plan to work from, and whether or not your dreams include moving from city to town or country. Bearing this in mind, we list below the most obvious options open to you:

1 stay where you are
2 stay in the same area but opt for a lower mortgage or rent
3 move to a smaller property or to a street in the same area where properties are cheaper
4 sell up and move to a new area
5 work from home
6 move into shared or communal accommodation

1: Staying put

If you, your partner or family are wedded to your present home then it doesn't make sense to leave when your aim is to achieve a happier, more balanced life. Instead, you will need to build all your plans around staying where you are. It is quite possible to downshift without moving, but you will have to make careful calculations about what you can afford.

If your rent or mortgage is high, and your family income is going to drop then you will obviously have to cut back in other areas. But don't despair! We have already pointed out how cutting out commuting costs and other work-related expenses can save people thousands of pounds a year.

Try and calculate all the money you have spent annually on your home and garden over the past two or three years. Then see how much of the expenditure covered jobs which you yourself could do in future. For example, you may have paid a gardener to cut the lawn or a plumber to do a simple job like replace a tap washer. You may have employed a weekly cleaner and you may have paid a decorator several hundred pounds to re-paint your living-room. All these are activities which any able-bodied home-owner could do given the time, the equipment and the patience. If you are prepared to take such jobs on in the future, you could reduce your annual housing costs substantially.

2: *Re-mortgaging or renting*

Of course, the biggest holes in your housing costs are made by your monthly mortgage, council tax and rent payments. But here, too, you'll be pleased to hear, there are ways of cutting your bills significantly.

With the housing market quiet for so long, and interest rates at an historic low, most building societies are offering very good deals to tempt people to switch their mortgages. In the 1990s, re-mortgaging has become big business with tens of thousands of families profiting by negotiating a lower monthly payment with a new lender. Most of these deals tie you in with a lender for at least five years. In return, house-holders receive a reduction of anything up to a third on their monthly repayments for the first few years of their new mortgage agreement. Although it is a hassle switching your mortgage, and you will be charged a couple of hundred pounds in administrative costs, the potential gains are substantial. If you are paying back, say, a £75,000 mortgage at £550 a month, you should be able to find a deal which cuts your repayments by up to £100 a month.

A word of warning, however. You need to act soon, before the pick-up in the housing market becomes so strong that building societies lose interest in attracting new customers through re-mortgaging deals. Getting advice from a financial expert on the best deals available – and possible pitfalls in the small print – is always a good idea if you can afford it. Otherwise seek advice from your local Citizens Advice Bureau and scan the business pages of the broadsheet newspapers. They all offer easy-to-read information on the best re-mortgaging deals going.

Another course of action would be to switch from owning your own home to renting. The monthly rent might be a similar amount to your monthly mortgage repayment and, of course, you still have to pay the bills. But all those expensive overheads – repairs, re-decoration and unexpected disasters such as a flooded bathroom – will be dealt with and paid for by the landlord. Renting is probably a good option to consider if you are flexible in your lifestyle and are looking to save as much money and reduce your responsibilities as much as possible.

3: Trading places

If you want to stay in the same area, but are happy to move home to suit your new needs, this is obviously an ideal opportunity to save money. Whether you live alone, in a couple, or as part of a family, sit down and work out systematically, room by room, how much space you really want or need.

It may be, for example, that you now have a guest bedroom which is almost never used. You may also have a junk room which you wouldn't need if you gave or threw away all that junk, which you never use anyway. You may have a garage, but do you really need it?

Once you have decided how much space you need, think about locality. If you are living in an expensive but small inner-city flat, you may be able to save substantially by moving to a less fashionable area a little further out of the centre. On the other hand, you could get somewhere bigger, if that's what you need, for the same price. In the same way, if you are living in a three-bedroomed house in an affluent suburb, you could save a lot of money by selling up and moving to somewhere smaller, or the same size in a less up-market neighbouring suburb.

Take some time visiting neighbourhoods in your area to see how you like them. Check with friends who live in cheaper localities what the advantages and disadvantages are. And make sure the new locality you have in mind has good local transport and shopping facilities which don't involve much more travel than at present, and preferably less. There's no point saving on the mortgage if you have to start using your car for work or driving five miles to get to a decent supermarket.

4: Pastures new

For many people, moving out of the city into the suburbs or, better still, the real countryside is a cherished dream. Since the early 1980s, hundreds of thousands of us have been fulfilling this dream by fleeing town for country. But, if you are planning to join this exodus, stop and think first. Remember that a downshifted lifestyle, including many 'country' pursuits such as growing some of your own food and getting involved in community activities, can be successfully created just as well in a town or city as in the countryside. And be aware that starting again in an idyllic rural setting carries disadvantages as well as advantages. Below, we offer a short list of pros and cons to living in both town and country.

Living in the country: pros
✓ Fresh air and natural surroundings.
✓ Life is usually quieter and slower-paced.
✓ Accommodation is often cheaper than the more affluent city suburbs and there is often more land or garden with the house.
✓ Children will probably have more and safer playing space; neighbours are likely to be friendlier and local activities may be easier to become involved in.
✓ Parking problems are rare and housing and car insurance rates are lower.

Living in the country: cons
✗ Choice of housing is much narrower than in cities and planning permission for home extensions and improvements may be restricted.
✗ Weather may be inhospitable in winter – cold, foggy, windy or snowbound; farm smells can be off-putting; tourist areas can be over-run by summer visitors.
✗ Isolated houses in exposed positions can be costly to heat and there may be no mains gas or sewage drainage.
✗ Street lighting may be poor and local transport sparse, while the GP's surgery, local hospital and schools, chemists and supermarket may be some distance away.
✗ Social life is likely to be much more restricted and, with local transport limited, it may be harder for guests to visit you.

Living in a town or city: pros
✓ More choice of neighbourhoods and houses; flats, limited in rural areas, are plentiful.
✓ More public transport, schools and health care are available.
✓ Shopping is much more diverse and convenient.
✓ More entertainment, leisure and sports facilities; children may benefit from having more youngsters nearby to play with.

Living in a town or city: cons

✗ House prices are higher; you may have to accept a smaller house and/ or garden than in the country and children's play space may be restricted.

✗ Closeness to neighbours may mean a lack of privacy, especially in terraced housing.

✗ Faster pace of living and higher noise levels from traffic, people, shops and factories.

✗ Health and welfare services are more likely to be over-stretched and large inner-city schools may have more discipline problems.

✗ Neighbours may be unfriendly and you may feel isolated in the midst of so many strangers. Friends may have to be made through your job or children's schools.

✗ Parking may be difficult and more expensive.

If you do decide to go ahead and move to a new part of the country, think through the lifestyle changes this will involve and how they will affect your budget. For example, it's not only your mortgage and council tax payments which may be much higher or lower. What about fuel bills if you are moving to a colder climate? And telephone bills? If you are moving away from your friends and work colleagues, you are therefore likely to be making many more long distance phone calls in future. Also, think through your new travel needs and the amount of routine upkeep your new home is likely to need. Again these items may substantially affect your budget either way. You may be saving even more than you thought by moving. Or you may find unexpected expenses to offset against the savings you have estimated that your new home will bring.

But, if you have decided to head for pastures new, how do you find your new home? House hunting in a new part of the country is not an easy business. Spending weekends or even holidays touring around looking out for 'For Sale' signs may be fun once or twice, but it soon becomes tiring, time-consuming and expensive.

There are several ways for you to get round this problem. Find out the names of the weekly or evening papers in the areas you are interested in and then order copies by post for the days that their property advertising comes out. If you are wired to the Internet, it is also worth a quick trawl. Limited accommodation listings are now provided for most of the country.

This initial research will give you a good idea of the range of accommodation available and how much it costs. Armed with this knowledge, you could then link up with an estate agent in the area, specifying what you are looking for. Members of the National Association of Estate Agents will provide a referral service for people moving from one area to another. Just walk into an agent's in your home town and tell them you want to take advantage of the National Homelink Service.

5: *Mixing business with pleasure*

Like many downshifters, you may be tempted by the idea of working from home. If so, you must think through the implications not just for your career, but also for your housing arrangements. Working from home, as we said in Chapter 13, can be a wonderful experience, allowing you more time with family and friends while saving you money on commuting and other work-related expenses. But it can also bring unexpected savings in accommodation costs.

If you work from home, you can set some of the costs of the room/s you use as a study or workshop against tax. So too can a proportion of your telephone bill. And when you want to buy a new piece of furniture, such as a desk or shelving, you can again claim back tax so long as the items are used, at least in part, for business purposes. If, as a self-employed person, you become VAT-registered, then you can also claim back VAT on office equipment, the cost of a business telephone line and other items you may tot up in the initial outlay of setting up a business from home. The financial bonuses can be substantial.

If you want to move, then work out how much more space you would need to work from home and then look for properties of that size in the area you're interested in. It may be that you will have to look in a slightly cheaper area than you'd originally planned in order to find a house with adequate work space which is within your budget. On the other hand, remember to calculate how much money you will be saving on commuting and other work-related costs, giving you a bigger monthly budget to cover your mortgage.

If you want to work from home but would prefer to stay where you are, be inventive about the space you have. Moving is a costly business, however efficiently you do it, and it may be that your home has unfulfilled possibilities. You may have a well-kept loft or cellar which could be converted into a study without too much expense. Or, if you need a large workshop, how about converting your garage or a garden shed? You may need to park your car on the street in future but that should be a small price to pay compared with the benefits.

If you are stuck in negative equity then a home conversion is a particularly good idea. Not only will it create the space for you to work at home, but it will raise the value of your property and make it easier for you to sell in the long run.

6: Sharing a roof

If you need to save money to create a new lifestyle then how about sharing accommodation? This could mean either opening your own doors to a lodger; moving into someone else's flat or house; or sharing a rented house with several other lodgers.

With the long slump in home-buying, renting has grown in popularity, but prices still vary enormously. In exclusive parts of London, renting a room in a flat can cost £250 a week, compared with £150 in a trendy but less expensive area and £75 in parts of the East End. Out of London and the south-east prices drop significantly. In parts of the north-east, you can rent an entire two-bedroom flat for £120 a week. The cheapest decent accommodation is usually rented out by housing associations and trusts which operate nationwide. Unfortunately the waiting lists tend to be enormously long.

If you own your own home, but want to dramatically reduce your outgoings, one option would be to sell your flat or house, pocket the profits and move to rented accommodation in a cheaper part of the country. Your rent may not be a huge amount less than your mortgage but all those overheads will disappear and with luck you'll now have decent savings in the bank to fall back on. Of course, such a change of direction would need to fit in with your employment and living plans. It is a course of action probably best suited to the young and single, or to couples without children. But there is no compelling reason why any of us should feel we have to keep our feet on the housing ladder if we have other, more pressing priorities for our money.

If, on the other hand, you are a home-owner who wants to live off less but would prefer to keep your property, how about renting out a room? Everybody has horror stories about the lodger from hell, but if you think carefully about the advertisements you place, making clear your likes and dislikes, and take your time vetting would-be housemates, you should be able to avoid making a bad choice. If you are very nervous about it, stipulate a three-month trial period and make them sign up to it on the dotted line. Then if things go quickly wrong, they'll be out before you know it. There is a big market for rented rooms and you should be spoiled for choice. But remember, to do it legally you will need to declare your earnings from rent to the tax man who will deduct tax at the same rate you pay on your salary.

For the bolder downshifter, another option may beckon: communal living. In the individualistic 1980s buying your own home became a national craze and communal living a national joke. Remember the cult TV comedy *The Young Ones*? But in the 1990s communal living, both legally and by squatters, has taken on a new lease of life.

One high profile example is the Findhorn community in Scotland which draws thousands of visitors and tourists a year to its holistic village. But, on a smaller scale, dozens of communes based in rented houses, tents or 'benders' (canvas stretched over tree branches) have sprung up in the mid-1990s, often precipitated by a protest against road-building or a new mining operation. To find out more about how communes operate and where to find one near you, contact the Brighton-based organisation Justice, listed in the Downshifter's Directory in Part Six.

PART FIVE

LIVING BETTER ON LESS

Civilisation, in the real sense of the term, consists not in the multiplication, but in the deliberate and voluntary reduction of wants. This alone promotes real happiness and contentment.

Mahatma Gandhi (1869–1948), Indian Nationalist leader

HOW TO USE THIS SECTION

In this section, we build on the 'strategic lifestyle planning' advice given in the previous section on finance, work, and housing. Now we are going to show you how ten aspects of day-to-day living can become happier and healthier with less money, but give you more time to enjoy what really matters to you. Some of the suggestions and ideas we offer are, individually, fairly modest steps, while others are more radical.

Nowhere in this book is it our intention to lay down the law, for downshifting is not a cult. It's simply a way of living, with a strong philosophical basis. All we want to do is set out the best information that we can find to help would-be downshifters or those already embarked on downshifting, and to give some suggestions and markers that simplify the process and make your goals easier to achieve. Only you can decide what steps amount to impossible sacrifices and which burdens you can happily shed. Only you know what is negotiable, and what provokes the response: 'That's ridiculous,' or 'Hmmm, well, maybe it's worth thinking about.' The radical downshifter, of course, will harbour no such doubts and will go the whole hog at every opportunity!

In each of the forthcoming nine chapters, we will show you examples of free or cheaper alternatives to the way you may currently eat, travel, run your households, and so on. But cost is not the only guiding principle underpinning our advice – better health, environmental sustainability, and ethics are equally important.

CHAPTER FIFTEEN

Food and Drink

By forcing the damn fool public to pay twice over – once to have its food emasculated and once to have the vitality put back again, we keep the wheels of commerce turning.
Dorothy L. Sayers, *Murder Must Advertise*, 1933

Never under-estimate the importance of good food – making enough time to shop for it, prepare it well, and, above all, to enjoy eating it. Your health and sense of well-being is critically dependent upon it, so if you cut the wrong corners you are simply cheating yourself and the people whose diets depend on you.

The whole business of eating and drinking should never be an after-thought. We are what we eat. With every mouthful, with every supermarket expedition, with every visit to your allotment, if you have one, it is your chance to get healthier and happier, but not only that. The way you spend your money on food and drink also shapes the livelihoods of other people, and so their health and well-being too.

Shopping is far from a trivial business. Like any other activity, it is a set of skills that can be learned, honed and improved. It is also about making political choices. We have a responsibility to get it broadly right. It's your opportunity to help to change the world and yourself. Your stomach, your brain and your wallet are inextricably linked, and it is for you to decide whether all three should benefit from this inter-dependence, or not. Here we suggest ways of reviewing your shopping, eating and drinking habits, changing some of them, and getting more from less money.

Before we outline our alternative plans, we offer some general thoughts on the art of shopping.

Where should you buy your food and drink?

Ask yourself whether the shops and other outlets you use deserve your custom, and whether their activities are consistent with your beliefs. You may worry, for example, about the quality of produce available in supermarkets and modern mass production practices. The ingredients of processed foods are often mystifying. The fruit and vegetables on offer often look better than they taste and their nutritional content may have diminished in transit. Do you have a decent market locally where you could save pounds on fruit and vegetables?

The Women's Institute runs superb little fresh produce markets around the country. See if there's one in your area, or a similar enterprise run by another voluntary organisation. If not, and you grow some food yourself, think about getting together with other like-minded souls and starting your own market.

Many people believe that eating well costs a lot of money. In fact, the key barrier to healthy eating is not simply the *price* of the food itself, but whether people have *affordable access* to it. An out-of-town supermarket may make all kinds of impressive claims about the quality, freshness and price of its food, but none of it is the slightest use to the person who is unable to get to it. The answer is not to encourage more car use, but to increase the incentives to shop locally. That sets off a positive chain reaction. If more people shop locally, the choice and quality of goods available will rise, and prices will fall. So community and neighbourhood life benefits, the environment wins because car dependence declines, and you save time and travelling costs because you can get good food round the corner.

Let us take the inspiring example of what has happened in the Herefordshire town of Leominster. Many superstore chains have started loyalty bonus cards, but Leominster thought it made more sense for individuals to carry a card that encouraged loyalty to their community. More than 60 retailers have got together and pledged discounts to carriers of cards that declare the holder is 'Loyal to Leominster'. Membership is free to local residents. Benefits include 10 per cent off a pint of beer for pensioners. Why not ask your local council to follow suit?

When is the best time to shop?

Avoid going shopping when you are hungry or thirsty or very tired. Your defences against subtle advertising, and the seductive atmosphere of a well-stocked supermarket, will be down. You will emerge with a trolley heaving with ready-meals, processed foods and other 'comfort and compensation' items that can waste your money. Meanwhile you may forget to get things that you *do* need. If you use a supermarket, try to go when it is likely to be quiet, and you are in a reasonably positive frame of mind. For many people, impulse-buying increases with stress levels. The quicker and more easily you can get around, the more rationally and cost-effectively you are likely to shop. One exception to this rule that could save you even more money is to shop when prices are cut on goods that are nearing or have reached their 'sell-by' dates. Saturday afternoons, and the hours before a shop closes for a public holiday, could be prime shopping times for downshifters with their new flexibility.

How can I best resist temptation?

With the benefit of a succinct shopping list. It helps you to cut down on impulse buying, and forces you to think about the next few days' meals in the relative calm of your home rather than in those temples to temptation where we tend to buy our food. If you need more reinforcements against temptation, then leave all plastic cards at home. Only take with you the cash you intend to spend at the shop. And a calculator to keep a running total as you cruise the aisles: it works every time.

Who to shop for food and drink with?

Ideally, no one. Shopping with small demanding children, who have yet to absorb the liberating philosophy of downshifting, is likely to present practical problems to anyone trying to save money and to buy healthy food. Some of the more enlightened supermarkets have supervised play-areas, where you can drop off the children, and some offer confection-ery-free check-outs.

Why shop for all your food and drink?

Think laterally. You could grow some of it yourself, barter with friends and neighbours, organise the delivery of locally-produced organic or conservation grade food to your door, and finally toast your success with some home-made wine, beer or lemonade. Food and drink is fundamental to our enjoyment of life. Why delegate so many decisions and so much of your spending power to unseen, anonymous, profit-driven supermarket chains and multi-national food producers? Might not eating and drinking become more pleasurable and meaningful when you know more about its origin, how the food was produced?

What sort of food and drink should we consume?

Most people need to eat more fresh fruit and vegetables to get the vitamins, minerals and fibre they need to stay healthy – five portions a day is the amount recommended by the World Health Organisation. Many should boost their consumption of starchy, fibrous foods: this means eating more bread, pasta, potatoes, pulses and cereals and building at least some main meals around these foods. These should make up about half your daily diet. Luckily for the downshifter, a healthy diet need be no more expensive than an unhealthy one, and may cost less although as we pointed out earlier you may have to travel further to get hold of the freshest ingredients.

Buy foods that give good nutritional value and are versatile – dried pulses are a great standby for making soups, casseroles and savoury bakes, they are cheap and they keep for months if stored in an airtight tin or jar. When you shop for groceries, try to cut down on the tinned and pre-packaged food. Supermarket 'own brands' are usually cheaper than other varieties and often just as good as their better-known counterparts. Processed food, such as cakes, biscuits, crisps, pre-packed pies, sweets, chocolates and tinned meats, can never match fresh, whole food for providing what your body needs to function well. These items also tend to be packed with saturated fats. Most people would benefit from eating less fatty foods. And don't forget, the longer food is kept, and the more it is cooked, the less nutritional value we get from it.

Now we accept that one person's meat is another's poison and that you will take much advice about your diet with a pinch of salt (no more than a few grains ideally). So we will focus on giving you a few facts so that you may draw your own conclusions.

Living off the fat of the land

As a nation we consume more fat than is good for our health. Most of this excess comes from meat and dairy products such as cheese, milk and butter, and the heart disease created by this excess kills thousands of people every year. Moreover, we are profligate in the way we use precious land to produce food. We spend £9bn a year on meat and meat products. Most animals reared for meat are fed on crops that could be eaten by people, yet livestock only convert a fraction of the crop's energy into food.

To yield one kilo of beef, you may need as much as 10 kilos of grain. If a one hectare field used for beef production was given over to bean and vegetable growing, it would produce ten times as much protein. So it makes sense for those concerned about the planet, their health, and their pocket to reduce their consumption of meat and dairy foods, and increase consumption of vegetables and pulses. Try substituting some of your meat-based meals with vegetarian ones. If you are already a vegetarian, and veganism holds no appeal, then you can concentrate on other ways of saving money. There are plenty to pick from, for most people.

From plot to plate

Britain has some of the finest and most fertile arable land in the world. Yet rather than grow most of it here, we prefer to fly in exotic fresh food, often produced by cheap labour in countries thousands of miles away. The pollution caused by transporting all this food on roads and by air is huge, and the produce loses a fair proportion of its goodness *en route*. Processed food is often well-travelled too by the time we eat it. The ingredients are sent to processing plants, perhaps in other countries, then on to warehouses, and then supermarkets, before finally being loaded into our cars. So food production cycles can measure several thousands of miles. Alternatively they can be a couple of miles, or even just a few feet. The aim of the downshifter, we suggest, should be *to shorten these distances between plot and plate*. Obviously, it is for you to decide how modest or radical this shortening should be. But remember, the fresher the food you eat, the healthier your diet.

Some like it hot

As a general rule, fruit and vegetables are best consumed either raw or lightly cooked. *Do* wash your fruit and veg, or scrub it very gently if it is dirty, but try to resist the temptation to peel the skin off everything, because the most nutritious elements are often in the skin or just beneath it. *Don't* boil away all the goodness. Try steaming vegetables or briskly stir frying. Instead of dribbling oil into your pan, you can now spray it in so that the oil goes further and you stay trim and gorgeous. There are now oil sprays on the market, which cost next to nothing, but will save you pounds in the long run. That way you can afford the tastiest and healthiest oil – extra virgin olive oil – *most* of the time, not just as a special treat.

It's the real thing: H_2O

There is only one liquid that our bodies really need in order to function well, and we do not drink nearly enough of it. Sales of bottled water have rocketed since the mid-1970s, partly because so many of us do not like the taste of tap water, but also because we tend to think of the bottled variety as healthier. This is not necessarily true. Many people worry about the nitrates content of their tap water, but it is quite possible that the level is even higher in some types of bottled water. Provided that your drinking water supply lies within legal safety limits, there is no real reason for buying bottled water other than on grounds of taste or fashion. A slice of lemon or lime in a glass of tap water can improve the taste enormously, so think seriously about whether it's really necessary to pay twice for your supply. Alternatively, consider investing in a water filter jug.

Tea, coffee and soft drinks

Tea and coffee contain caffeine, a chemical that stimulates the metabolism. These drinks may be habit-forming, but there is no credible evidence that they are addictive. The question for downshifters is whether they might wish to substitute at least some of the cups of tea and coffee they drink for something rather less stimulating, such as fruit or herb teas or cereal-based drink. If you want to take steps to slow the pace of your life, you will probably want to cut down on stimulants like caffeine that would otherwise charge you up again. What might help you do this is to buy real coffee, not instant, and loose tea instead of teabags. It will take longer to make so you will probably drink less of it! As for soft drinks, fruit juices, with no added sugar or sweetener, are healthier than canned fizzy drinks such as colas.

Alcohol

Scientific studies have shown that moderate drinkers sustain less heart disease and have lower levels of cholesterol than those who drink to a greater extent. Most independent health experts regard drinking up to two units a day for women and three for men as moderate. A unit is the equivalent of a glass of wine, a half pint of beer, or a single measure of spirits. Beer and wine contain certain vitamins and minerals. The downshifter has three main options on the question of alcohol: to become teetotal (perhaps you are already); to save money by drinking less; or to save money by making their own beer or wine.

If you want to go the whole hog

Here are five more tips for people who wish to downshift more radically:

1 ONLY buy organic fresh produce. Most shop-bought vegetables and fruit are sprayed with pesticides which can cause environmental damage.

2 ASK your friends and neighbours whether they would join you in a local produce marketing scheme. A local organic farm would deliver produce direct to one householder who then distributes it to other members of the group. There are many variations on the theme. The Ryton Organic Food Club, based near Coventry, for example, charges £6.50 a time for a weekly bag of seasonal organic vegetables, which members collect from a local shop.

3 CUT your supermarket visits to one a fortnight, then once a month. Increase visits to shops that you can walk or cycle to. Find the nearest good wholefood shop and start stocking up on pulses, such as chick-peas and lentils – amongst the cheapest and best sources of protein available. With pulses, vegetables and herbs, you have the core ingredients for the most delicious soups, casseroles and bakes that cost very little and are packed with goodness.

4 SAVE restaurant visits only for really *special* occasions. Anyway by now your home cooking will be improving in leaps and bounds, so you are less inclined to go out to a restaurant. Make sure your family or your friends are taking their turn at the cooking, so you get a break from it. Get into the habit of taking picnics, or packed lunches, when you go out for the day.

5 DO a food and drink audit of your kitchen. Read one of the ethical consumer books, such as Karen Christensen's *The Green Home*. They will tell you whether you are a regular consumer of an item that is not produced ethically. If so, stop buying it. Write to the manufacturer or distributor and tell them why. If you bought it at a supermarket, tell the customer care department – they won't want to lose your custom, and their feedback to the supplier will certainly be listened to. If you feel strongly enough about it, start a campaign. Write to your local newspaper, or link up with an existing protest.

Further reading and contacts
Find out where you can obtain organic produce from the Soil Association (see page 247 for details).
Recommended reading: *Food for Free* by Richard Mabey, Collins, 1972.

CHAPTER SIXTEEN

Transport

Motoring is promoted as a glamorous male hobby that offers legitimate opportunities for excitement and risk.
Cosmopolitan magazine

Travelling in the late twentieth century has never been easier – or more complex. We get around on foot, by car, bicycle, bus, tram, train, ship, ferry, hovercraft and aeroplane. The choice is liberating and phenomenal. So much so that we have become lazy and unthinking in our habits. We take the car for the shortest of journeys when we could just as easily walk. Instead of jumping at the opportunity of getting fit by cycling, we prefer to drive everywhere. Then we go to the gym – and work out on bike and running machines! And when we take a foreign holiday we crisscross the globe in jets without a second thought for the huge amounts of energy consumed and the pollution created.

Those of us not scraping by on low incomes and benefits also tend to forget or ignore the costs of transport, just as we ignore the cost to our time of sitting in rush hour traffic jams. We reason that we deserve the luxury of our personal space and would rather be stuck in a queue than on public transport.

The average British family spends 14 per cent of their weekly budget on transport, compared with 12.6 per cent on eating at home. Yet we think much less about cutting back on travelling costs than we do about saving on other essentials such as food and housing. Transport is therefore a living expense ripe for reform by budget-slashing downshifters. And the good news is that finding cheaper ways to get around can be fun, healthy and nothing like as inconvenient as you might imagine. Below we suggest seven ways forward, ranging from the easy and obvious to the much more radical.

Step 1: cheaper driving

Two-thirds of British households own cars, so let's assume you own one or maybe even two. You may be one of the millions who commute to work every day or you may just use it for leisure, shopping and school trips. Either way, you probably believe that your car is indispensable or that you can't bear to part with it. If this is the case, the priority is to cut down your car maintenance costs. There are many ways of doing this:

Ditch the second car

If you are a two-car family, then seriously consider selling one. Even if one partner had to switch to a long commuter train journey, the expense would be highly unlikely to outweigh the annual cost of a second vehicle.

The Environmental Transport Association estimates that for people who travel less than 2,000 miles a year, the fixed and running costs of motoring work out at £1.24 a mile, making it cheaper to travel the full 2,000 miles by taxi! For those covering 5,000 miles a year by car, ETA estimates the total cost per mile at 47p. If their owners sold their cars and travelled a third of the mileage by taxi, a third by train and a third by bus, they would each save £450 a year. So, if you're trying to save money, running two cars doesn't make sense unless you are both working in places so inaccessible that they are impossible to reach by any other means.

Choose a cheaper model

The next step is to consider changing down a gear in your choice of car. If you've bought your latest model for speed or fashion status, regardless of your actual needs then trade it in. Cars with rapid acceleration and top speeds up to 120mph drink up petrol and you can hardly ever make use of what you've paid for unless you break the speed limit. Instead, buy a car whose hallmarks are safety and reliability, and which has cheap spare parts. Safe, reliable cars are generally considered a low risk by insurers, and this will help keep your annual premium low.

Also be careful to buy a car no bigger than you need. If you're one of the many people who think they must have a car which can take the whole family plus luggage on the annual holiday, think again. It makes much more sense to choose a car which matches your day-to-day needs. It works out cheaper to hire a car for a fortnight once a year than to drive around most of the time in an almost empty gas-guzzler.

Another must is to shop around for the best deals. If you live in London or the south-east, it might be worth a trip to the north of the country where saleroom prices can be considerably cheaper. You will almost certainly get a better deal if you sell your current car privately rather than trading it in. Finally, try and choose a fuel-efficient model which doesn't burn up the petrol. Depending on their engine size, BMWs drink up between 9 and 19 litres to travel 100km in urban areas, while a bottom-of-the-range Ford Escort uses up 8 litres and a Fiat Uno only 4.6 litres. Over a year it will make a sizeable difference to your pocket.

Keep it running

Now you've got a car which is reliable and cheap to run. The next priority is to keep it on the road for as long as possible. The longer you own a car, the slower the depreciation rate. To help keep your car healthy:

- find a garage mechanic you like and trust, and stick with him – you're more likely to get a good cheap service that way
- repair little ailments such as fan belts and worn tyres as they come along, to avoid bigger bills later
- check your oil level frequently and make sure you change it when the owner's manual suggests
- get your car tuned regularly. Badly tuned vehicles drink up petrol as well as being highly polluting

Drive cheaply and safely

Set a personal speed limit, preferably below 60mph. Driving at 50mph (80kph) on motorways rather than 70mph (112kph) burns up far less petrol and cuts emissions substantially.

Don't leave an idle engine running. A stationary engine uses up fuel and pumps out unnecessary pollutants. Never leave your engine running for more than 60 seconds and switch it off when stuck in a traffic jam.

Step 2: consider car pooling

Car pooling or sharing – for commuter journeys, school, shopping and leisure trips – is an excellent way to save money while helping to reduce the number of cars on the road. By sharing trips you will help both to reduce pollution and congestion and to speed up your own journeys. Car sharing is still in its infancy in Britain but has taken off in Germany and Holland where extensive networks help people find suitable partners to commute or travel over distances of hundreds of miles. The average commuter car in Britain carries just 1.2 occupants, or six people for every five cars. Not surprisingly, the roads into every major city in the country are jammed with monotonous regularity every rush hour.

To make car pooling work successfully, you need to find one or more colleagues who live nearby, work in the same building or close by, and who have inflexible, identical working hours to your own. Mutual goodwill is obviously crucial to making the arrangement succeed. For example, if one of you wants to stay behind in town one evening, the other either has to make similar social arrangements or one of you will have to get home by another means. It may take a little effort to get started, but the benefits – halving your commuter costs and the time you spend behind the wheel in stressful rush hour traffic – are substantial.

Car sharing between neighbours and friends for domestic journeys, school runs, shopping trips and so on is much more widespread than commuter pooling. Suggest to your neighbours that you might like to co-ordinate your weekly shopping trip, taking it in turns to drive. Do the same with the parents of your children's classmates. It's an easy and sociable way to cut down your driving costs. For women based at home in one car families, where the man takes the car to work, you could offer a neighbour free babysitting, or fresh vegetables from the garden in return for lifts to school or the supermarket. Car pooling is especially useful in rural areas where bus services can be very limited.

Step 3: get into cost-free travel – rediscover walking and cycling

Most of us get into our cars for the shortest of journeys without thinking. Three-quarters of journeys in Britain are under five miles long, half are less than two miles. Yet a staggering 69 per cent of these journeys are made by car. Within 50 years, it seems, most of us have forgotten how to use our feet and legs. If you are one of the culprits, try stopping to think every time you reach automatically for the car keys. If your journey is only half a mile away, it's a fine day and you have plenty of time, then walk or cycle. Gradually build up the distance and the number of trips you make without driving. You may even end up walking or cycling to work. If you do, don't worry that you will have to set aside more time to get there. Government statistics show that a 7 kilometre (4.4 mile) rush hour journey takes 41 minutes by car, 51 minutes by bus, 45 minutes by train or tube, 51 minutes on foot – and only 22 minutes on a bicycle. We use our cars even more for shopping trips than for commuting but here, too, bicycles are a good substitute. Major bicycle outlets now sell attachable bike trailers made of a light alloy metal frame lined with a tough plastic which can easily carry a week's shopping for a family of four.

Not only will walking and cycling save you money, it will make you fitter. The Sports Council and Health Education Authority recommend regular aerobic exercise as essential for healthy living. Walking and cycling both fit the bill perfectly, improving strength and stamina, lowering the risk of heart disease and helping you to stay a trim, healthy weight.

Step 4: rediscover public transport

If your job or children's school is too far away for you to walk or cycle, try rediscovering buses and trains. Many local authorities are now actively trying to revitalise public transport networks, after years of neglect, to reduce the number of cars on the road. You may be pleasantly surprised by the standard and frequency of service. To save money, always find out about cheap weekly, monthly or annual tickets and about non-premium times to travel – usually after 10 a.m. – when prices are much cheaper. Invest in a copy of the British Rail/Railtrack national timetable so that whenever you're planning a business trip or a weekend away you can look up your destination and decide whether to let the train take the strain instead of driving. For those living in rural areas where public transport is scarce, seek advice on organising alternatives from the Community Transport Association, 211 Arlington Rd, London NW1 7HD.

Step 5: *give up your car*

It may seem difficult, especially if you live in remote countryside, to get around any other way, but if you re-think the way you live, it is possible to greatly reduce your car dependence and get around instead by foot, bicycle, public transport and the occasional taxi.

First investigate public transport alternatives for getting to work and for other essential trips like shopping and school runs. Then decide which journeys you can feasibly make by public transport, walking or cycling and which, if any, are out of the question. If you conclude that it will be very difficult to make many of your present journeys without driving, think how you could alter your lifestyle to make your car less essential.

This sounds dramatic, but may well fit in with the changes you are already contemplating. For example, if you are deciding to work from home in your new downshifter's lifestyle, then one knock-on effect would be that you would no longer need a car to commute.

Similarly, if you were prepared to switch your shopping habits from a superstore to local shops, a car would again seem much less indispensable. Home shopping, which is beginning to take off in Britain, is an even better option. No transport is needed because your supermarket order is delivered to your door (see also Chapter 15, Food and Drink). Likewise, if you are planning to move to a new area, make the choice partly on whether essential facilities such as schools and a hospital are in easy cycling, walking or taxi distance. If you are planning to stay where you are, then investigate the public transport. On the surface, it may seem cheaper to run your car than use a bus or local train service, but don't forget to factor in the big annual lump sum costs of tax, MOT, annual service, depreciation, and so on. The Environmental Transport Association calculates that, for those travelling 5,000 miles a year by car, the running costs total £578 and the fixed costs a whopping £2,256. If the distances involved are not too great, then invest in a bicycle which will cost only a tiny fraction of your annual driving budget. Major bicycle outlets these days boast a wide range of choice, including folding bicycles which can be easily stored in trains, buses or the back of cars. And don't overlook tandems for couples. If you have young children, family bicycles, which can carry up to four people, are now on the market.

For those living in areas with poor public transport, another route is to join or start up community initiatives. These could include lobbying the Post Office and local councils for Postbus services to take on passengers as they now do in many rural areas. Another option is to get a group of residents together who agree to share local taxis for weekly trips into the nearest town, and so on. It is already quite common for taxis to offer cheap daily school pick-up services between rural villages.

Step 6: co-own a car

A more radical alternative to sharing trips with other car owners is to jointly buy and run a car with other individuals or families. Again, this is a practice which is in its infancy in Britain but has taken off on the Continent, particularly in Germany and Switzerland. The Sainsbury's Family Trust and the environmental pressure group Transport 2000 are now putting together British pilot schemes.

For eager pioneers, the Environmental Transport Association is producing an innovative scheme under which they will insure co-owners of a single vehicle. The benefits of such a scheme are obvious. Depending on how many people co-own a car, you dramatically reduce your daily transport costs and the costs of any repairs or accidents. Of course, you will need to carefully negotiate the days and/or times of day when the car is yours to use.

Step 7: choose as 'green' a car as possible

If, when buying a car, you want to think beyond saving money to protecting the environment as well, then read on. First, let's be clear. There is no such thing as a truly green car. Walking and cycling, which are pollution-free, will always be much more eco-friendly as well as cheaper and healthier. Luckily for us, at present 60 per cent of the world's people use their feet to get around, while 14 per cent cycle, 20 per cent use buses or trains and only 6 per cent use cars as the normal mode of transport. However, if a car is essential for your lifestyle, an energy and fuel efficient model which is regularly tuned and uses a green fuel undoubtedly causes far less harm than a gas-guzzling top-of-the-range executive car.

The basic rule of thumb when trying to choose a reasonably green car is to go for a catalytic converter; low engine capacity and power;

economic fuel consumption of miles per gallon; and a low top speed. Unleaded fuel is obviously far preferable to leaded. Diesel was thought until recently to be a green fuel as it produces very few oxides of nitrogen. But it is now known that diesel emits a high level of tiny dust particles known as particulates which exacerbate lung and chest diseases.

The Environmental Transport Association, which is Britain's green AA/RAC, produces a comprehensive annual car buyer's guide for the concerned motorist. It gives star ratings, depending on eco-friendliness, to 350 different models, including diesel fuel and automatic transmission versions of popular cars. To give you some idea, its 1995 list of the top and bottom ten cars is as follows:

Top 10		Bottom 10	
1	Fiat Cinquecento	1	Lamborghini Diablo
2	Fiat Punto 55	2	BMW 850 CSi
3	Fiat Panda Selecta	3	BMW 750 iL
4	Fiat Uno 1.0	4	Range Rover 4.6 HSE
5	Subaru Vivio 2WD	5	BMW M5
6	Peugeot 106 Diesel	6	Porsche 911 Carrera 993
7	Suzuki Swift 1.0	7	Nissan Patrol GR
8	Nissan Micra 1.0L	8	Jeep Cherokee 4.0L
9	Ford Fiesta 1.1CFi	9	Lotus Esprit S4s
10	Citroen AX Debut	10	Toyota Supra Turbo

If enough people choose cars on the grounds of environment-friendliness rather than speed, design or sex appeal, it could make an enormous difference to the development of cleaner motoring worldwide. Already, General Motors, Volvo, Volkswagen and Renault have all developed a prototype engine which will do 60 miles per gallon/21km per litre in city traffic and 70 miles per gallon/25km per litre on a motorway. But without popular pressure, car manufacturers are unwilling to invest in the new machinery needed to turn these prototypes into mass-market vehicles. Meanwhile, don't be put off secondhand cars. About a quarter of the impact a vehicle makes on the physical environment is in its construction, the rest is in its use. So whatever model you choose, you are reducing the impact substantially just by opting not to buy a new car.

Further reading and contacts

Which Car? available from most newsagents, is a helpful, comprehensive guide to value-for-money vehicles.

The Environmental Transport Association can be contacted at The Old Posthouse, Heath Rd, Weybridge, Surrey KT13 8RS. Its car buyer's guide costs £3.95 and the association also offers a breakdown recovery service for bicycle owners.

The Cycling Touring Club provides advice on the full range of bicycles and accessories now available. Write to Cotterell House, 69 Meadrow, Godalming, Surrey GU7 3HS.

For information on folding bicycles contact The Folding Society, 19 West Park, Castle Cary, Somerset BA7 7DB.

CHAPTER SEVENTEEN

Health

Within every patient, there resides a doctor and we physicians are at our best when we put our patients in touch with the doctor inside themselves.
Albert Schweitzer (1875–1965), French theologian and missionary surgeon

Many people take much better care of their financial and material assets than the ones that really count in life. They would not dream of neglecting a hole in the roof of their house, or dent in the side of their car, but they would put off a visit to the doctor when the pain in the chest refuses to go away, perhaps until it is too late to treat. Men are particularly good at ignoring painful symptoms. Taking good care of ourselves is neither a luxury nor an indulgence. It is our ultimate responsibility. Think of your responsibility to others, if you are uneasy about focusing so much attention on yourself – your partner, parents, children, employer, customers or your cat. They all depend on you.

Perhaps the most precious and enduring gift that downshifting will hand you is better health – mental, physical and maybe spiritual. 'I feel *so* much better these days . . .' was a common and very emphatic response among those downshifters we interviewed for this book, when we asked them about the advantages of slowing down and simplifying their lives.

Downshifting is good for you!

Many of the steps we are suggesting for successful downshifting have an automatic pay-back in health terms. You will have noticed that eating better on less, for example, is also about eating healthier and more nutritionally rich food. So just dwell for a moment on all the benefits that you are storing up for yourself. Getting fit and staying healthy will not only transform your outlook on life; it will also help you save money. You will become more resistant to infection, so you will spend less on prescription charges, over-the-counter cough mixtures, cold and flu 'remedies', aspirin and boxes of paper tissues.

Naturally, if you can persuade your family to downshift with you – or at least apply its healthy living spin-offs to their own habits – then the savings multiply pretty quickly. This is not to suggest that you won't ever need doctors or pharmacists, but given long NHS waiting lists and the high cost of private health care, it is wise to take all the precautions you can against getting ill in the first place. Prevention is always better than cure.

Taking more exercise is an unavoidable and hugely enjoyable consequence of reducing our dependence on cars for getting around. Almost everyone needs to become more physically active to prevent illness and to stay in good shape and it is virtually impossible to be a couch potato *and* a downshifter. Your new lifestyle is almost certain to make you more physically active.

Get out of that armchair now!

We have dealt with eating your way to healthier, more cost-effective living. Here are ten tips to living better through more *physical activity*.

1   Walk or cycle to places that you currently use a car, taxi or bus to reach. Try and integrate each of these activities into your daily routine for work, shopping, socialising, study or leisure.

2   Use stairs or steps instead of escalators or lifts.

3   Indulge your dormant curiosity about the world around you. Get to know the area you live in by foot or bicycle – you will notice all sorts of interesting features, and people, that you miss from a car or a bus.

4   Consider joining a health and fitness club. Yes, it will cost you money, but you do sometimes have to spend in the short term to save in the long term. Many local councils now run very good gyms, often inside a leisure centre or municipal swimming pool. They tend to offer hefty discounts on annual membership cards for local

residents and off-peak use. The more you use the facilities, the more cost-effective it becomes.

5   Work out the pros and cons of using a club or gym near where you live, or close to where you work. The advantage of the latter would be that you could go there during lunch breaks or before work if you do flexible hours. The activity would give you a mental and physical boost and so help you work more efficiently. Don't rule out joining a private health club. Go and see its facilities, and if you are impressed, ask whether the management could work out a corporate member-ship deal with your employer so you would pay a reduced rate.

6   Take up another active sport or pastime, if the idea of joining a gym does not appeal. It could be swimming or Scottish dancing, provided it is cheap or free, and you can do it without too much paraphernalia or travelling.

7   Try to think of housework, gardening and DIY not as chores but as health and fitness opportunities! There are bound to be days when you would prefer to make your house gleam instead of sit down and work. Bad for your short-term cash flow, but good for your health.

8   Plan six walks that you would like to do when you get the chance either on your own or with company. Borrow some books from the library or leaflets and maps from the council leisure department to help you work out suitable routes along public footpaths.

9   Roll your sleeves up and do some practical voluntary work. Spend a weekend laying hedges, repairing stiles or stone walls for the British Trust for Conservation Volunteers (BTCV). It costs very little – you are giving them free labour after all, and sometimes the accommoda-tion is somewhat basic – but you will be well-fed. If you want a completely free active weekend away, then maybe make time to go WWOOFing. Willing Workers on Organic Farms (WWOOF) charges members £10 a year. For that you get lists of organic farms that need extra pairs of hands for weekends or longer periods, and a brief description of the type of work they will want you to do. Give them your labour and they give you free bed and board. All you have to pay is your travelling costs.

10 Borrow a dance video from your local library or dance centre. Learn whichever dances or step routines you fancy and practise them in the kitchen while waiting for the kettle to boil, the toaster to pop, or the microwave to go 'ding!' Having fun matters more than style and choreographic niceties. And don't worry about the strange looks your cat will give you – who's he going to tell?

If you have followed all that advice, you might appreciate some suggestions for relaxing and winding down from either hard physical or mental activity. The following tips will be just as important to your health as those concerning exercise. Taking a decision to change your life, even to slow it down, is not necessarily without its stresses and there are bound to be times when you need to switch off and treat yourself to some slow, sensual pleasure.

Slow down, switch off and chill out

Here are ten ways to relax and practise stress relief that cost little or nothing.

1 Yoga

This is a system of exercises that creates a sense of calm and relaxation, but also improves the body's strength and suppleness. If practised regularly, it can be an extremely effective way of eliminating stress and anxiety and enhancing one's sense of physical and mental well-being. There are several different types, but hatha yoga is probably the most widely practised as well as being the oldest. It is best to attend classes run by a qualified yoga teacher to learn the basics. But once you can perform the postures safely, there is no reason why you should not practise yoga at home on your own, preferably for a few minutes every day.

2 Meditation

This is easy and free. The psychological and emotional benefits of meditation have been well-known for centuries. As the theme of this book is simpler living, we'll give you the simplest version. Here's what you do:

- Take an alarm clock or a kitchen timer into a quiet room where no one will disturb you. Set the clock to go off in 15 to 20 minutes time.

- Sit down on a straight-backed chair, with your hands in your lap or on your knees.
- Close your eyes and relax. Breathe through your nose rhythmically and slowly, taking each breath deep down into the abdomen. Let an image flow into your mind and hold it there. It can be a face, a leaf, a pattern, or whatever you like. When it drifts away, try to draw it back and hold on to it again.
- When the time is up, stretch slowly, open your eyes and look around. Do not stand up quickly, because your blood pressure will have dropped. You should feel relaxed, refreshed and calm.

3 Listening to music
This can energise or relax you, so find something soothing on your radio or stereo, lie back, and drift off.

4 Get some more sleep!
If you go to bed late, find it hard to get up in the morning, and tend to lack energy during the day, you probably need to change your daily routine. Try going to bed earlier. Instead of having a big meal in the evening, sink into a hot aromatic bath. The chances are that you will sleep better and wake up feeling more relaxed and refreshed.

5 Treat yourself to a massage
Better still ask your partner to join you in learning the art of massage so that you both benefit from the highly relaxing and enjoyable experience of giving and receiving a massage. It can be done with or without essential oils (see 7, below).

6 Put on a face mask
It's very hard to do anything but relax when a cleansing mask is hardening on your face. Talking can be particularly difficult, as can seeing if you normally wear spectacles. Might as well have a lie down.

7 Aromatherapy
Add a few drops of essential oils to your bath or to the water receptacle of a candle fragrancer. Make sure you choose one that has relaxing properties, such as lavender, neroli, geranium, marjoram or ylang-ylang, or blend together two or three of these. The aroma will make you feel more tranquil. Using one of these candle fragrancers in the bedroom should help you sleep better, but ensure you extinguish the flame safely before nodding off. Oils can also be used in massage to great effect.

8 Have a good laugh

Laughing is wonderfully therapeutic because it releases tension and helps you to wind down. It is also infectious. So next time you borrow a book or a video from the library, choose something you are likely to find funny. Cinemas often offer half-price admission one night a week. Look out for the next comedy, and take a friend or partner.

9 Give your cat or dog a stroke

Very relaxing for you and your pet. People who work from home or live on their own are likely to find the company of a cat or dog particularly rewarding and relaxing.

10 Visualisation

This is a good technique to master if you are prone to anxiety. Essentially, it is about mobilising your imagination to help deal with difficult situations or physical illness. It may help dispel fear about a forthcoming event – a wedding maybe, or an actor's first night in a play. What you do is make a mental image of your own triumph in facing down these fears. So to beat wedding day nerves, you might visualise your guests fêting you and your partner with confetti and congratulations. Actors might imagine a cheering, packed theatre of fans demanding encores. Some leading cancer specialists encourage patients to use the powers of positive thought to help fight their disease.

There are probably as many sceptics as advocates of this type of self-help therapy. But there are a fair number of respectable medics who believe that there could be a sound physiological basis to the benefits of visualisation. Anyway, it won't cost you a bean, so is probably worth a try. You need to be totally relaxed, preferably lying down on the floor or sitting comfortably in a quiet room, and it is important to get the right image for you, so do experiment.

Spontaneity

When was the last time you acted on impulse? When did you last do something really silly, joyous, daft or slightly childish. It is quite possible that you cannot remember, because you have been so busy aspiring, achieving and earning, or indeed caring for others. Yet marriages founder for the lack of it; and conformity and competition squeeze it out of our working lives. Resurrect the spontaneity of childhood memories in every area of your life, in work, play and personal relationships. It is not only healthy, spontaneity is creativity in its purest, simplest form.

Further reading
The HEA Guide to Complementary Medicine and Therapies by Anne Woodham, Health Education Authority, 1994.
Stress: The Aromatic Solution by Maggie Tisserand, Hodder & Stoughton, 1996.

CHAPTER EIGHTEEN

Household Management

Have nothing in your houses that you do not know to be useful, or believe to be beautiful.
William Morris (1834–96), English designer, socialist and poet

Clutter is the enemy of efficient household management. In this chapter we are going to help you get rid of what you don't want or need, by recycling or selling it. We will also give you some tips on cutting your heating, water and lighting bills, to save you money and help the environment.

Clutter spreads like a virus, and you are unlikely to summon all your powers of decisive action to dispose of it unless you establish exactly what it is, and why you allow it to accumulate. Try this practical exercise. Inspect the contents of each room, drawers, cupboards. Just look at everything you have and list every item that fails to pass the 'William Morris Test'. Don't forget any sheds or attics, well-known breeding grounds for this insidious species that colonises our domestic worlds.

We will recognise most things as either useful or not, but a significant minority will fall into a grey area that we could sum up as: 'Well, You Never Know, It Might Come In Handy.' This grey area is actually stuffed full of clutter.

If in doubt, throw it out

Once you have your own clutter report, think about how you came to have all these items still lying about the place. That should help you stop it all building up again after the clear-out we suggest you now undertake. When you are busy, it is all too easy to ignore clutter and find a drawer

194

that you can still open to store your most recently acquired knick-knacks. Then there are all the broken items that you always meant to repair, but never did. In addition, there will probably be items that you strongly suspect you will never use again, but you simply cannot face making a decision about their future.

Here is a five-point plan to help you transform your clutter list into a satisfying achievement, and an act of altruism to your fellow man and woman. Do not despair, panic or prevaricate. The chances are that you will suffer absolutely *no* withdrawal symptoms, but will feel *liberated* by creating a new, more spacious habitat in which to enjoy the delights of simple domesticity. Remember, it means less to keep clean and to insure, less to lug around the country when you next move home, and less to worry about!

1   **GET** some cardboard boxes. Place in them all the items on your list that you know are incapable of being recycled – tins of congealed paint for instance, and long dead paintbrushes. Take them to your local council tip, or arrange for someone from the council to collect them. On the same trip take all the recyclable bottles, cans and newspapers that are lying about to put in the 'eco-banks' that you generally find at these official tips.

2   **GATHER** together all the things that you simply hate, or no longer need but which others may be able to use, or even find aesthetically pleasing. It might be worth offering first refusal to relatives and friends before making any irrevocable disposals!

3   **GENERATE** some income! Car boot sales thrive on gatherings of people who are undertaking clear-outs. You can make some money by taking your unwanted paraphernalia to one. If there is room in your car, take your neighbour's unwanted items too. Alternatively, you can contact a dealer in secondhand furniture and knick-knacks, who will come round and offer you a deal.

4   **GIVE** it away! Take it to charity shops, and such virtuous behaviour will be its own reward. Make sure it really is in good condition, otherwise you are simply passing on your responsibility to junk your junk to someone else. If you don't want the hassle of travelling to such shops or the logistics are too difficult, then it is worth phoning them, telling them what you have got and ask

whether they will collect. Some areas have charity or volunteer-run recycling centres. Check if there is one near you, and again they may collect if you can persuade them that it would be worth their petrol money.

5   **GO ON** recycling, every day week and month, not simply as part of the annual domestic clutter audit that we urge you to undertake. Make it part of your life, enjoy being part of an endlessly replenishing loop of renewal and regeneration.

What happens to your rubbish?

By now we hope you are convinced of the need to recycle and cut down on the volume of rubbish you put out each week for the binmen. In case you still harbour doubts, let us give you some facts about what is in the rubbish we create and what happens to it. Here is a breakdown of household rubbish that Britons simply discard – i.e. they *don't* recycle or give away:

Material	%
Paper and card	33.2
Organic waste matter	20.2
Glass	9.3
Dusty particles and other 'fines'	6.8
Plastic bottles and other dense plastics	5.9
Steel cans and other ferrous metals	5.7
Plastic film	5.3
Textiles	2.1
Aluminium cans and other non-ferous metals	1.6
Miscellaneous	9.9
	100

Where does it go? Mostly it is put in holes in the ground, or landfill sites, as they are technically known. Some 86 per cent of British domestic waste is disposed of in this way. As the waste decomposes it produces massive quantities of methane gas. This is highly explosive gas which can and does contribute to the greenhouse effect or global warming. Potentially, it can be contained and diverted into some useful purpose. The Department of the Environment has reported that some 1,400 waste disposal sites in the UK leak some of this noxious gas into the atmosphere. At least 600 *urgently* need the installation of gas control equipment to stop the discharge of methane into the atmosphere.

As if the release of methane was not bad enough, there is also a liquid called leachate that can seep into underground streams and rivers, and finally into surface water that causes pollution. Then consider the pollution caused by lorries taking the waste from your front gate to the landfill sites. You can see the environmental damage piling up.

If you recycle or compost more of your waste, the planet gets less polluted. Sure, yours is only a negligible amount in the grand scheme of things, but multiply it by the number of families in your street, then by the number of streets in your neighbourhood. If everyone gave the same thought, and made the same effort as you are making in your life, it would make a serious difference. Waste can be burned to create a renewable source of energy, but only about 9 per cent of waste is currently disposed of in this way.

Remember the four planet-friendly 'Rs' that you should try to integrate into your new household management routines:

- **Reduce** what comes into your home, or at least ensure that what you buy is durable and really useful. Cut back on short-life items such as disposable razors, ordinary batteries and kitchen roll.
- **Re-use** products and their containers, if possible. Start buying washing powder and liquids in containers that can be refilled. Use yoghurt pots to grow seedlings for the kitchen garden, or indeed to make your own yoghurt.
- **Recycle** your kitchen and garden waste as new raw materials for yourself or others.
- **Replace** worn out products with ones made from recycled materials especially stationery, glassware or even clothes.

Five ways to keep in touch on less

You may be spending more on phoning, faxing and postage than you need.

1 Send mail second class, unless it is important that it gets to its destination the next day.

2   Pay as many bills as possible through your bank or building society: doing so is usually free if you have an account, so you save postage costs.

3   Make calls and send faxes in the evenings, when it's cheaper.

4   You may be paying more than you need to call, so check the prices of alternative telephone service providers such as the cable companies. Often, you don't have to sign up to cable television as well.

5   Sending e-mail messages is by far the cheapest way for you to communicate from a distance with friends, family or work contacts. So if you don't already have a computer, this might be a good reason why you should.

Shedding light on saving energy

If every household in the country replaced their ordinary lightbulbs with low energy bulbs, it would save enough energy to close down a nuclear power station. If we don't take drastic steps to cut current levels of consumption, global warming will get worse. Taking steps to save energy is one way you and your family can help to make such avoidable environmental problems less likely and less serious. It will save you money too, which is good news for the downshifting fraternity. But don't stop at using energy efficient lightbulbs – consider 'greening' your entire home.

Looking and lagging: the energy challenge

Households are being asked to join a national campaign to save money and energy. Those who have followed a long-term energy action programme devised by a Government-backed environmental charity, Global Action Plan (see The Downshifter's Directory for details) have saved an average of 9 per cent on their fuel bills, with the potential of saving much more over time. Now everyone else is being invited to join the drive. Here is a shortened version of the plan.

Week 1   Inspect your **hot water tank** and what it is wearing. Buy it an 80mm thick insulation jacket if there is none or the one

198

it has is wearing thin. A good thick layer can cut your heat loss by 75 per cent, and will pay for itself in a few months.

If you have a boiler and a hot water tank ensure the **pipes** between them are well lagged.

Make a note to replace the next 100 watt ordinary lightbulb that you unscrew with a **low energy bulb**. It will last eight times as long as the one it has just replaced and uses 75 per cent less energy.

Week 2 How good is the **draught-proofing** in your home? If you feel chilly near closed windows and doors, the chances are that your home is leaking heat. Make a note of the worst offenders, and deal with them first. **Outside doors** will need robust, waterproof, draught-proofing material. Spend some time looking at the variety of possible materials available at DIY stores. Don't forget the **letterbox**, the **keyhole** and the **cat flap** – they too can be insulated these days! Less robust draught-excluding materials will suffice for internal doors.

What you need to draught-proof **windows** will depend on their type and the way that they open. Those that open like a door can be fitted with brush seals. Sash windows that open up and down on cords are best sealed by fitting a brush strip to the frame. Heavy lined curtains that reach down to the floor or just below the window sill make excellent insulation material. Just make sure curtains do not hang over radiators, otherwise none of the heat will reach you before it disappears out of the window!

A word about **ventilation**. Don't draught-proof kitchen and bathroom windows, as condensation is likely to build up. Also ensure adequate ventilation in rooms that have a fuel-burning boiler or fire, unless you have one with a balanced flue where the air for combustion is drawn directly from outside, and waste gases are expelled directly.

Week 3 Next check out your loft, if you have one. **Loft insulation** could cut your heating bills by one-fifth, and pay for itself within two years. If your loft is already insulated check how thick the material is. It needs to be 200mm deep to be really effective. Top it up if necessary.

Get more warmth out of your **radiators**. Attach sheets of kitchen foil to the wall behind them. Moreover, if you fix shelves above your radiators (allowing space between them to let warm air circulate), more of the warm air will be deflected into the middle of the room instead of rising to the ceiling.

In your kitchen, check that you are using your cooking and cooling energy efficiently.

Try to introduce at least five of these tips into your everyday life at home:

- use well-fitting lids on pans
- heat only the amount of water you need in kettles or saucepans
- don't have gas flames on so high that they lick the side of saucepans
- use a pressure cooker
- keep the fridge at 2–3°C, and the freezer at –15°C, and defrost regularly
- turn off the television set at the set, not on the remote control. A television on stand-by is not actually switched off
- if you have a home computer, keep it switched off when not in use. If it has a fax program, get into the habit of telling contacts to phone you before they send you a fax so that you can switch it on
- switch off lights. Don't leave them all on when you go out in the evening. Consider getting a security timer for table lamps
- try to make sure the washing machine is full when you use it
- dry clothes naturally if possible rather than using a tumble drier

Now are you in control of your heating controls? Ensure your system has a timer or programmer so the house and water are heated only when you need them to be. Turning down your thermostat by 1°C could cut 10 per cent off your heating bills, and you probably would not notice any temperature difference.

Week 4   Just when you thought you had insulated everything bar the cat and the kitchen sink, there are two other important areas we have not mentioned so far – floors and walls. More domestic heat is lost through uninsulated walls than through any other route. Most houses built since the early 1930s have outer and inner external walls, with a small cavity in between. Older properties tend to have solid external walls. You can usually tell by measuring the width of a wall at a window or door opening (exclude external rendering). Solid walls are usually 9 inches (230 mm) thick. Cavity walls are at least 10.5 inches thick (260 mm). Cavity wall insulation should be done by a specialist. Solid wall insulation could be done by a competent DIY person.

Floors can account for 15 per cent of heat loss. The easiest way to reduce that loss is by covering the floors over. Choose from felt or rubber underlay, layers of newspaper, carpet with foam backing, wood blocks or cork tiles.

It will take longer than four weeks to implement your plan, but you can probably make quite a bit of progress in that time. People on benefits and pensioners may qualify for grants from the Home Energy Efficiency Scheme (HEFF). For more information about grants ring Freephone 0800 181667.

Routine household maintenance: greening your cleaning

How can downshifters best keep their homes clean and save money? Luckily, as is the case with so many areas of downshifting, these two objectives are completely compatible, provided you add in plenty of elbow grease. The less money you spend, the less demands you are likely to make on precious natural resources.

SUBSTITUTE some of your chemically-based household cleaners for gentler alternatives, but think about whether your house really needs all the time-consuming pampering so many of us lavish on our homes.

TURN your home into a toxin-free zone. You can do most of your cleaning with the following: distilled vinegar, salt, bicarbonate of soda (buy a big box from your chemist, not the tiddly little tubs used in baking), soap and elbow grease. Make your own furniture polish from beeswax. Floors rarely need polishing, if at all. Life is too short.

RUMMAGE around your local shops, and ask the owners or managers to consider stocking more eco-friendly household items.

USE tea tree oil as a disinfectant, but go easy on it. Many of us were brought up to believe that our homes were teaming with harmful bugs, and that we had to wage war against these invaders with every bucket, mop and bottle of bleach we could muster. In fact, most bugs are either harmless or positively beneficial. Our bodies' immune systems are designed to cope with bugs. As long as you obey the basic rules of hygiene, you will be safe from harm.

DECORATE your home with traditional, non-toxic water-based paint. You may find that it is more expensive than the solvent-based paints that most of us use, but think of all the money you are going to save by following our *other* tips! Water-based paint comes in a range of gorgeous colours, and leaves no nasty smells while it is drying out. If you find it hard to obtain locally, a number of firms provide a mail order service. These include Fired Earth plc, Twyford Mill, Oxford Road, Adderbury, Oxon OX17 3HP. Tel: 01295 812088; and Farrow & Ball, 249 Fulham Road, London SW3. Tel: 01202 876141.

CHAPTER NINETEEN

Keeping Up Appearances

Vanity of vanities; all is vanity.
Ecclesiastes 1:2

In the modern post-war consumer world the fashion and beauty industries have become more powerful and pervasive than ever before. Seduced by advertising, both British women and men are spending more and more on trying to achieve the body beautiful. In 1995 we spent a total of £3,553m on cosmetics, toiletries, hair and skincare products, more than double what we spent, in real terms, a decade earlier. In the 1990s fashion mania across the world has reached new heights.

This mania is fuelled by different motivations. One is sheer habit: we go shopping, see something we like and buy it. Often we don't bother to think through whether it will match the other items in our wardrobe. If it doesn't, the new purchase either languishes in a bottom drawer – or we feel compelled to buy something else to go with it! Another reason is the pervasive presence of fashion advertising on television and the radio, in newspapers and magazines, on the Tube, the bus and the hoardings in the street. Buying under influence, we often end up wearing clothes which we don't need, which don't suit us and which go against our natural instinct and style.

A third powerful motivation is competition. For women especially, but also for men, wearing clothes which are up-to-date, smart and expensive-looking can make a big difference to their confidence and sense of self-worth. In many workplaces women are still judged by the way they look – their face and hair and the kind of clothes they wear. And it is not just men who label women frumpy, sexy, unadventurous, and so on, according to their attire. Women often judge each other by the same criteria.

Fourth, we buy clothes, beauty products and make-up as a form of retail therapy. If you are downshifting because you're over-worked and stressed-out then it's likely you've been indulging in a little extra clothes buying simply because you feel you deserve a reward.

Pretty or elegant clothes and attractive make-up are, of course, great fun to wear and help to make us feel good. We are not suggesting for one minute that men should throw out their expensive suits or women renounce face-paint for good. But take fashion and beauty too seriously and they can tyrannise your life, and make a deep hole in your pocket. So, if you've decided to re-balance your life, why not throw your wardrobe and bathroom cabinet into the scales?

Wardrobe changes

Let's start in the bedroom. Below we suggest four easy and enjoyable ways to take a fresh approach to clothes and clothes buying.

Bin it Empty your wardrobe, cupboards and drawers of all your clothes and shoes. Take a long, hard look at them. Those you haven't worn for months and you know you will never wear again put in a pile to give away immediately to friends and charity shops.

Bag it Put all the clothes and shoes you haven't worn for months but can't bear to throw out in a bag marked with the date six months ahead. Mark the date in your diary. Then put the bag in an easily accessible clothes cupboard. When the alloted day arrives, if you haven't felt the urge once to open the bag, then take it to a charity shop or car boot sale without stopping to peek inside.

Mix and match Assuming that you have been too busy to give your wardrobe an appraising eye, spend a few enjoyable hours mixing and matching in front of the mirror. You may be pleased and surprised to find that the blouses, skirts and jackets you bought in different colours several years apart actually go quite well together. This applies as much to men's shirts, trousers, jeans and shorts as it does to women's more varied wardrobes. With any luck this exercise should provide you with several untried outfits which feel brand new.

Shop with care and flair

Of course, this pared-down, mixed and matched wardrobe won't last you forever, so how should you go about choosing new clothes when you're on a tighter budget? Here are a few useful rules of thumb:

- If you're used to buying expensive new clothes every season, spend some of your new-found extra time shopping around for similar designs at less expense. Pick out the winter or summer outfit you covet most and then look for them in the cheaper range of stores. Next, Marks & Spencer and Warehouse, for example, all do a very good range of mass-market versions of catwalk clothes. If you're a real fashion addict, there's no reason to deprive yourself. Just shop around and lose that obsession for designer labels.

- How 'new' does a new outfit have to be? Many secondhand and nearly new clothes stores offer a very good range of cheap, well-kept clothes for the bargain-hunter. Often they are also stocked with unusual, authentic clothes from past decades which look and feel much better than the modern imitations. Apart from the specialist secondhand stores, charity shops, too, are worth a look-in. Many have raised the quality of their clothes substantially in recent years and there is the added bonus of giving your money to a good cause.

- Go for simple colours and classical design. Black, white, cream and grey are all fantastically interchangeable and you can brighten them up with splashes of your favourite bright colour. You will find mixing and matching a small wardrobe much easier if your clothes don't come in a mass of prints, checks, stripes and Paisley patterns. Equally, a hip-length black or white jacket and a skirt cut a couple of inches above the knee will last the seasons much better than a tiny mini or a long, sweeping Victorian-style skirt. You can always make your classic clothes suit the trend of the day by adding an inexpensive new item such as a T-shirt, scarf or piece of jewellery.

- Look for durability of fabric first when buying anything new. You don't want to spend your money on flimsy clothes which will soon wear out or on outfits so delicate they need to be expensively dry-cleaned every time you wear them. Natural fibres are generally more adaptable and longer-wearing than artificial fibres. So pick cotton and wool, rather than nylon, rayon or viscose. Check that seams are well-made and zips well-fitted.

- If you have the time and inclination why not have a go at making some of your own clothes? Many local authorities run dressmaking evening classes, and there are easy-to-follow books available in libraries. An easier alternative is swapping clothes with friends when you are bored with your wardrobes, either on a loan basis or for good. Or you could swap another service, such as home-grown fruit or vegetables or a few nights' babysitting for a friend's or neighbour's outfit. You'll be surprised how much fun it can be!

Going for broke

For those who want to drastically reduce their wardrobe as part of a conscious effort to live a simpler, less cluttered life, or who can't afford more than a minimal wardrobe, it is of course possible to exist comfortably on a very small range of practical outfits. The Californian downshifting guru Elaine St James, a 52-year-old former businesswoman, recommends the following Spartan wardrobe, based on her own: two skirts, two pairs of trousers, two warm jumpers, eight T-shirts, six turtleneck tops, one pair of black loafers and one pair of boots.

Ms St James could easily afford more. But she doesn't need it so she doesn't buy it. Thousands of enthusiastic American converts are following her example, emancipating themselves from retail slavery and dumping their designer dresses on the doorsteps of the delighted Salvation Army.

Keen to be green

For people who not only want to save money, but are also concerned about the environmental implications of the clothes they wear here are a few simple ground rules:

- Avoid artificial fibres which are mostly made from oil products.
- Support the charities and small fair trade companies which sell natural

fibre clothes by sending off for their mail-order catalogues. You can buy clothes direct from Oxfam (Oxfam House, 274 Banbury Rd, Oxford OX2 7DZ) or from Traidcraft (Kingsway, Gateshead, Tyne and Wear NE11 ONE).

- When you've finished with your clothes either give them away or take them to a textile recycling centre. If you put them in the dustbin they will end up in a landfill site. Bear in mind that not all clothes need to be washed after wearing just once, and always use the minimum amount of detergent necessary. Hang your clothes on the washing line or a clothes horse rather than using a tumble dryer.

Toiletries and cosmetics

How much beauty care do you really need? Obviously the answer depends very much on individual taste, but doctors and dermatologists will tell you that normal healthy skin only needs to be kept clean and moist to stay looking good. In one of his columns for *The Observer Magazine*, Dr John Collee told readers that a good moisturiser was the only vital ingredient for facial care, and that there was often little to show between the cheap and the expensive brands. The other vital ingredients to a good complexion are not miracle skin-lifters and tonics but lots of sleep, a good diet and not too much alcohol.

Cosmetics is much more a matter of personal taste and style. Some women wear little or no make-up, others don't feel dressed without the full works, especially if they feel their jobs demand it. But it is interesting to note that many make-up artists asked what they put on their own skin will admit that they don't bother with the foundation creams and powders they so liberally slap on to other people's faces. Beauty treatments are also, of course, another great form of retail therapy. Your new lifestyle should mean less stress, less tiredness, fewer bags under the eyes and therefore less need for expensive trips to the salon. Below we list a few easy ways to cut back.

Cut down Take a long, hard look at all your toiletries and decide which ones you think are really essential or are definitely doing your body good. Then next time you run out of a cream or gel which is not essential, don't replace it. Try just buying a skin cleanser and moisturiser, soap, shampoo and deodorant and see whether your skin really feels any worse for this new minimalist approach.

Trade down If you buy expensive brands of toiletries, try less expensive ones. Many of the cheaper ranges, such as Body Shop and Boots own-brand, use the same 'booster' ingredients such as vitamin E to help revive as well as moisturise the skin. If you don't like the change, you can always swap back.

Try DIY Attempt a major beauty routine at home rather than in a salon. Instead of booking in for a facial, cleanse, exfoliate (by rubbing your face vigorously with a warm flannel) steam and face-pack – while having a long, luxurious bath. Use home-made beauty treatments wherever possible. Cold tea bags or slices of cucumber over tired eyes can be just as effective as expensive creams, for example.

If you want to be a green and ethical consumer you can use your buying power to make a difference. Remember that the chemicals used in many toiletries sold daily in Britain end up flushed into rivers and groundwater, adding to a cocktail of pollutants which harm wildlife. Also remember that most cosmetics still contain ingredients which have been tested on laboratory animals.

Thankfully, more than 100 companies, including chainstores such as Boots and Tesco, now sell 'cruelty-free' and 'green' product ranges. The huge success of the Body Shop, which recycles its bottles, supports environmental causes and uses ingredients which have not been tested on animals for at least five years, has led the way in a cosmetics revolution. As a result, the lucky consumer no longer has to seek out hidden-away health food stores to do his or her ethical shopping. Still, the proliferation of these new products can be baffling. Just because a bottle of bath foam is called 'Rainforest Glades' doesn't mean that most of its ingredients are not, in fact, unnatural man-made chemicals.

Careful scrutiny of ingredient lists will help you to choose the better brands, essentially those made up of fewer chemicals than natural ingredients. Companies are not required to state whether or not their products' ingredients have been tested on animals. So the best bet is to stick with those that state categorically they are cruelty-free.

Think carefully before you buy any new toiletries and cosmetics. Most come in over-packaged boxes and bottles which are a waste of natural resources as well as expensive. Many chemical-based products can also cause allergies to people with sensitive skins, and chemical factories producing ingredients for the beauty industry cause pollution. The greenest beauty option of all is to stop using all but the most basic products.

Further reading and contacts

The British Union for the Abolition of Vivisection lists 100 cruelty-free companies in its free *Good Products Guide*, many of which have mail-order catalogues. Write to BUAV, 16A Crane Grove, London N7 8LB. Tel: 0171 700 4888.

The Body Shop produces a range of information, available from the head office at Watersmead, Littlehampton, West Sussex BN17 6LS. Tel: 01903 731500.

CHAPTER TWENTY

Growing Your Own

Many gardens and allotments of the villagers had already received their spring tillage, but the garden and the allotments of the Durbeyfields were behindhand. She found, to her dismay, that this was owing to their having eaten all the seed potatoes . . .
Thomas Hardy, *Tess of the D'Urbervilles*, 1891

Growing at least some of your own food is one of the greatest delights of downshifting. Whether your home is in a tower block, a bedsit, a suburban semi or a rural smallholding, gardening will enhance your life. It's healthy, sociable and it will save you money. Not only that but if you garden organically, as we suggest you do, you will be helping to create a healthier planet too. This is because you will be creating a balanced eco-system to match your newly balanced lifestyle.

Newcomers to gardening first need to size up the opportunities for growing. You may want to start in a small way first, with perhaps a few seedlings in pots on a window sill, just to see how it goes. Those who fancy growing out in the fresh air can exploit patios, backyards and window ledges if there is not much space elsewhere. Maybe the idea of an allotment appeals, in which case register your interest with the council quickly. In some parts of the country, available allotments are rare, so get your name on the waiting list while you are still thinking about it. You can always drop out later if you change your mind – there will be plenty of others after your plot!

Having room to grow flowers, shrubs and produce is frequently a major reason why people want to move house, sometimes out from an urban area to a rural one. However, it must be emphasised that if and when you catch the gardening bug you will find happiness and satisfaction in your gardening wherever you are. We aim here to give some advice to beginners and more advanced gardeners, who may be interested in switching to organic methods. More importantly we want to inspire and galvanise those of you who tend to think that gardening is what retired people do. Think again, you are never too young or too old to enjoy it. Gardening is for life.

It's cool to compost

Composting creates an excellent natural fertiliser for all your gardening and growing. You can recycle in this way at least 20 per cent of your household waste that would otherwise end up being driven by a gas-guzzling lorry to a distant landfill site. Once you get in the habit, you will find composting is fun, and your garden produce will be all the better because of it. It takes a while for your kitchen and garden waste to decompose to the point where you can spread it on your flowers and vegetables, so there's no time like the present to start a compost heap or bin. Don't forget, you don't need a garden to make compost.

Warm to a worm: your best flexible friend!

Indoor gardeners need not lose out in the composting stakes. You just need to come to terms with worms – or even make friends with them. They will see you right just by doing what comes naturally. All you need is a wormery. Yes, you will probably need to buy one rather than try to make one, but this is sustainable expenditure, so it's well worth the investment. You can obtain one through Original Organics Ltd [details below]. The wormery is supplied complete, ready to start producing top quality compost. It stands 30 inches high, and has a 90 litre capacity. There is a junior version with a 23 litre capacity, designed specifically for flat dwellers or single person households. You get special Tiger worms, a bin with all the fittings, shredded paper for worm bedding and worm starter food. Give them your kitchen vegetable waste and in return, they will produce beautiful rich compost for you, which you can put on your houseplants, window boxed vegetables or patio tubs. For more details of the Original Wormery, as it's called, write to Original Organics Ltd, Units 4/5, Farthing's Lodge, Business Centre, Plymtree, Devon EX15 2JY. Tel 01884 277681.

Composting in the great outdoors

People with gardens need no paraphernalia to compost, except for a piece of old carpet or thickish polythene to keep the rain from washing it away. Those who like paraphernalia can buy or make a container for it from wood or recycled plastic. An old dustbin is perfect, provided you punch some holes in the sides and stand it on bricks so that air may circulate. The more varied the composting input, the richer and more nutritious the output. So start with some stemmy material, such as prunings, to help the air circulate at the bottom, then alternate layers of soft and tougher material. Most organic waste can be usefully composted, but here's a rough and ready guide. These items are ideal:

- vegetable and fruit peelings, or raw whole pieces if they are beginning to decompose in your rack or larder
- tea leaves or bags
- eggshells
- undiseased plant remains
- grass clippings
- small amounts of wood shavings
- waste from rabbit and guinea-pig hutches or hamster cages
- shredded newspaper

Avoid the following:
- cooked kitchen scraps, even cooked vegetables
- raw meat or fish – they can attract vermin or make nasty smells
- any non-plant based artificially-made material, such as plastic, metal or glass
- cat and dog faeces
- persistent weeds such as bindweed, couch grass and ground elder

It can take several months for the first batch to compost. It depends on the ingredients, how you mix them and the temperature. The original material should be unrecognisable when it is ready to use. It should be crumbly, dark or black, sweet-smelling and earthy in texture. The longer you leave it the better it will be, and so will your home-grown produce, shrubs and flowers. Don't forget, every time you compost, you are renewing your connection with nature, and giving it a helping hand. Don't worry too much about the technicalities like layering – it is better to just have a go and get on with it than concern yourself about perfect layering. When you have got your compost going, what next?

The answer lies in the soil

Those of you with gardens need to become better acquainted with soil. Use one of the home-testing kits you can buy at garden centres to find out what will grow best in it, in short, whether it is alkaline or acidic. You should be able to tell from digging a fork into your soil and handling it whether it is mainly clay or chalky or sandy. Sew and plant accordingly. One of the best aspects of gardening is that you can do it all year round. In the case of vegetables and herbs, which we are mainly concerned with as downshifters, there should always be something delicious and nutritious to pull, wash, chop and serve at the dinner table. You don't have to buy a lot of books, although there is a huge variety to choose from if you feel so inclined. You can borrow from the library, join a local gardening club, or just ask a gardener.

Complimenting your neighbours on their impressive-looking leeks or carrots is a great way to get to know them better, and to glean some valuable information to start you off on this exciting journey. There is nothing an established gardener or grower likes more than being complimented on his or her produce, and being asked: 'Tell me, how could I grow some like that then?' Before you know it you will have a fund of knowledge which you can later pass on to some other curious gardening innocent, a bagful of free produce and some cuttings and seeds. This precious commodity of gardening knowledge and enthusiasm is passed on free, from one to another like a never-ending Mexican wave. Books can do this too, if your nearest neighbour lives a few miles down the road! So can television and radio, even the Internet.

If you don't have much space, one idea is just to grow herbs in pots on sills and ledges. Get into the habit of using them every day in cooking or salads. Perhaps you have plenty of space outside but the ground is covered by weeds. This is not a problem; it is what gardeners call a challenge. You can save the nettles for composting or for nettle water to spray on aphids. While clearing away the weeds – ask others to help you – start designing the garden you want to create in their place.

Imagine what different styles would look like, and how much work each would require of you. Think seriously about whether you want a lawn. Many people have decided that it is simply not worth the time and effort they put into creating and maintaining an immaculate lawn. The prospect of global warming, highlighted by some exceptionally dry summers in certain parts of the UK in the mid-1990s, has caused more gardeners to question the quintessentially English love of lawns. What are the alternatives?

Design your own downshifter's garden

Simplicity, balance, eco-friendliness and a degree of edibility! These must be the essential features of a downshifter's garden. Whether you are starting from scratch or you have inherited someone else's plot, try bearing those four features in mind when designing and planting. Here are ten tips that will help you create a downshifter's garden:

1 **Trees and large shrubs**
   These will give shade, shape, character and privacy to your garden, so try to include some in your designs if there are few or none at present. We should try to plant new trees where and when we can.

2 **Dig a pond**
   A pond will attract wildlife, in particular frogs, which will eat some of the pests that would otherwise eat your plants.

3 **Grow less grass**
   Think about what else might grow where your lawn does. You could get rid of it altogether and turn it over to wild flowers and vegetable growing. Or you could make it into a small circle at the centre of your garden, and part-pave the surrounding area leaving random or designed gaps between the stones for herb-growing.

4 **A place to sit**
   Watch how the light and shade changes in your garden, and decide where would be the best place for a seat or table and chairs. Build this into your plan.

5 **The compost heap**
   Decide where the compost heap will go. The closer it is to the house the more often you will use it. If the end of the garden is the only available place, keep a minibin, with cover, in the kitchen so you don't have to go out in the rain.

214

6 Catch that rain

Acquire or buy a water butt, to catch the rainwater run-off from your roof. Maybe you could convert a large plastic barrel or drum. This way you may still garden and grow while others' activities are stalled by drought-induced hosepipe bans. Rainwater is soft and may be better for your plants than tap water.

7 Which plants to grow?

When deciding what to plant, chose plants that require little or no watering. These include lavender, lilac, tulips, sunflowers, carnations, wall flowers, jasmine, holly, broom, buddleia and crocus. Plants that need a lot of water include willow, elder, bamboo, clematis, primula, and azalea. Incorporate plenty of organic matter, such as compost, into the soil. It will condition the soil and help keep moisture around the plants' roots.

8 Which plants to keep?

Remove from your garden anything that you hate, or that obscures one of your treasured plants. Remember the 'William Morris Test' that we suggested you applied to your home in Chapter 18? Well, repeat it in your garden. Bear in mind that what you may find irksome now, may look glorious in six months. So just draw up a hit-list at this stage and monitor those plants that you list. One year from now, get out your list and only then decide which plants can no longer justify their existence. Give an offender a stay of execution – ask a neighbour or a gardening contact if they would like it. If there are no takers, then dig it up. Where practicable, shred it and put it on the compost.

9 Water with care

Water your plants in the evening, and surround the stems with a layer of mulch to reduce evaporation. Cut the bottom out of plastic bottles and push them, top first into the ground next to those plants that need plenty of water. When watering just fill the bottle from your watering can. It will take the water directly to where it is needed, wasting virtually none.

10 Share the work and enjoy the results

Gardening can be solitary and some people like it that way. There are ways of making it more sociable, even if you cannot interest other family members or it is not feasible to join a club. If you have a friend who gardens, maybe you could arrange for him or her to come and help you with your gardening and for you to do the same in return. You could alternate the sessions monthly or weekly. It would give you a sounding board for your gardening plans, an extra pair of hands, and an instant cuttings and seed-swapping partner. It may be fun to dream up some joint projects – like growing some plants to give away as birthday or Christmas presents. After a couple of hours of hard labour, you can then sit down with a cup of tea, catch up with each other's news, and admire your joint handiwork.

Bring your garden into the office

Gardening can be a great adventure, so be bold in your vision and think laterally. So many millions love gardening, so bring your new-found knowledge and enthusiasms into other areas of your life. Make new connections through gardening, meet new people, get to know colleagues and acquaintances better. Who knows what new doors will open for you?

Let's imagine you are still working at your career or job and are wondering how you can downshift without leaving your employer for whom you have toiled long and hard. Here's an idea for making your working life more enjoyable and for getting your boss to allow you to go part-time or flexitime, or to do more of your job from home. Put a notice on the office noticeboard (or e-mail your colleagues if you can), inviting them to join you in a 'Gardener's Question Time' session. You could hold it in the function room at the pub round the corner, or in the company's board room, if your boss agrees.

Everyone brings along a cutting or some seeds to swap, or else a gardening problem that one of your green-fingered colleagues could probably solve. This is an excellent wheeze for bonding with colleagues and bosses alike. Office politics will be cast aside as you have a jolly good chat about Nina's sweet peas or David's problem with honey fungus, and you leave with something new and intriguing to put in your window box or garden. If you can relate to the colleagues around you at work as people, gardeners preferably, the easier it will be to negotiate that switch to part-time or home working, or win that sabbatical you have always hankered for. If your question time session goes with a bang, you then have the makings of a workers' gardening club. Remember, you don't need to be an expert to garden successfully and enjoyably. You need only genuine curiosity, a demonstrable enthusiasm for gardening, and a few social skills.

Allotment contentment

Parks are often described as the green lungs of urban areas, but so too are gardens and allotments. There is a distinctive romantic appeal about allotments, these hidden havens of DIY food production, mutual support and co-operative endeavour. Visitors accustomed to a built-up environment are also often struck by the vast expanse of sky that suddenly opens up above them, but also by the friendliness and character of allotment holders. A sensible first step is to contact your local council to get some general information and advice. They should be able to put you in touch with allotment associations in the area. Alternatively, the nearest allotments association is likely to be listed in your phone book or *Yellow Pages*. A plot will cost a few pounds a year to rent, and provided you put in enough effort, it will give you and your family virtually free food. Moreover, you will never be stuck for a gift!

If you hanker after something bigger than an allotment – a smallholding in the country for example – we advise you to try allotment gardening first, for this will help you decide whether you are temperamentally suited! As you will have read in our interview in Chapter 9 with downshifters Dan and Bel in remote rural Wales, smallholding has unique rewards, but it is also fraught with possible difficulties, requires tremendous energy and is potentially isolating. Do plenty of research before putting your house on the market!

Further reading
The Allotment. Its Landscape and Culture by David Crouch and Colin Ward, Faber & Faber, 1988.
Running Your Own Smallholding by Richard and Pauline Bambrey, Kogan Page, 1989.
Moving to the Country by David Green, Kogan Page, 1990.

CHAPTER TWENTY-ONE

Leisure and Pleasure

For a long time, leisure was for the rich, while slaves or the working classes did the work. Now we can all have leisure and we have to decide how to spend it.
Michael Argyle, *The Social Psychology of Leisure*, 1996

'In our day, we didn't have television – we made our own entertainment,' so millions have been told by their parents or grandparents. Now that television is probably the most widespread leisure activity of the modern world we will use this chapter to explore some alternatives. The person who has no TV is regarded as an eccentric curiosity by almost everyone else, but he or she may be leading a fuller and happier existence.

If you have ambivalent feelings about your television, it might be worth logging how much time you spend watching it and pondering whether life might be better without it. Consider doing what your parents or grandparents did. Make your own entertainment. The enthusiastic downshifter will take this message to heart more than most!

He or she will give *serious* thought to the following idea: swap or sell your television set and video, or cancel your agreement with the rental company. That way you will have much more time to try any or several of the options outlined in the preceding chapters, or to pursue your own alternative leisure ideas.

Ten ideas for cheap thrills, and lasting pleasure

1 Readers and borrowers
Half the adult population read books regularly and about one-quarter use public libraries at least once a month. Britain's *free* public library system

has to be one of the jewels in its crown. It is greatly cherished by those who use libraries, but perhaps there is a tendency to take them for granted. At various times in the past few years there has been talk of privatising libraries. This is unlikely, but greater commercial involvement in their running is almost a certain bet in the early years of the next century. Despite the best efforts of their champions, there has been a 10 per cent fall in the numbers of books taken out on loan since 1990. Some critics complain that libraries are boring, fusty places that need a thorough overhaul.

Others claim that the middle classes are deserting them as the price of books in the shops falls and alternative ways of gathering information – from videos, audio tapes, computers, and CD-ROMs – becomes increasingly accessible and affordable. One can expect campaigns over the coming years to spruce libraries up, for they have certainly not all benefited from advances in technology in the way that other public services have.

The changes we can expect over the next few years will probably protect library books from charges. Mercifully, the three main British political parties still appear to regard free book borrowing as sacrosanct. However, existing borrowing charges for audio tapes, videos and other media could well increase. Much will depend on users themselves and their resourcefulness as lobbyists. Downshifters, we respectfully suggest, should be in the vanguard of such campaigning.

The reference sections of libraries are nerve-centres for downshifters. These are free information points for local, regional and national activities and organisations. They should be able to help you track down most of the addresses and phone numbers you need to find out about hang-gliding, spaniel-breeding or whatever new leisure activity you plan to pursue. Don't forget the British Library, London, which is seeking to create a 'virtual library' for the future, not only of the written word, but of computer graphics, even architectural drawings. The idea is to make increasing amounts of information available over the Internet.

Finally, a word about library staff. They are generally extremely helpful, and often respond heroically to courteous requests for help. What's more, most of their services are free.

2 Volunteering

About one quarter of British adults do some voluntary work each month, according to an analysis in 1992 of 15 previous surveys. Whether they shake a tin in a shopping centre for charity, do committee work, visit

219

prisoners or hospital patients or help out with their child's playgroup, volunteers are the backbone of any community. We dealt with some aspects of volunteering in Chapter 13.

Many voluntary and charitable organisations report shortages of volunteers these days. If you can spare some time on a monthly or weekly basis, then decide to whom you would like to offer your services. This might be a national charity that you already support financially, or a new organisation. The chances are that you have read or heard about one recently that has struck you as particularly worthwhile. Decide whether hands-on practical work suits you, indoors or out, or whether you'd be happier doing committee work and report writing.

One idea is to find out if there is a Groundwork Trust in your area. This is a voluntary body that employ volunteers, and some paid workers, to regenerate the natural and built environment in run-down or derelict urban areas. Sustainable development is the common thread running through its projects, so both the environment and the local community benefit as jobs are created.

3 Buy less, make more, do it yourself

As we have seen, rat racing leaves us with little personal time, so we end up buying clothes, food, furniture and furnishings that at one time we and our families would have made ourselves. We 'contract out' domestic and household services far more than we used to, for the same reasons. Clearly, it would be unrealistic to expect more than a very small minority of people to aspire to total self-sufficiency. However, inherent in the downshifting philosophy will be a hankering to do some of the work ourselves that we currently farm out.

The trick is not to think of it as work, but leisure with attitude, leisure with purpose. What you can do is think now of one or two jobs that need doing around the house or garden, or items that need replacing. Then pick out those that you fancy having a shot at doing yourself. It can be jam-making, particularly if your garden has a fruit tree, making a lampshade, a brick wall, or laying a patio. You have to really want to do it, otherwise you probably won't get around to it, or you won't accomplish the task as well as you might. Motivation is all-important. Maybe you could rope in some friends to help you, other downshifters perhaps, whom you could repay in kind at a later date.

Another secret of successful DIY is to set yourself generous deadlines, or not to set them at all. Many of us have had a basinful of deadlines, enough to last a lifetime. Let your leisure activities evolve at your pace, no one else's. Those jobs that need doing urgently, which you don't really have the time or inclination to do, are probably best given to someone whom you pay.

4 Use the Internet to meet other downshifters

You may be geographically separated from other downshifters, but if you have a computer, or can arrange to use a friend's machine or visit a tele-cottage, you can still network with them. If you think a 'website' is somewhere that ducks congregate, then you probably need a lesson or two on how to surf the Information Super-Highway, perhaps at your nearest cyber-café. Trust us, such places really do exist, and eventually you will understand the cyber-babble used by those who run and inhabit these centres. Now, once you have mastered it, use this technology to swap information and gossip.

5 Get to know your mother's father's Uncle Horace

Researching one's family history could become a fascinating and reward-ing lifetime's project. If you write it up into a narrative, complete with family tree, you and your family will have a unique record to keep and ultimately pass on to the next generation. Circulate chapters of your *magnum opus* as you complete them as Christmas or birthday presents. Don't wait until you have finished the whole work because if you do it properly, it will probably take years. Some of your relatives may not live that long! Writing up a family history will give a new focus to your relationship with your kith and kin.

Older relatives will probably be only too pleased to be asked to rummage around for letters, photographs and family documents for you to borrow and glean interesting material. Don't forget to 'interview' them too – getting your parents' or grandparents' memories recorded. You can spread this over several sessions, each one focusing on a different era or major life event. To make it easier you can use a tape-recorder, or even a video-recorder. Encourage your willing participants to make their own video diaries; you provide the technology, they will provide the mem-ories.

Of course, the whole enterprise will have to be handled with tact and diplomacy, especially if there are a few skeletons rattling in the family cupboard. But most families are likely to be grateful that one of their number has agreed to undertake this task.

6 Set up a reading circle

Libraries are not the only sources of free or cheap reading matter. Another one is reading circles. Get together with a few friends, agree on a book that you would all like to read. Take it in turns to borrow or buy the book then pass it on to the next person, and so on until everyone has read it. Then meet up in each other's homes to discuss what you liked or disliked about it. Start all over again with a different member suggesting the book you all read. Obviously it makes sense to keep the numbers fairly small – half a dozen or fewer, and ensure you live quite close together.

7 Write a novel, short story or play

Everyone has a story to tell – their own – and it can provide the basis of any piece of fiction, or simply inspire it. Many overlook shorter forms of creative writing in pursuit of the novel, which is fine if you have the self-discipline, staying power and the talent to sustain such a long piece of work. If you want to get your work published, you are probably more likely to strike it lucky if you divide your writing ambitions into more manageable chunks. There are plenty of writers' workshops and creative writing courses to choose from. One excellent way to start is to read the guidelines published by BBC Radio for new writers of drama and short stories. For other markets, look out for the *Writers' and Artists' Yearbook* or the *Writer's Handbook*.

8 Become a dog-walker

To have all the pleasure of being a dog owner and none of the responsibility, you can offer your services as a dog escort to elderly or disabled neighbours or their carers. You will suddenly assume great popularity, especially if you live near a park!

9 Enjoy your parks

Treat your local park or open space as an extension of your garden or its substitute, if you do not have one. If there is some aspect of it that puts you off, such as vandalism or excessive litter, do something about it. Form a local Park Watch group, perhaps through an existing organisation such as a residents' group or a Neighbourhood Watch Scheme.

10 Giving to the person who has everything

Present-giving and entertaining friends, relatives or colleagues can be a delightful, life-enhancing experience, or it can be a time-consuming, duty-laden ritual for both donor and recipient. It can be extremely expensive, but the money spent does not necessarily equate with the enjoyment had.

Why don't we give each other more pleasant experiences as presents instead of buying things? Why don't we go and spend more time with the people we care about instead of compensate for our long periods of absence by handing over beautifully wrapped objects that they may neither want nor need. A walk in the country and a picnic; organising a home-made dinner, get everyone to bring a different course or dish – it will save you time and money, and possibly be more fun for everyone; or arranging a surprise visit to or from a mutual friend or relative is likely to be a far more memorable and meaningful way of marking a birthday or an anniversary. We all long for more spontaneity and serendipity in our lives, but we don't use our imaginations or make the time to make these things happen.

We prefer to spring our surprises on others in the form of purchases, which are just as likely to disappoint as to thrill unless we have asked some pertinent and searching questions in advance. If the best things in life really are free, why do we behave as though they cost a lot of money, and that the more we spend the better they are? The answer, in many cases, is that we don't stop and take time to think about it often enough, or that we do know it to be true but are too busy to act on it. So maybe the next time you want to do something nice for someone who has 'everything' give them something that they almost certainly have not had enough of recently; your time. Essentially, you don't have to be more generous with your money to make life better for you and the people you love. You simply have to be more generous with yourself.

Further reading
Writing for BBC Radio available from BBC (send large SAE to the BBC, Broadcasting House, Portland Place, London W1A 1AA. Tel: 0171 580 4468. Fax: 0171 765 3561.
Writers' and Artists' Yearbook (A & C Black) and *The Writer's Handbook* (Macmillan) are each published annually and are indispensable guidebooks to new and established writers in all market areas.

CHAPTER TWENTY-TWO

Holidays

*One of the symptoms of approaching nervous breakdown is
the belief that one's work is terribly important and that to take
a holiday would bring all kinds of disaster.*
Bertrand Russell (1872–1970), English philosopher and mathematician

As we near the end of the twentieth century our opportunities for global travel and tourism have never been greater. And we Britons, always an adventurous race, are taking up the challenge in our millions. Most of us now take two or three holidays a year within the UK and more than a third also abroad at least once a year. Between 1985–95 spending on holidays, including air and sea fares, rose by 93 per cent in real terms to a staggering £18 bn. And by the year 2000, we will be spending another 10 per cent again on our holidays, forecasts the market research company Mintel.

As a nation, the much-predicted move towards a more leisure-oriented society has yet to materialise. Instead we have an overworked majority and an idle, jobless, impoverished minority. But if you belong to the ranks of the overworked, switching to a downshifter's lifestyle should allow you more time for both leisure and holidays. And instead of spending your precious time off lying flat out on a beach recovering from a stressful job, you will be able to explore new, more fulfilling ways of spending your leisure time.

Of course, your new downshifter's lifestyle may also mean you have less money to spend. But having an enjoyable holiday doesn't have to mean splashing out a thousand pounds on a week-long skiing trip or a rushed visit to Florida or the Caribbean. There are many cheap, exciting alternatives which just take a little more time and energy to explore. Read on to find out what they are.

Cheap packaged paradise

Most of us take package trips for our annual holidays which we often book several months in advance. While this is a safe, hassle-free approach, especially when we only have a few precious weeks a year, it is much more expensive than waiting for last minute bargains. For those who don't mind which particular resort or even country they are visiting but just want a beach with sunny weather or a good skiing centre, then waiting for late deals is a good investment. And if you have flexible working patterns or are self-employed then taking a last minute holiday is much easier than when you have to clear dates with bosses and colleagues weeks in advance.

Most High Street travel agents advertise last minute package and flight bargains throughout the year, with prices down to as low as a third of the original price. Or you could scan the newspaper travel sections or trawl through the holiday listings on Ceefax and Teletext in the comfort of your home. Look out in particular for the growing number of travel agencies which specialise in cheap late bookings. Last minute packages to the Caribbean out of the peak season can sell for as little as £450, two week trips to Kenya for as little as £400 and packages to Goa, India, can drop as low as £300. One word of warning, however. Do make sure that whoever you book with is a member of ABTA or ATOL, the two trade associations, just in case your last minute holiday goes wrong. If you are misled by your agents about your destination, you want to have a legal comeback.

Shoestring travel

If you want a more adventurous time than a fortnight's package deal will offer but have restricted funds, then take advantage of the range of very good budget guides now on offer. These are a very good investment, guiding the shoestring traveller to the best sites and cheapest decent hotels in the farthest-flung corners of the world. Among the best and best-known are the Lonely Planet travel survival kit guidebooks and the Rough Guide series, both available from major bookstores. They provide in-depth city-by-city information on budget transport, accommodation and restaurants in every country they visit as well as lots of cultural and historical background. Once you have covered the expense of your air fare, it is quite possible to live much more cheaply than at home in many foreign countries, especially those in Asia and Africa. If you're planning to travel for several months rather than weeks, another way of eking out your funds is to take temporary work abroad. English is by far the most-used of the international tourist languages, so English-speakers are particularly in demand for bar, restaurant and hotel jobs in resort areas the world over. One good, comprehensive guidebook to help you along is Susan Griffith's *Work Your Way Around the World.*

House swaps at home and abroad

For the less adventurous who don't fancy roughing it in cheap foreign hotels, house-swapping could be the perfect answer. Since the recession, house-swap holidays have grown in popularity as families desperate for a break, but unable to afford splurging out on two weeks in a hotel, began advertising their homes in national and overseas newspapers and magazines. Most swaps take place between families living in different parts of the UK, although swaps with second homes in France, Italy and America are also growing in popularity.

Agencies have now sprung up to help the process along and to offer back-up to families nervous about opening their homes to strangers. Usually all you have to do is supply a description and photograph of your house and details of the type of area you want to holiday in, seaside, mountainous or whatever, and they will put you in touch with a suitable householder on their lists for a reasonably small fee.

If you would prefer not to go through an intermediary, try advertising in national newspapers or in the local papers of the area you want to visit. This should only cost you £20 or so a time. The advent of the Internet has also produced new opportunities to find houseswap partners the world over. You can scan through a comprehensive list of holiday homes across the UK at your leisure or advertise your own home to interested parties in Britain or overseas. We recently heard of someone who advertised to swap his North London home for a family house in Boston for two weeks. He received three inquiries and telephone numbers within a week!

226

Activity holidays

Try a more active holiday than those of the beach and sightseeing variety. Your vacation should turn out to be cheaper, healthier and at least as rewarding. Activity holidays can allow you to indulge a favourite hobby or to try your hand at something new you've never previously had the time for. They include long-distance walking and cycling, hiking and bird-watching, fishing and canoeing. All of these can be pursued either within the UK or abroad, and the growth in specialist holiday companies means there is plenty of advice on hand.

Just look up advertisements in newspapers and magazines and then ring up for the brochures. You can either opt for a ready-made package, which is likely to be quite expensive, or cull the company brochures for information on good locations for your activity and then go it alone, hiring bicycles, canoes, or hiking equipment and staying in bed and breakfast accommodation or small hotels.

Other agencies also offer impartial advice on activity holidays. The Sports Council, for example, in the interests of public fitness, publish a register of firms offering guided walking holidays. The National Trust also provides a long list of nature walks around Britain (it owns 57 nature reserves and over 400 sites of special scientific interest), while the Youth Hostels Association has compiled a comprehensive directory of walks to suit all ages and interests.

Camping and caravanning can also be classed as activity holidays in that they involve more physical effort – and more personal freedom and adventure – than booking into a hotel. Both are still very popular in Britain, particularly, but not exclusively, in the summer months. Both caravan and camping sites cost peanuts compared with hotel prices, especially for families. If you're looking for a site near a nice clean beach, the best bet is to invest in a copy of the annually-produced *Good Beach Guide* or to look it up in your local library. The guide gives beaches star ratings depending on the cleanliness of the water and the sand and the quality of the amenities. Then check whether camping and caravanning is available on or near the beachfront.

Working holidays

Working holidays may sound like a contradiction in terms, but they are cheap and can be great fun. They also offer a good opportunity to get away from it all and contribute to a good cause at one and the same time.

Many farms around Britain offer working holidays with free food and lodging in return for a good day's work in the fields, helping to harvest crops or fruit-picking. For those who want to work in the wider countryside the British Trust for Conservation Volunteers (BTCV) – details in the Downshifter's Directory – organises a wide range of conservation holidays from dry-stone-walling to re-planting hedgerows and ponds at very reasonable rates. Accommodation is often communal but prices are cheap and holidays or weekends such as these are a great way to meet like-minded people.

Holiday at home

This may sound like another contradiction in terms, but think about it. We don't mean literally stay confined to the house, but use your time off from working or household duties to get to know your locality better. It's much less hassle and requires much less organisation than preparing for a trek abroad. Take time to sit down and enjoy simple pleasures such as listening to music and reading books. Catch up on the gardening you've been falling behind with and the exercise you haven't had time for. Discover, or revisit, local beauty spots, garden centres or wildlife havens. Most cities and large towns now have city farms or nature activity centres on their fringes. Then there are all the films or plays you've been wanting to see, the friends you haven't had time to visit and the new restaurant which you were saving for a special occasion. The week or fortnight will fly by in no time, and you'll feel relaxed and refreshed without having left the comfort of your own home!

Be a green tourist

Now we've given you lots of ideas about how to holiday more cheaply and – we hope – more enjoyably, how about taking a little time to think about the impact your wanderings make? Tourism now ranks as the world's third largest industry and its impact on the environment is enormous and growing. Many beautiful parts of the world have been ruined by overdevelopment, with little of the travel companies' huge profits being ploughed back into the local economy in compensation.

But concern is growing about damage from tourism, fuelled by the growth of green consumerism. If you count yourself among the latter, here are a few guidelines on how to choose a holiday which allows you to tread lightly on the Earth.

1: Don't take a mainstream package holiday

They may be cheap, but package tour holidays operate in a cut-throat, cut-price industry where protecting landscapes and beaches from environmental degradation comes close to the bottom of the priority list.

2: Support green tour operators

As an alternative a growing number of travel companies are jumping on the green bandwagon and are offering eco-tourist holidays and/or are making contributions to conservation efforts either in Britain or in the countries where they operate. Many of these more specialist firms are members of the Association of Independent Tour Operators, which has a useful database of green-minded companies. For the adventurous, canoeing and kayaking have little environmental impact. Canoeing holidays in two-seater canoes are common in America and Canada, and takers are usually rewarded by coming close to a rich array of wildlife.

While on your travels, watch out for the sale of products made from endangered species, such as elephant ivory trinkets and tortoiseshell jewellery. Consumer power is the quickest way to stamp out such activity and help protect the remaining animals in the wild.

3: Holiday in the UK

Travelling abroad, either by plane or boat, uses large amounts of energy and creates pollution. So the serious eco-tourist should take holidays within Britain as much as possible. And there's plenty to see. Our ten national parks, for example, offer a great variety of holiday opportunities amid spectacular natural beauty. For those wanting to spend their time off in actively green pursuits, there are now lots of opportunities including working holidays and field study tours.

Bird-watching is another activity holiday with a decidedly green tinge. Most specialist firms are conservation-minded, limiting the size of their tours so as not to over-disturb the birdlife and its habitat. They also often hire conservationists to give lectures to tourists.

Further reading and contacts
British Tourist Authority, Thames Tower, Black's Rd, London W6 9EL. Tel: 0181 846 9000.
Association of Independent Tour Operators, 133A St Margaret's Rd, Twickenham TW1 1RG. Tel: 0181 744 9280.
Youth Hostels Association, Trevelyan House, 8 St Stephen's Hill, St Albans, Hertfordshire AL1 2DY. Tel: 01727 855215.
National Trust, 36 Queen Anne's Gate, London SW1H 9AS. Tel: 0171 222 9251.
The Readers' Digest Good Beach Guide, David and Charles, 1996.
Work Your Way Around The World, Vatican Work, 1997.

CHAPTER TWENTY-THREE

Making a Better Community

No man is an Island, *entire of it self* . . .
John Donne (1571–1631), English metaphysical poet

We are often told that Britain is in terminal decline and it certainly sometimes feels that way. No longer does Britannia rule the waves, or lead the world in manufacturing output. Undoubtedly, it has lost its colonies, lost its way, lost its self-confidence and cohesiveness as a nation. But scratch beneath the surface, open your eyes and look around you at what is *still* good, or *better* than it was. In many ways, Britain remains – perhaps is *more* than ever – a thriving collection of fascinating and diverse communities, bubbling with creative energy, citizenship and extremely good ideas. They may be situated in beautiful valleys, identikit suburbs or inner-city tower blocks. But the common thread linking them is that they are full of people with vision, dynamism and hope. We don't always hear about them quite enough.

Many of these havens of common sense and mutual support live rather quiet, low-profile lives, and they probably like it that way. These places are simply light years away from the depressing diet of violent crime, Royal rows, television soap star marriage break-ups and the Westminster or Euro-shenanigans that fill the pages of our tabloid national newspapers; and which can give a misleading impression of contemporary Britain.

Bishop's Castle – a town at ease with itself

Bishop's Castle (pop. 1,600), Shropshire, is one of these havens of quiet, common sense, full of life and vigour. It is England's smallest town, set in one of the country's least populated areas, south Shropshire, a friendly unassuming sort of place, steeped in fascinating historical features.

No way is Bishop's Castle set in aspic, living entirely off its past for the benefit of visiting tourists and historians, however. This town is bristling with life and exciting plans for the future. Like many rural towns and villages across Britain it strives consciously to strike a delicate balance between the livelihoods of residents who need to earn a living, and the visitors who come on holiday or for weekend breaks from Manchester, Birmingham and the Black Country. Its story, its people and its experience can inform, inspire and educate all of us.

Bishop's Castle has more than 30 community groups and associations. It has four dance groups, two theatre groups, six music societies, two art galleries and two museums. In addition Bishop's Castle has 13 sporting organisations, from Badminton to Women's Hockey. It boasts no fewer than a dozen support networks from Amnesty International to the Visually Impaired Club. It heaves with small businesses. What's more it has two breweries!

Bishop's Castle has a highly impressive local economy, perhaps not in terms of traditional manufacturing employment as measured by Gross Domestic Output, but certainly in terms of models for balanced, community living.

Positive news

Shauna Crockett-Burrows is the editor of *Positive News with Planetary Connections*. It is published in Bishop's Castle, and prints about 60,000 copies every quarter. However, it is read or scanned by up to 300,000 people, because the paper is distributed to schools, hospitals, surgeries and libraries. This is a rare newspaper, because it publishes nothing but good news. But don't be too quick to dismiss it as cranky and marginal. Shauna explains: 'We were created about three years ago to try to restore some balance to the negative news reporting that we saw in the media.

'The media teaches by what it omits as well as what it chooses to write about. So we cover news in terms of people trying to create a positive future for themselves, trying to take charge of their lives. We don't consider positive news as soft news, but simply giving people the material need to make informed choices about the future.'

There is no standard annual subscription fee for recipients of *Positive News*. People just donate what they feel they can afford. What can they expect for their donation? In issue number 10, published in the summer of 1996, there were news articles and features about the kind of issues we have covered so far in this book, and more. Everything from the Oxford Rickshaw Company, offering low interest loans to rickshaw drivers in India, to a man in Kent who has invented a gadget that turns ordinary radios into solar-powered radios.

Trading without money

When Carole Salmon first moved to the area two years ago, she went to a fruit and veg market in the market hall. After getting what she wanted, the stallholder asked her: 'Do you want to pay in Onnies?' What she was being asked was whether she wanted to barter goods or services instead of pay using conventional money. Carole used money: 'As a mother looking after two small children, I was worried that I wouldn't have time to contribute to the bartering scheme.'

Bishop's Castle has a thriving barter economy, partly because the average income is well below the national average. The barter economy is run via the Castle Local Exchange and Trading System (LETS). More than 200 people are active LETS members – at least one in eight townspeople. Each member lists the goods and services they offer to trade in the local LETS directory. There is everything from locally-produced organic food, and catering services to house and cat-minding, and spinning wheel hire. There is a Children's Corner, where youngsters may advertise their talents for raking up leaves and suchlike.

Requests for certain goods and services – helicopter flying lessons even – are also logged. These offers and request then are traded in the form of 'Onnies' – the name given to the local unit of exchange. The transaction price is agreed between buyer and seller and a 'cheque' written out in the local currency is issued. This amount is then credited or debited to the person's account held on a central register. Selling your services clocks up credit that helps to eliminate your debt.

The local LETS treasurer sends out regular statements of members' accounts, just as a bank would. No coins or notes are issued, no interest is charged or paid. Carole is now an active member of the Castle LETS scheme, after she started drawing up 'life charts' for people wanting help with planning their lives. 'It took me a long time to realise that actually there was a service that I could contribute,' she says.

'Let's set up a LETS'

In the early 1990s, very few people had heard of local currencies and LETS. By mid-1995, there were about 400 schemes across Britain, with an estimated 30,000 members and an annual turnover equivalent to £2.1m. By mid-1996, there were nearly 40,000 members. On average each scheme has about 85 people signed-up, so the Bishop's Castle scheme must be one of the biggest, per head of population, in the country. Manchester's 'Bobbin'-based LETS scheme has the most members at 550. Women make up more than half of all LETS members, nearly one-third of members are unemployed and nearly three quarters of them rank themselves as 'green', according to a survey of local LETS administrators in 1995.

The unemployed element has grown considerably according to Colin C. Williams of the Centre for Urban Development and Environmental Management at Leeds Metropolitan University: 'Although the early schemes are rightly caricatured as playthings of the "environmentally-conscious middle class", more recent examples have many more jobless and fewer greens.'

Enthusiasts see bartering as an important mechanism for communities to re-assert themselves in the face of increasing external control over local economic affairs. The most commonly cited reasons for setting up LETS schemes are to:

- rebuild 'localised economies' which are more inter-linked and less reliant on external goods and services
- develop a sense of community
- help those excluded from employment to take part in productive activity, to improve self-esteem and quality of life

Bartering is also diversifying into new areas. A new business LETS is due to be set up in Hounslow, west London in 1997, and there are now several schemes where members 'trade' in counselling and other mental health services. Why not investigate whether there is a LETS scheme in your area? If so join it, and get involved in the running of it if you can. Consider setting up a LETS scheme in your area, if there isn't one already. The national co-ordinating body for these schemes is Letslink UK, listed in the Downshifter's Directory.

There are countless ways of contributing towards a richer, stronger community life. Tenants of Apple Tree Court, a Salford tower block, used to stare out on to a bare patch of grass in front of their flats. They decided to create a garden when management of the block passed from the local council to the tenants themselves. Thanks to the help of a charity, the Arid Lands Initiative, and a government grant in 1995, the tenants were able to plant and grow an orchard with 20 varieties of traditional fruit and nut trees, had organic vegetables growing on their allotments, and had earmarked part of the land for a wildflower meadow and woodland.

10 ways to build a better community

1   **GET** to know your neighbours, if you don't already. Showing a courteous, friendly interest in your neighbour's affairs is not busy-bodying – it's good citizenship, and the first essential step to becoming involved in your community. At best you will make a new friend by making the first move and at worst you will get to know your enemy if he or she turns out to be the neighbour from hell.

2   **JOIN** your local residents or tenants association and see whether there are any skills you could offer to keep the wheels turning. It's a quick and easy way to get to know people in the area and find out what community projects are worth pursuing or setting up.

3   **STAND** for your local parish or borough council. You do not have to be a member of a political party, nor indeed harbour party-political ambitions. Some of the best councillors sail under their own 'independent' flag. How about standing as the Downshifter's candidate or the Simple Lifer candidate?

4 **START** planning a street party or a whole programme of community events to celebrate the Millennium. It does not have to be anything grand or lavish. Consult your residents or community association to see whether it already has plans in hand. Alternatively, leaflet your street or estate about the idea, call a meeting and see what happens. Have a few ideas of your own ready to put to your neighbours about potential projects – turning a piece of derelict or neglected land into a garden growing fruit and vegetables, or planting some trees there. The ideas will probably come thick and fast once you all get going. The point is getting people together to talk about their common interests.

5 **BECOME** a school governor, or volunteer for hospital or prison visiting.

6 **BUY** and read your local paper to find out what are the burning local issues. You may want to get involved. Write letters for publication in local and national papers – it's an easy way of contributing to political debates at all levels, and you don't have to leave the comfort of your home.

7 **SUPPORT** your local theatre or arts group. Even if you are not interested in performing or exhibiting work, you can be helpful behind the scenes.

8 **BECOME** an adult literacy tutor – help adults who left school without knowing how to read and write: most libraries will have details of local schemes.

9 **MAKE** better use of a spare room if it is empty for long periods – get in touch with your local college or university to see whether they could use it to accommodate students or visiting youngsters on exchange schemes. If your town, village or suburb is twinned with another overseas, your local council should be able to put you in touch with the local town-twinning organisers.

10 **CONSIDER**, if you have young children or elderly relatives, setting up a baby-sitting or granny-minding circle, so you can get out more and get stuck into wider community involvement.

Further reading
If you need funds for a community project, it could be well worth buying or borrowing *A Guide To The Major Trusts*. It lists around 700 grant-giving trusts which between them fund projects worth £100m each year. Entries give details on contacts, favoured areas of funding, exclusions and applications procedures. Published by the Directory of Social Change, 24 Stephenson Way, London NW1 2DP. Tel: 0171 209 5151.

PART SIX

THE DOWNSHIFTER'S DIRECTORY

In this section we set out details of 50 organisations who can offer further information, inspiration and ideas to help you achieve your downshifting ambitions.

Finance

The Co-operative Bank
Head office: 1 Balloon Street, Manchester M60 4EP

This is the banking arm of the Co-operative Movement, founded more than 100 years ago. It takes a robust ethical stand in all its operations – no investment of customers' money in oppressive regimes, the export of weapons to such regimes, in activities that needlessly or illegally damage the environment or companies involved in animal experimentation for cosmetic purposes. It *does* actively encourage and support organisations that monitor their impact on the environment and that help people to help themselves, such as *The Big Issue*, the magazine that is sold by homeless people and Groundwork (see below). Above all, it regularly canvasses opinions from customers about what the bank should and should not be doing. It offers an 'armchair banking' service to transfer funds, pay regular bills, request statements and standing orders over the telephone. Compared with the main High Street rivals, it is small but it is the best known bank that espouses 'small is beautiful' principles. At the same time, it claims to be Europe's biggest issuer of gold Visa cards. A wholly-owned subsidiary Co-operative Bank Financial Advisers offers investments and pensions planning. Ask at local branches for more details, or phone 0345 212212.

Ecology Building Society
18 Station Road, Cross Hills, Near Keighley, West Yorkshire BD20 7EH
Tel: 01535 635933

The society was born in 1981 out of concern about the impact of existing lenders' preferences and practices on the environment. In cases where a lot of renovation was required, the lender tended only to release part of the funds needed or even retain the whole advance until the work was completed. This meant that borrowers were often pushed into taking on costly bridging loans and contractors to carry out the work swiftly. The net result of this, says the EBS, was a lending policy that devalued self-reliance, repair and renovation and encouraged the wasteful use of natural resources. The EBS advances 'up front' the bulk of the purchase price, so bridging loans are not needed – and much of the work can be carried out by borrowers themselves. It promotes green house-building technology and ecological lifestyles.

Ethical Investment Research and Information Service 'EIRIS'
504 Bondway Business Centre, 71 Bondway, London SW8 1SQ
Tel: 0171 735 1351

The ultimate ethical sleuths. Established by a group of Quakers and other churches in 1983 to help 'socially responsible' investment funds to screen potential investments, EIRIS (pronounced 'iris') provides information rather than makes moral judgements about the companies it analyses. It does the research and lets the individual investor decide whether to put in money or not. It offers three main services: (1) An *Acceptable List* of all company groups in the service's index that meet the criteria specified by the investor. (2) A *Portfolio Screen* that analyses all the company holdings in a portfolio to ensure that they meet all the criteria specified by the investor. (3) *Factsheets* that can provide all the information available on its database about a given company.

Triodos Bank
Brunel House, 11 The Promenade, Bristol BS8 3NN
Tel: 0117 973 9339 Fax: 0117 973 9303

A 'social' bank that only supports businesses and projects that are socially, ecologically and financially sustainable – projects that benefit the community, enhance the environment and respect human freedoms. Its wide range of 'green' savings accounts for individuals, businesses and charities include an 'Earth Saver' account which promotes investment in renewable energy, a high interest cheque account and Tax Exempt Special Savings Accounts (TESSAS). Triodos comes from the Greek word '*trihodos*' which means threefold path – a view of society that emphasises education and culture, human rights and economics.

Work and Learning

Crafts Council
44a Pentonville Road, Islington, London N1 9BY
Tel: 0171 278 7700 Fax: 0171 837 6891

A independent Government-funded organisation that promotes the contemporary crafts in Great Britain. It organises a continuous programme of exhibitions and events. The council provides start-up grants for makers who are within two years of setting up a business and whose work meets the scheme's criteria. Every two years it produces a free guide, the *Crafts Map*, which lists craft shops and galleries selected for the quality of the work on display. To receive regular information on Craft Council exhibitions, send your name and address to be included on the council's mailing list.

Department for Education and Employment (DFEE)
Training Information Service, PO Box 200, Timothy's Bridge Road, Strat-
ford-Upon-Avon CV37 9HY
Tel: 01345 665588

Free information packs entitled *Free Your Potential* are available for
individuals over the age of 18. It contains factsheets giving addresses of
all Training and Enterprise Councils (TECs), which offer information
and guidance on local training schemes and courses; on national
vocational qualifications (NVQs), and how to claim tax relief on
training leading to NVQs; and on modern apprenticeships.

Home Run
Cribau Mill, Llanfair Discoed, Chepstow NP6 6RD
Tel: 01291 641222 Fax: 01291 641777

A magazine published ten times a year. Available by subscription only.
It aims to bring homeworkers useful and timely advice to help them
work more effectively and to provoke fresh thinking. How to recover
debts, and increase your chances of swift payment; how to find new
clients and keep abreast of the latest technology are typical subjects
covered. There are plenty of case studies and interviews with people
who work for themselves from home, giving their own secrets for
success and pitfalls to avoid. Money saving offers tailored to the needs
of homeworkers usually included.

New Ways to Work
309 Upper Street, London N1 2TY
Tel: 0171 226 4026 Fax: 0171 354 2978

The leading organisation in the UK that helps people to find viable
alternatives to conventional full-time employment. It advises on
flexible working hours, part-time work, job sharing, term time
working, career breaks, voluntary reduced work time, sabbaticals and
working from home. It encourages employers to adapt employment
practices to ensure that they can recruit and retain workers with
domestic responsibilities. Publishes books, leaflets, and a quarterly

newsletter and runs seminars and training sessions for employers and personnel officers. But it also works with individuals, employers, trade unions, researchers and the media. It says: 'Demographic changes will lead to a marked reduction in the number of school leavers over the next decade. Employers will need to look to other groups for recruitment – particularly women with children and older workers.'

Ruskin College
Walton Street, Oxford OX1 2HE
Tel: 01865 310713 for prospectus

Founded in 1899, Ruskin was the first residential college for working people and its courses are designed for adults who missed out on full-time further education. Each autumn entrants arrive from a wide variety of backgrounds. They leave with formal qualifications and go on to further study or return to the world of work. Few have any qualifications when they arrive, but all have an interest in society, past, present and future. The prominent Labour MP John Prescott, who spent his early working life as a steward on ocean liners, is a former student. Entry to Ruskin is by interview and is only for students who are over the age of 20. The college is residential. State bursaries are available.

The Telework, Telecottage and Telecentre Association (TCA)
Freepost CV2312, WREN, Kenilworth, Warwickshire CV8 2RR
Freephone 0800 616008

The world's largest association of teleworkers – those who work for a geographically remote employer or customer, and using computers and telecommunications to bridge the gap. Members include the self-employed, company employees working from home and also companies introducing teleworking into their organisations. Benefits include a network of 150 telecottage resource centres, teleworker training, lobbying force to promote interests of teleworkers, group discounts on home office insurance, stationery, computer equipment and software, and an advice line.

Trades Union Congress
Congress House, Great Russell Street, London WC1B 3LS
Tel: 0171 636 4030

The TUC has produced a range of publications to help people in flexible or part-time jobs make sure their rights are recognised. It is also campaigning for part-timers to receive the full range of benefits such as holiday entitlements, sick leave and pay, and redundancy arrangements. And it gives advice to employers on the recruitment and assimilation of part-time workers. The TUC can also advise you on which union to join or seek advice from if you are planning to switch career.

Worker's Educational Association (WEA)
Temple House, 17 Victoria Park Square, London E2 9PB
Tel: 0181 983 1515 Fax: 0181 983 4840

The largest voluntary provider of adult education in the UK, with more than 650 branches nationwide providing 10,000 courses. The voluntary and democratic traditions of the WEA make it unique in the field. The association was founded in 1903 on a particular concern to help the economically and educationally disadvantaged, and on the belief that education can do much to create a more democratic and just society.

Food and Growing

Henry Doubleday Research Association (HDRA)
The National Centre for Organic Gardening, Ryton-on-Dunsmore, Coventry CV8 3LG
Tel: 01203 303517 Fax: 01203 639299

The national centre for organic gardening. A mine of information that all organic gardeners should consider joining or at least visiting its HQ just outside Coventry. It has an inspiring demonstration organic garden on its 22 acres, an excellent shop selling books, guides and everything you will need to garden without pesticides and chemical fertilisers. It also has a café/restaurant.

Permaculture Association
PO Box 1, Buckfastleigh, Devon TQ11 0LH
Tel: 01654 712188

It promotes the spread of permaculture – self-empowerment through living in balance with nature whether in town, city or country. Provides information to raise the profile of sustainable development. A separate organisation publishes the quarterly *Permaculture Magazine*, which is full of good advice, tips and news for downshifting enthusiasts wherever they live. Send £1 in stamps for a sample copy to Permanent Publications, Little Hyden Lane, Clanfield, Hampshire PO8 0RU.

The Soil Association
86 Colston Street, Bristol BS1 5BB
Tel: 0117 929 0661 Fax: 0117 925 2504

The national organisation that regulates and promotes organic farming and growing in the UK. It sets standards that producers must meet to be able to label their food as organic. The association also gives helpful advice and information to consumers. An extensive range of books and other publications are available, including the *Directory of Organic Farm Shops* and *Boxed Food Schemes*.

Shopping and Household

The Good Deal Directory
PO Box 4, Lechlade, Gloucestershire GL7 3YB
Telephone hotline: 01367 860016

The directory is the ultimate guide to discount shopping, providing a comprehensive list of factory shops, bargain outlets, sales and secondhand stores around the country. Its range covers both designer fashions and everyday clothes as well as accessories, gifts, children's wear and home furnishings. The directory is updated every year. To get a copy, send a cheque to The Good Deal Directory at the above address or call the hotline to make a credit card payment.

Out of This World
52 Elswick Rd, Newcastle upon Tyne NE4 6JH
Tel: 0191 272 1601

Embryonic ethical supermarket chain owned by its customers opened in 1996 and based in Bristol, Newcastle and Nottingham. Four more are planned for London, Cardiff, Edinburgh and Altrincham, Cheshire. It presents a direct challenge to destructive consumerism and is aimed at anyone who cares about social and environmental issues and would like to use their spending power to change the market. It sells a range of 3,000 products, mainly food and drink. Some products are available mail order. For a minimum investment of £250 members can become stakeholders and can choose the rate of interest they wish to be paid up to a maximum of 10 per cent.

Sustainable Agriculture Food and Environment Alliance (SAFE Alliance)
38 Ebury Street, London SW1W OLU
Tel: 0171 823 5660

The alliance campaigns and lobbies at a national level for a greater awareness of environmental and development issues in British farming and consumer policy. It also provides information on consumer co-operatives and organic farming outlets. One of the main issues it campaigns on is that of 'food miles' – the distance travelled by the produce we eat before it reaches our shops and dinner tables. A *Food Miles Action Pack*, helping consumers to identify how far different foods have travelled is available from the address above, price £5. The aim is to help consumers make informed choices about eating truly local food.

Community

Common Ground
Seven Dials Warehouse, 44 Earlham Street, London WC2H 9LA
Tel: 0171 379 3109

Set up in 1983 to offer ideas, information and inspiration to help people learn about, enjoy and take more responsibility for their local area. Common Ground encourages people to cherish and enhance local distinctiveness whether it is an apple orchard or hedgerow or a town clock. It works with artists and sculptors, and helps to organise exhibitions of creative community efforts such as drawing up parish maps. 'A greater care for local distinctiveness could help us to re-invigorate our sense of domestic attachment and to reweave the local world,' it says. In 1994, Common Ground won one of the 21 Schumacher Awards to celebrate 21 years of the publication of *Small Is Beautiful.*

Justice
Prior House, 6 Tilbury Place, Brighton BN2 2GY
Tel: 01273 685913

Justice is a counter-culture information centre, set up in 1994 to campaign against the Criminal Justice Act. It provides advice and address lists on squatting and communal living around Britain and recently set up an official squatter's housing agency, helping to find suitable squats for individuals. It also produces a weekly news-sheet packed with information on counter-culture events – protests, street parties, raves and so on – around the country.

KAIROS (Centre for a Sustainable Society)
The Rectory, Glencarse, Perth PH2 7LX
Tel: 01738 860386

Supported by the Scottish churches, Kairos promotes a programme of education and policy formation called Vision 21. It embraces a citizens' initiative in community education on how to live sustainable lifestyles and produce local development which doesn't harm the environment. The programme aims to involve communities throughout Scotland.

The Land Is Ours
Box E, 111 Magdalen Road, Oxford OX4 1RQ
Tel: 01865 722016, Spokesman: George Monbiot

Another direct action movement. It campaigns against the ascendancy of private property in Britain. It has staged high profile sit-ins on disused land owned by wealthy private landowners and by companies such as British Gas. Its several thousand supporters plant trees and vegetable gardens and set up 'holistic villages' on these derelict sites until they are moved on. It also lobbies local authorities and national politicians over land policy, arguing that derelict land in towns and cities should be turned into urban oases, providing green spaces and sustainable accommodation for local people.

The National Association of Citizens Advice Bureaux
Myddelton House, 115–123 Pentonville Rd, London N1 9LZ
Tel: 0171 833 2181

Almost every town in Britain has a citizens advice bureau staffed mainly by trained volunteers who help members of the public who can't afford expensive legal advice. Their expertise covers a huge range of areas including debt, housing and mortgage difficulties, family break-up problems, rights for the employed, the self-employed, the sick and the jobless, and so on. The national association's public information unit holds a central register of all offices nationwide and can provide general information on the services offered by its branches.

National Federation of City Farms
The Greenhouse, Hereford Street, Bedminster, Bristol BS3 4NA
Tel: 0117 923 1800 Fax: 0117 923 1900

There are 63 established city farms throughout the UK and new ones planned in Portsmouth, Bath and Gloucester. They give a new lease of life to derelict pieces of land and are run by management groups drawn from local communities. Most farms have animals and about 5,000 school visits are made to them each year, raising awareness of agriculture and food production among children in urban areas. Many city farms have shops selling their produce to local people. On a wider social level, they have acted as catalysts in reviving community spirit and activity in areas suffering varying degrees of disadvantage and dereliction. A wide range of training activities are undertaken, in co-operation with official schemes such as Youth Training and Employment Training. Some farms actively promote local community gardening initiatives and allotment-holding. The National Federation of City Farms acts as a support and development organisation for community-managed farms. All the farms rely on volunteers to keep going.

Neighbourhood Initiatives Foundation
The Poplars, Lightmoor, Telford TF4 3QN
Tel 01952 590777

A national charity, specialising in community participation, training and development. It works with local authorities, voluntary agencies and community groups to empower people to shape the future of their neighbourhoods and improve the quality of life for everyone living there. Much, but not all, of the foundation's work is in disadvantaged areas.

Reclaim The Streets
PO Box 9656, London N4 4JY
Tel: 0171 281 4621

Reclaim the Streets was set up in 1995 by some of the leading direct action protesters who had fought the extension of the M11 through East London. The organisation has staged a number of non-violent demonstrations against the car culture by setting up street parties in busy London roads and by car 'bouncing' – picking up illegally parked cars and dumping them on pavements. There are now Reclaim the Streets groups in several other major cities. For advice on staging direct actions or information on activities in your area contact the number above.

United Kingdom Co-operative Council
c/o The Co-operative Bank plc, PO Box 101, 1 Balloon Street, Manchester
M60 4EP
Tel: 0161 829 5290 Fax: 0161 832 9707

It provides support and encouragement to existing and potential co-operative endeavours, and promotes the interests of co-operative enterprise generally to the government and other bodies. Member organisations include the Association of British Credit Unions Ltd, the Confederation of Co-operative Housing, the Co-operative Women's Guild and the UK Institute for the Social Economy.

The Volunteer Centre UK
Carriage Row, Eversholt Street, London NW1 1BU
Tel: 0171 388 9888

The national centre runs a variety of training courses for both would-be volunteers and employers. They include volunteer induction training, courses on staff-volunteer relationships, and courses on the role of volunteering in specific social areas such as care in the community. The centre also publishes *Volunteering*, the only UK-wide magazine devoted to the subject, which comes out ten times a year. It provides a news and information service and costs subscribers £20 a year.

Women's Royal Voluntary Service (WRVS)
234–244, Stockwell Road, London SW9 9SP
Tel: 0171 416 0146 Fax: 0171 416 0148

Runs social centres and clubs for elderly, disabled and others in need. One of its prime objectives is to carry out non-medical welfare in hospitals, including psychiatric and mental handicap hospitals. It runs playgroups in children's wards and crèches in outpatient departments; does flower arranging for patients and operates library trolleys. Helps to organise transport and other support services for people being discharged from hospital.

Environment

British Trust for Conservation Volunteers (BTCV)
36 St Mary's Street, Wallingford, Oxfordshire OX10 0EU
Tel: 01491 839766 Fax: 01491 839646

It began in 1959 when a group of 42 volunteers, including David Bellamy, went to Box Hill in Surrey to clear a vast expanse of dogwood to encourage native chalkland plants to grow. Now the UK's biggest practical conservation organisation, with 85,000 volunteers, the Trust runs courses, working holidays and volunteer groups. The Natural Break working holidays are focused on learning new skills, meeting new people and saving wildlife. Laying nature trails, clearing ponds, and hedge-planting are typical activities. Often the conservation projects are within national parks or nature reserves, although Trust staff and volunteers also work on improving landscapes in towns and cities.

Centre for Alternative Technology
Machynlleth, Powys, Wales SY20 9AZ
Tel: 01654 702400

The best-known green technology showcase of its kind in Britain, CAT offers visitors a wide variety of displays on non-polluting ways of living. These include demonstrations on the use of solar, wind and water power. The roof of the centre's main office building was itself fitted with solar panelling in 1996. The centre also offers short courses on renewable energy, low energy building, organic gardening, healing herbs and woodland skills. It is open all year round but hours are restricted during the winter months.

Global Action Plan
42 Kingsway, London WC2B 6EX
Tel: 0171 405 5633

GAP has helped over 7,000 households to save money and do something positive for the planet. Its six month programme gives participants practical household advice on how to cut down on what they spend and consume. As a result, families throw away 33 per cent less rubbish and reduce their domestic energy use by 9 per cent, their water use by 13 per cent and their petrol use by a tenth. GAP also successfully operates in North America and across Western Europe. There are a growing number of volunteer GAP groups in Britain. To find out if there is one in your area, or to find out how to set one up, call the GAP office on the number above.

Groundwork Foundation
85–87 Cornwall Street, Birmingham B3 3BY
Tel: 0121 236 8565

Established in 1981, its mission is to bring about 'the sustained regeneration, improvement and management of the local environment by developing partnerships which empower people, businesses and organisations to maximise their impact and contribution to environmental, economic and social well-being'. The foundation helps to improve housing estates, parks and other public amenities, and is active in 120 towns and cities across the UK.

Willing Workers On Organic Farms (WWOOF)
19 Bradford Road, Lewes, Sussex BN7 1RB

WWOOF was set up in 1971 to help people learn organic farming methods at first hand. Volunteers receive board and lodging and a basic grounding in organic horticulture and agriculture in exchange for a weekend's work. Weekends are arranged through a regional organiser who puts volunteers in touch with host farms or smallholdings. Transport can be arranged to and from the nearest BR station. Those who have satisfactorily completed two weekends can opt to receive a Fix-It-Yourself List for the UK and overseas, so that they can organise further weekends, or longer breaks, themselves. Some farms will take children, by arrangement. Send a 9 × 6 SAE to the above address for membership details.

Transport

Environmental Transport Association (ETA)
10 Church Street, Weybridge, Surrey KT13 8RS
Tel: 01932 828882

The ETA is Britain's greenest road rescue organisation. Members can join for £20 a year to help the Association's active campaigning for more environmentally-friendly transport systems. Its activities, financially supported by conservation groups such as the World Wide Fund for Nature, include running a nationwide Green Transport Week event once a year. In addition, the ETA offers a full range of breakdown and home start-up services on a sliding scale, depending on the vehicle's age. It is also the only vehicle breakdown organisation to offer a rescue service for cyclists – personal cover costs £18 a year.

Pedestrians' Association
126 Aldersgate Street, London EC1A 4JQ
Tel: 0171 490 0750

Founded in 1929, it campaigns for measures not only to make walking safer but to make roads less intimidating and more pleasant for pedestrians. It works with central and local government to discourage car dependence, and encourage more people to walk shorter journeys; and it helps local communities to lobby their councils for better footpaths and for pedestrianisation schemes in town centres.

Sustrans
35 King Street, Bristol BS1 4DZ
Tel: 0117 929 0888

A national civil engineering charity which has built hundreds of miles of traffic-free paths for cyclists and walkers, often by rivers or on disused railways. It aims to create a 6,500-mile National Cycle Network passing through the centre of most major towns and cities in the UK, within two miles of more than 20 million people. Its ambitious target was boosted in 1996 with a generous grant of several million pounds from the Millennium Commission. For details of cycle routes near you or in areas where you would like to go for a cycling holiday, contact the address above. Members also receive details of fund-raising and social events and a newsletter.

Health

Association of Tisserand Aromatherapists (ATA)
PO BOX 746, Hove BN3 3XA

Robert Tisserand runs one- and two-day seminars for people who want guidance in practising aromatherapy safely and effectively at home. You can also write to him at the above address if you would like to train as a professional aromatherapist. The association provides a list of recommended practitioners.

Natural Medicines Society
Market Chambers, 13a Market Place, Heanor, Derbyshire DE75 7AA

Promotes consumers' rights to safe, effective complementary and alternative medicines and remedies, and campaigns for their integration into mainstream healthcare. The society has led moves to set up a UK Forum for Alternative and Complementary Medicine. For more information, send a large SAE.

Yoga Therapy Centre
Royal London Homeopathic Hospital, 56–57 Great Ormond Street, London WC1N 3HR
Tel: 0171 833 7267

It runs clinics for people suffering various long-term chronic ailments such as diabetes, asthma, hypertension and back pain. It trains yoga therapists and can put enquirers in touch with trained yoga therapists throughout the UK.

Bartering

Letslink UK
61 Woodcock Road, Warminster, Wiltshire BA12 9DH
Tel and Fax: 01985 217871

The first national LETS agency founded to develop, monitor, design and popularise methods of organising Local Exchange and Trading Systems and local currencies. Most emerging LETS groups use its *Information Pack* to get themselves off the ground, to maintain themselves and to grow. The organisation also publishes a quarterly magazine *Lets-Link!* and other literature to help enthusiasts and attract new converts. For more information on LETS and your nearest local contacts, send six first class stamps.

Media

Positive News
The Six Bells, Church Street, Bishop's Castle, Shropshire SY9 5AA

A paper that reports only good news – about the local, national and international green scene. Send a stamped addressed label for sample copy.

Holidays and Leisure

The National Trust
PO Box 39, Bromley, Kent BR1 3XL
Tel: 0181 315 1111

Founded in 1895 to preserve places of historic interest or natural beauty, the Trust protects and opens to the public more than 200 historic houses, 160 gardens and 25 industrial monuments. It owns

240,000 hectares of Britain's most beautiful countryside and 550 miles of coast. The Trust and its properties enjoy unique statutory protection. None of its land can be sold, mortgaged or compulsorily purchased against the Trust's wishes without special parliamentary approval. The National Trust relies on armies of volunteers to carry out its work.

The Ramblers' Association
1–5 Wandsworth Road, London SW8 2XX
Tel: 0171 582 6878

A membership organisation and lobbying group that aims to promote rambling and access to open country, to protect rights of way and the countryside in general. Local groups organise regular walks and the Association offers a wide range of rambling holidays in this country and abroad.

Skyros
92 Prince of Wales Road, London NW5 3NE
Tel: 0171 267 4424 Fax: 0171 284 3063

Undoubtedly a European leader in personal development or alternative holidays. It offers holidays for 'the mind, body and spirit' on the quiet, beautiful Greek island of Skyros. There are two centres on this island – the Skyros Centre in the main village, a 25–60 person community where you can take part in writers' workshops, personal and spiritual development, painting, health and healing courses. Stay in the centre itself or in the village. Alternatively, you can stay at Atsitsa, nine miles from the village, which is a 50–100 person community right by the sea. Courses range from wind-surfing, dance, yoga and t'ai chi to dreamwork, massage, theatre and music. Accommodation here is in bamboo huts or in the stone villa overlooking forest and sea. Writers' workshops have been led by Sue Townsend, Andrew Davies and D.M. Thomas.

Futures

The New Economics Foundation
1st Floor, Vine Court, 112–116 Whitechapel Rd, London E1 1JE
Tel: 0171 377 5696, Director: Ed Mayo

NEF is Britain's leading think-tank on alternative economics. It introduced Local Exchange Trading Schemes to this country in 1985 and developed the concept of a social audit of the impact made by companies, which progressive firms such as Body Shop is now using. The foundation campaigns for a new economic approach centred on people and the environment rather than consumption and growth. They advise both organisations and individuals on all aspects of new economics. Details of membership, at £18 a year, are available from the above address.

The New Road Map Foundation
PO Box 15981, Seattle, Washington 98115, USA
Tel: 001 206 527 0437, President: Vicki Robin

The inspiringly-named New Road Map Foundation is a non-profit-making charity at the heart of the American downshifters' network. It offers its members ways and means to adopt low-consumption, high-fulfillment lifestyles and produces literature on the links between such personal choices and global survival. Its founders, Vicki Robin and Joe Dominguez co-wrote the best-selling *Your Money or Your Life* which has helped hundreds of thousands of Americans to escape from the credit trap.

Real World
Real World, c/o the Town and Country Planning Association, 17 Carlton House Terrace, London SW1Y 5AS
Tel: 0171 930 0375 Fax: 0171 930 3280

A coalition launched in early 1996 by 32 campaign and research groups with more than two million members drawn from the environmental, social justice and development fields. Set up to try and force these neglected issues on to the national political agenda, their aim is to work for environmental improvements, the eradication of poverty, community regeneration and the promotion of democracy both in Britain and internationally. Real World has challenged the three major political parties to sign up to a 12-point action programme of reforms before the next general election. Details of campaigning activities in Britain are available from the above address.

The St James's Alliance
St James's Church, 197 Piccadilly, London W1V OLL

The alliance seeks out new approaches to promoting social justice, economic sustainability and a way of life that can fulfill the needs of everyone in society. It believes that by bringing out the common spiritual and psychological values that motivate everyone wanting to transform the political agenda, it can attract steadily-widening support from large numbers of people in all parts of the country. The Alliance draws together people involved in politics, economics, ethics, religion, psychotherapy, environmentalism, education, the media and non-governmental organisations.

SustainAbility Environmental Consultancy
49–53 Kensington High St, London W8 5ED
Tel: 0171 937 9996

An environmental think-tank and business consultancy specialising in sustainable lifestyles and environmental management, strategy and communications. It has launched three successful national public campaigns: Green Consumer Week (1988), Green Shopping Day (1989) and the Greenest School Competition (1990). Its co-founders John Elkington and Julia Hailes wrote the best-selling *Green Consumer Guide* which helped to turn environment-friendly shopping into big business. It advises many businesses on corporate strategies for a sustainable future.

POSTSCRIPT

In 1891, William Morris published his futuristic fantasy *News from Nowhere* where the narrator dreams that he finds himself in a crafts-man's paradise of simple living, spawned by a revolution in 1952 against industrial mass production. The Houses of Parliament are used for storing dung, since there is no need for politics any more. Money has been abolished. 'England was once a country of clearings amongst the woods and forests,' Morris wrote. 'It then became a country of huge and foul workshops . . . it is now a garden, where nothing is wasted and nothing spoiled.'

Like his contemporary British successor to the mantle of socialism, Tony Blair, Morris had grave doubts about the *concept* of socialism. State socialism was incompatible with true society, Morris believed. 'It is the business of socialism to destroy the State and put Free Society in its place,' he wrote. So what *was* Morris's vision of a happy balanced society?

> 'Free and full life and the consciousness of life. Or, if you will, the pleasurable exercise of our energies and the enjoyment of the rest which that exercise or expenditure of energy makes necessary to us . . . Therefore my ideal of the Society of the future is first of all the freedom and cultivation of the individual will, which civilisation ignores.' (From the journal *Commonweal,* 1889.)

One century on, Morris's ideal remains hard to beat, but its practice somewhat limited. Indeed, it will seem extreme and thoroughly anarchic from the perspective of those successful and rich entrepreneurs who have done very well selling us products whose built-in obsolescence was instantly apparent to others.

People who espoused Morris's ideals went quiet for a few decades, but they never went away. Perhaps their time will come again, and the best of socialism and capitalism will survive to be distilled into a far more potent and lasting political movement than either of them, one with a vision that no one has yet managed to articulate clearly enough to inspire electoral success. The longing for such a movement is among us, but has yet to find political expression.

BIBLIOGRAPHY

Michael Argyle, *The Psychology of Happiness*, Methuen, 1987

Michael Argyle, *The Social Psychology of Leisure*, Penguin, 1996

Alison and Richard Barr, *Which? Way To Buy, Sell and Move House*, Which? Ltd, 1993

Ulrich Beck, *The Risk Society*, Sage Publications, 1992

Robert Blatchford, *Merrie England*, London, 1893 (reprinted by Journeyman Press London, 1976)

Richard Nelson Bolles, *The 1995 What Colour Is Your Parachute? A Practical Guide for Job-Hunters and Careers-Changers*, Ten Speed Press, Berkeley, California, 1995

John Button, *How To Be Green*, Century Hutchinson, 1990

Mihaly Csikszentmihalyi, *Flow: The Psychology of Happiness*, Random Century Group, 1992

Karen Christensen, *The Green Home*, Judy Piatkus (Publishers) Ltd, 1995 (first published as *Home Ecology*, Arlington Books Ltd, 1989)

Ros Coward, *Our Treacherous Hearts*, Faber & Faber, 1992

Crafts Council, *Crafts in the 1990s*, The Crafts Council, 1994

Joe Dominguez and Vicki Robin, *Your Money or Your Life*, Penguin, 1992

Alan Thein Durning, *How Much Is Enough?* Earthscan Publications, 1992

Duane Elgin, *Voluntary Simplicity: Towards a Life that is Outwardly Simple, Inwardly Rich*, William Morrow, 1981 (reprinted 1993)

John Elkington and Julia Hailes, *The Green Consumer Guide*, Victor Gollancz, 1988

Nicholas Evans, *The Horse Whisperer*, Bantam Press, 1995

Friends of the Earth Europe Report, *Towards Sustainable Europe*, Friends of the Earth, 1995

Charles Handy, *The Age of Unreason*, Arrow Books, 1989

Charles Handy, *The Empty Raincoat*, Arrow Books, 1994

Dennis Hardy and Colin Ward, *Arcadia for All*, Mansell Publishing Ltd, 1984

Fred Hirsch, *Social Limits to Growth*, Routledge & Kegan Paul, 1977

Will Hutton, *The State We're In*, Jonathan Cape, 1995

Richard Greensted, *Go It Alone*, Pan Books, 1995

Susan Griffith, *Work Your Way Around the World*, Vacation Works, 1995

Michael Jacobs, *The Politics of the Real World*, Earthscan Publications, 1996

P. Macnaghten *et al., Public Perceptions and Sustainability in Lancashire*, Centre for the Study of Environmental Change, Lancaster University, 1995

Merck Family Fund Report, *Yearning for Balance: Views of Americans on Consumption, Materialism and the Environment*, Merck Family Fund, 1995

Mintel Marketing Intelligence Report, *British Lifestyles*, The Mintel International Group, January 1996

Mintel Marketing Intelligence Report, *Changing Work Patterns and the Consumer*, The Mintel International Group, May 1996

William Morris, *News from Nowhere*, Reeves and Turner, 1891

Ray Pahl, *Patterns of Urban Life*, Longman, 1970

Ray Pahl, *After Success: Fin de Siècle Anxiety and Identity*, Polity Press, 1995

R.E. Pahl and J.M. Pahl, *Managers and their Wives*, Penguin, 1971

Ian Phillipson, *How To Work From Home*, How To Books, 1995

Faith Popcorn, *The Popcorn Report: Targeting Your Life*, Doubleday, 1991

Laurens van der Post and Jane Taylor, *Testament to the Bushmen*, Viking, 1984

John Ruskin, *Unto This Last And Other Writings*, Penguin Classics, 1985

Juliet Schor, *The Overworked American: The Unexpected Decline of Leisure*, Basic Books, New York, 1992

E.F. Schumacher, *Small Is Beautiful*, Blond & Briggs, 1973

Russell Sparkes, *The Ethical Investor*, HarperCollins, 1995

SustainAbility Report, *Who Needs It? Market Implications of Sustainable Lifestyles*, SustainAbility Ltd, 1995

Nick Vandome, *How To Spend A Year Abroad*, How To Books Ltd, 1992

Pam Walton, *Job Sharing: A Practical Guide*, Kogan Page, 1990

Martin J. Weiner, *English Culture and the Decline of the Industrial Spirit 1850–1980*, Cambridge University Press, 1981

Michael Young, *The Metronomic Society: Natural Rhythms and Human Timetables*, Thames & Hudson, 1988

INDEX

Entries in **bold** denote entries in the Downshifter's Directory.

Index

Index

Index